Love Me Later

1, Volume 1

R.A. Cambel

Published by Quill Your Darlings, 2024.

LOVE ME LATER

First edition. April 8, 2024.

Copyright © 2024 R.A. Cambel.

ISBN: 979-8224009589

Written by R.A. Cambel.

THE BAD NEWS

I barely slept when I heard the alarm.

Crap!

I opened my eyes to the unfamiliar surroundings, and it dawned on me.

Today is my first day in Ashton Greene's home. I dragged myself to the bathroom as my mind played the conversation between me and my parents last week before they left to attend a series of business dealings abroad.

"Natasha, honey?"

I paid attention to my 45-year-old dad, Jeremy Collins. My father stands at 5'10". He started growing his gray hair in his late 30s and has kept the same short hairstyle since his hairline started to recede

I noticed how his hazel-brown eyes pleaded. I knew that I might not like whatever he was going to say.

"Uhm...yes, dad?"

He glanced at my mom. She is busy putting a slice of my favorite red velvet cake on the plate.

"You guys are killing me. What is it?" I asked impatiently.

"Well, honey. You know how online shopping platforms helped to expand our business?"

I knew my dad was serious when I noticed the crease between his brows. Then, he pressed his lips together before he threw a pleading look at my mom.

I rolled my eyes when he did not answer.

"Yes. The technology paved our way to the global market... so?" I feigned a smile.

I wondered where this conversation was going.

I am in my last year as a Business Administration and Marketing student. Our family's online store was originally a product of a marketing project I had in one of my classes.

"And?" I looked at my mom, Julia Collins.

Julia is the same age as my dad, a brunette who stands at 5'7" and has eyes the same light brown color as mine.

If my memory serves me right, I have not seen her hair grow beyond her shoulders. She has had her hair colored, straightened, and curled. But they were almost always the same length.

"The global market demand is constantly increasing. We wanted to explore the possibility of expanding abroad." my mom smiled at my dad.

"Well, isn't that good news?"

I still don't understand where this conversation is heading. My dad interrupted my thoughts.

"Well, honey. We are flying abroad and might be gone for at least six months. You know, to attend a series of meetings with possible local suppliers. We also have to comply with the other business requirements of the country."

"We also need to supervise the establishment of the local office and the shop. Not to add the training and the hiring of local employees." My mom added.

Tears began to well up in my eyes.

At least six months? The longest they've been away for a business trip was two weeks, nothing more than that.

"Mom, do you need to go too?"

"You know your dad, dear. He's more of a baby than you are."

My dad rolled his eyes.

"Besides, honey, as much as we love you and want you to stay with us, you're graduating this semester. And we don't want to mess with that, do we?"

My mom put her hands into mine.

"Maybe this is also the best time for you to learn some independence." she waved her hands in the air, looked at my dad, and then continued, "And probably explore the management of our business?"

My heart sank. It is partly true. All my peers live in an apartment, work part-time, and pay their bills. On the other hand, I am a 23-year-old woman who still lives in my room at my parent's house.

Though I have started "working" as part of the administrative staff in our company since graduating from high school, I have heard gossip about how my salary was probably just my allowance. They said I earn way better than the senior administrative employee.

"I understand," I said with a playful smile. I leaned over the counter and teased, "How soon can I invite my friends to weekend parties?"

I grinned. My parents exchanged worried glances.

I sensed the hesitation in my mom's voice when she spoke.

"Well, dear. Though I trust that you will not do anything of that sort, I'm afraid you can't do that."

Dad scratched his balding forehead. Then he said, "No, honey. Your mom is right. You can't do that." He glanced at my mom again, widened his eyes, and said, "Not with Ashton around."

My jaws dropped.

"What? Do you mean Ashton, your friend's son Ashton Greene?"

I looked at my mom.

"Mom, I thought you said this is to learn how to be independent?"

"Well, dear, Ashton is a family friend. The one we trusted the most. So we figured that while we want you to be independent, he seems the right person to look after you while we're gone."

"He's our business partner too." My dad added. "So while we're away, we asked him to teach you about our business operations."

"I am 23! An adult! I don't think I need a guardian at this age." I let out a desperate sigh.

My dad took another worried look at my mom.

"There's more to this arrangement, right?" I asked.

"I am sorry, dear." My mom grasped my hands. " We know you can be a little rebellious, and should we say immature? So, we thought Ashton should stay with you and use one of our rooms."

My dad smirked. "But he said he can't."

Yes!

I might have rejoiced prematurely. Dad shook his head amidst his chuckle.

"Honey, I wouldn't be too happy if I were you." He pressed his lips again. "While he can't move here, he asked if you can live in his house instead. You know, his house, his rules."

I felt nervousness creep into my system. "Please tell me you said no."

"And we said yes." My mom answered.

"What?" I said it louder than I intended to.

Did I hear them right? How can they say yes? Do they trust Ashton that much?

"Mom...Dad! Ugh! Do you realize that you're leading me straight to the lion's den, right?" I pouted my lips. "Sometimes I wonder if you love me."

"You know we do, honey. You know we do." My dad pulled me into a hug and kissed my forehead.

"I'm sorry, dear." Mom approached me and gave me an embrace.

I heard hurried footsteps outside my room, which took me to the present time.

I glanced at the door, sighed, and looked at the ceiling again. I kicked my feet in the air, frustrated by the situation.

WE MEET AGAIN

I finished my bath quickly and then wrapped myself in a bathrobe. I headed towards the dresser and reached for the moisturizers. I walked to the bed, raised my left leg at the edge, and applied the lotion.

The door to my right took me by surprise when it burst open.

There, I saw the 33-year-old Ashton Greene, his eyes widened in shock. I docked behind the edge of the bed and tried to block his view of my almost naked body.

"Jesus Christ! I know this is your house, but don't you know how to knock?"

I felt the heat shoot up to my face. I knew that I was probably blushing from embarrassment.

"Well, good morning to you too. I thought you were ready because the door wasn't locked." He said as he leaned on the door frame. " I also want to remind you that I don't want us to be late. Come down when you're done. Breakfast is ready.

He put his hands on his waistband. His sleeveless sweatshirt exposed the toned muscles on his biceps. He furrowed his brows, and a smirk appeared on his face.

"Stop with the blushing, will you? I didn't see anything!" He said as if he was teasing me.

I grabbed a pillow and threw it at him. "Ugh! I can't believe I am going to spend six more months with an asshole like you."

He caught the pillow with his hands and threw it back on my bed.

"Watch your mouth, lady. I won't tolerate that behavior in my home." He was about to get out, then he paused. "And I am also happy to spend more than half the year with you."

He winked, then he reached for the door. He pointed at the lock on the knob and locked it before he pulled it close.

I am not used to locking my bedroom door. Neither of my parents gets in without knocking. Not even the house helpers.

I continued what I was doing. I dried my shoulder-length hair, put on light makeup, and prepared everything I needed for the day. I zipped my bag as I dashed out of my room.

I headed to the stairs and was about to grab the main door when I heard Ashton behind me. I turned around and saw that he was also ready to leave.

"And where are you going?" he asked. Ashton glanced at me, still buttoning the sleeve on his left wrist.

I furrowed my brows and wondered how quickly he had changed into a white long-sleeve shirt, which he tucked into his black pants.

Did I take that long to change?

I shook my head to yank the thoughts away and answered with irritation, "To school, I guess? Where else should I go? I have a 9:30 class."

Ashton glanced at his watch. "Good. It's barely 8 AM. Let's have a quick breakfast." He grabbed me by my shoulders and turned me towards the kitchen.

"Uhm.. thanks. But I am good. I am running late." I turned around and took a step backward.

"This place is closer to the university than your parents' home. You'll get there in half an hour." He grabbed me by my wrist and pulled me to the dining table." Your shenanigans won't work. I know when I am being lied to."

Ashton pulled out a chair before he put his hands on my shoulders. "Now, sit."

"Look, I have to go. I will appreciate it if you treat me like an adult and allow me to go."

He just smirked

"How about I'll treat you like an adult if you act like one?" He grabbed my shoulder again. Ashton did not put much force into it but pushed my shoulders down to make me sit. "We will have this breakfast. I cannot finish all these."

In front of me is a plate of bacon, some scrambled eggs, and two slices of bread. I can also smell the coffee brewing from the countertop.

Hmm. Tempting

I looked around for a food container and found them in the cupboard. I grabbed one, made myself a sandwich, put it inside the container, sealed it, and then put it inside my bag. I glanced at the Nespresso machine and contemplated whether I should pour myself a cup of coffee or not

But then I decided against it. If I did that, I would have to wait for the coffee to cool down. I can also put ice on it but I still have to spend awkward minutes with Ashton at the dining table.

Nah, I can't do that. However...

It looks like Ashton's cup of coffee has been sitting on his cup for a while. It's not just Americano. He put something else on it. I tilted my head.

From what I remember, Ashton had always preferred black coffee. I shoved him aside and studied his coffee closer.

Ashton cleared his throat. He nodded at me as if he was asking what.

Unknowingly, my lips stretched into a playful smile.

Ashton looked down at his coffee as if he understood my thoughts. He grabbed the handle before I did but I slapped his hand and took the mug from him. I took the lid closer to my mouth. The rich vanilla scent wafted in my nose.

Ah! Caramel macchiato.

I took a sip from it. His coffee is too sweet, and the taste of caramel lingers on my lips.

Ashton likes his coffee sweet? This is more like a coffee I would make for myself.

I heard Ashton call my name, but I did not pay him any attention. I walked back to the cupboard, still holding the mug. I reached out for the tumbler that I saw earlier. I moved back to the table and put the coffee down. I opened the tumbler's lid and smelled it. It was then that I saw Ashton trying to snatch his coffee back.

"Uh-uh. Mine." I slapped Ashton's hand.

Ashton shrugged his shoulders, smiled, and answered. "Yours."

Then he pulled out a chair to sit on. "That's clean. Why do you need that?"

I ignored him. Instead, I went to the fridge, filled the tumbler with some ice, returned to the dining table, and poured the coffee in. I took another sip. Already satisfied with it, I closed the lid tightly.

"Problem solved. Enjoy your breakfast. Ta-ta!" Ashton dropped his jaw. I heard him chuckle as I zipped my bag and turned away, carrying the tumbler in my other hand.

"Unbelievable!" I heard him say.

When I turned to look, I saw him laughing and running his hand through his hair. I sprinted and made my way through the door.

ASHTON'S POV

I knew Natasha would refuse to have breakfast with me. I won't let her outsmart me. I already know her daily schedule. Her parents have also left me with a to-do list which I didn't pay much attention to. I even teased them because they made it seem like I was babysitting a toddler.

However, I did pay attention to what Natasha likes to eat and drink. Julia said Natasha rarely eats breakfast at home. She prefers to carry them to school and have them with her friends.

But I know too that she will not voluntarily take the breakfast with her even if I put it in a container. I need to trick her into taking it.

I looked around my dining area and thought about where I could strategically place the containers without them being too obvious. The top left of the cupboard is just a step away from the dining table. I placed the container and the tumbler there.

The rest is easy. I know she can't refuse bacon and coffee. I learned from Julia about the coffee flavor that Natasha wants. I even prepared the same brand. I laughed at how she acted the way I thought she would.

Satisfied with what I did, I took another mug, poured espresso shots and hot water into it, took a sip, and enjoyed the rich taste of black coffee. I absent-mindedly smiled at the proud look on Natasha's face when she darted into the hallway.

WHO IS ASHTON GREENE?

Once I reached the university, I headed to my college cafeteria and searched for my friends. I saw them waving at me at one of the tables.

I sat beside Timothy Clarkson, a campus heartthrob, though I don't exactly see why. Tim has rare green eyes that suit his reddish-brown hair. Though cut short, his hair has bangs that cover parts of his forehead. Tim is muscular but only stands 5'9", shorter than what I would call a hunk. On him is a plain blue tee over his denim pants that runs above the length of his ankle. He partnered it with a pair of black slip-on loafers.

For comparison, Ashton is 6'3" and dresses more handsomely and neatly than Tim.

Memories from earlier flooded my thoughts. I shut my eyes tightly and hushed my brain.

"So, spill!" Vea giggled.

"Did you two share a bed?" Camille asked with a playful smile on her lips.

I gasped and threw a crumpled table napkin at my friends. I have known Vea Montgomery and Camille Vasquez since we were in middle school.

Vea stood at 5'3". She held her copper brown hair that ran to her shoulders into a loose bun, some of it fell on the sides of her small, round face. She has thick lashes and winged liners that accentuate her big, honey-brown eyes, small and high-bridged nose, and thin lips that sometimes show her upper canines. Coupled with fair skin that is almost pale, Tim nicknamed her the vampire chick or the vamp.

Her family owns the Montgomery General Hospital. Everyone in her family expected her to pursue medicine, like her parents, both surgeons. To her family's dismay, she took Creative Arts. Growing up, Vea has always been the creative one. But to us, Vea's career choice wasn't a surprise.

Vea used to give us personalized greeting cards for our birthdays and other occasions. When we were 13, Vea gifted me with a charcoal portrait drawing of myself, and it still hangs on my bedroom wall.

I noticed she had one of her denim jumper pants over a white shirt. Vea has lots of them and wears them even if some have paint stains. On her wrists are layers of black and brown leather bracelets.

My eyes followed Vea's hands as she handed Camille a clean sheet of table napkin to wipe off the mayo that spilled in the corner of her mouth.

Camille Vasquez is a 5'5" Mexican-American whose family runs a small law firm. Her father also works as a Legal Consultant for my family's furniture business. Though she never told us directly, Camille wanted to follow in her father's footsteps. She said before that she took the Business Administration course to become a business lawyer later.

Camille tied her naturally black and curly hair in a half pony. She has a square jaw face, dark, bushy brows, and black, round eyes surrounded by thick, curly lashes. Camille got a small, but round nose with a bulbous tip and naturally full lips.

Camille smacked her lips and said, "Hey, you, chica. Are you gonna tell us anything, or are you just gonna stare at my lips?"

"Please! Can we just eat? I have nothing to spill!" I pulled the food container from my bag and put it on the table. Vea threw me a doubting look.

"Wow! Looks like the dashing Mr. Greene does not want our girl to starve."

I rolled my eyes. Tim glanced at us as if he was watching a tennis match. By the confused look on his face, I knew he was having difficulty trying to figure out what was going on.

"Okay. So your parents left for abroad and will be gone for at least half of the year." He said facing me. "Then they left you under the care of Mr. Greene, who you said is a family friend?"

I nodded my head.

"I'm sorry. But how old is Mr. Greene again? And why are they teasing you about him? Do you guys have a history or something?"

Unlike Vea and Camille, who were my friends since the third grade, I met Tim at the university. He was my classmate in one of the subjects during our freshman year. We became close when we worked on a project together. I introduced Tim to Vea and Camille later on, and surprisingly, his personality also clicked with them. Tim is a varsity athlete and only hangs out with us whenever he's not busy with training.

Whenever Tim hangs out with us, we always do random things together. We play video games or go out to see the latest movies. All of us like Marvel movies. And whenever a new one comes out, we know we all have to schedule it and go. Tim also does some exercise with us like jogging, going to the gym, or trekking. Sometimes, he also invites us out of town with a couple of his other friends.

But we seldom talk about the past or any previous relationships around him. We don't discuss girly stuff or anything that Tim would find boring. That's like one of the unspoken rules of our friendship. If we ever have to mention it we talk about it in passing. So it's natural for Tim to be clueless about Ashton Greene. After all, Ashton was supposed to be a thing of the past.

"Ashton was his first love." Camille interrupted my thoughts.

"Wow! So you're not a lesbian, after all!" Tim exclaimed.

I hit him in his arms.

"Really, Tim? You thought I was a lesbian? Well, not that I have a problem with them or with any members of the LGBT.

But really?!" I slapped his arms after every sentence that I finished.

"You know I was kidding. But then, hey! Look at you!" he gestured toward me, trying to emphasize how I looked.

I do not have classes that require me to be in business attire today. So this morning, I chose to wear a dark gray tee, faded jeans, and a pair of high-cut sneakers. I let my hair down as it was still wet from the shower earlier. Now I am sure that my hair is everywhere. I grabbed the pony on my wrist, combed my hair with my hand, and tied it in a messy bun.

"Why don't you just say I am not as attractive?" I moved my hand from Vea to Camille to stress that I didn't look cute like my friends.

Tim snorted, "You know that's not what I mean." He took a bite from my plate. "Is it just me or are you just being too sensitive?" He nodded with his brows and then nudged my arm.

Vea and Camille continued chatting about 'the great' Ashton Greene while I decided to finish my meal. I allowed the girls to tell Tim about my embarrassing love confession to Ashton Greene. I cut them to react until my thoughts drifted back to that day, five years ago.

REVISITING THE PAST

IVE YEARS AGO

My mind drifted back to the events from five years ago.
He was 26 and I was 16.

Ashton Greene is just twelve years younger than my parents. His family has been friends with mine even before I was born. My earliest memory of Ashton was when I was about three or four.

Ashton lives across the country and only comes to stay with us every once in a while. We sometimes spend our family vacation in his home too. Every time he comes, he always has a gift for me. On the tag, he always writes, "For baby Tasha."

We used to be close until I turned 16. That's when things suddenly become awkward between us. I remember that afternoon when I came home from school. No one told me that Ashton was coming that day to stay a few days with us.

As I reached the living room, I saw him sitting on the sofa, with a guitar. He looked rugged in his gray cotton shirt and torn pants. I loved how he tied his long, wavy hair in a man bun. His husky voice filled the room as he sang to *Stolen* by *Dashboard Confessional*. I noticed how he slightly tilted his head to the side, as his fingers strummed the strings. Right then, the moment touched an emotion I could not fathom.

I got a little startled when I realized he already felt my presence. My gaze met his blue eyes.

"Ah, finally. My baby arrives."

I felt blood rush to my cheeks.

Why does the word 'baby' suddenly feel different?

"What now, huh? I can't call you my baby now?" He teased me by nudging his elbow to my side. Then he pulled me in for a playful hug. I can't tell if I was relieved or sad when he finally let me go. My heart started to thump crazily against my chest.

Then he handed me the guitar. Sweat started to form in my hands as I felt uneasy and hesitant. But I took the guitar from his hand anyway. He led me to sit on the sofa before he sat next to me. I felt his left hand brushing against my shoulder as he positioned my fingers on the fingerboard. Then he grabbed my other hand and taught me how to strum.

I did not understand a single word he said. All I could think of was his masculine scent that wafted on my nose. I felt dizzy as the whirlwind of emotions ran through me. Confused, I got up abruptly. I excused myself and went straight to my room.

I heard Ashton calling out to me, but I was too embarrassed to come back. I knew something was happening to me, but I did not understand it. Or maybe I do understand, but I do not want to accept it.

I decided to just lay in my bed and stay in my room. I can still hear Ashton strumming on his guitar and singing random songs.

What is this? Is he having a concert or something?

Ashton sings so well, that it feels like I am being transported somewhere. When he started to play another song, I decided to climb out of bed and focus on something else. I walked to my study table. I turned on the computer and thought about sending a message to my friends in our group chat. But my mind just went blank.

What am I going to tell them?

I have been staring at my screen but do not know where to start. In the living room, Ashton is now singing another song. I leaned my back on the chair and closed my eyes. My thoughts brought me to a few months back almost automatically.

I think it all started on my 16th birthday, just months ago. The party was close to over and I haven't seen Ashton. I was confused when the light dimmed and the DJ played a mellow song.

Then from the crowd, a semi-disheveled Ashton came out. He got a stem of a red rose between his teeth as he was still buttoning the pale blue shirt that he left tucked out of his jeans.

"Sorry, I am late." He extended his right hand toward me and handed me the rose.

He pulled me up from my seat as I laid my hand on his. Then he pulled me close to him, letting his hand rest on my waist. The beat of the music wasn't exactly slow. It's like the DJ is playing a remix version or something. Ashton kept on twirling me around and then pulling me in. The steps felt almost awkward. But he laughed. I giggled. Happiness filled us.

At one point, I looked up at him. I noticed the small strip of plaster on his chin. My hand automatically touched it.

"It's uneven, I know," Ashton murmured against my cheeks.

"What?" I moved my face away so I could read his lips.

"I hadn't shaved for weeks. I did it quickly before I went here." Ashton ran his hand to his chin and then he smiled sheepishly. "I don't want to look too old for this dance.

Ashton is right. He looks only about four years older than me without his beard. I nodded. Ashton kept cracking jokes as we danced and I kept smiling and laughing at them. When the song was about to end, he whispered something in my ear. And Ashton said it at about the same time the DJ switched the music to something louder and more upbeat. I am uncertain if I heard him right, but it's about keeping someone waiting.

Whatever he said bugged me since that night. And I regretted it so much that I got too shy to clarify what he said.

Did he say sorry if he kept me waiting? No. I'm sure he meant he was the one waiting.

Maybe it was the romantic ambiance, the music, or his endless laughter ringing in my head. It was a strange feeling when he held me in his arms. Maybe it was all of those things.

The memory lingers. Since that night, I have been thinking about what he could have said. Unconsciously, I have been assuming and daydreaming about him confessing to me. And whenever I think I could be wrong and realize it's inappropriate, I dismiss the thoughts.

Ashton did not stay that night as he used to. I guess that added to my confusion. It was like he was the last to arrive at the party but also the first to leave. To make things more bizarre, his texts become less frequent too. The more I wanted to reach out to him, the more he built an imaginary barrier between us.

And then without saying anything, he is here in our house. He is in the living room, dashing, strumming his guitar, and playing the songs I love.

Is it just me? Was I overthinking?

A scream from downstairs brought me back to the present. The voice sounded like some teenager gushing over a K-pop idol.

Who was that?

I pushed my chair towards the door to listen, but the wheels stuck in something. The force made me fall forward to my knees.

"Ouch!"

"Hey, honey? Are you okay?" I heard my mom coming from the stairs. Soon enough, she's at my door.

I crawled up and opened the door to let my mom in.

"Hi, mom! Yeah. I'm fine. Why did you ask?" I didn't realize I was bending forward and rubbing my knees.

"Well, Ashton is downstairs. Have you seen him?"

"Ah, yeah. I saw Ashton a while ago. I just had to do something so I stayed in my room.

"Are you sick? You look a little flustered." She felt my forehead.

"No, mom. I'm fine." I turned my head away.

"Are you sure?" She still looked worried.

"Yup." I stretched my lips into a forced smile.

"Okay. Dinner will be ready in a while. Come down in a bit, okay? And you might want to change clothes. We have a guest."

Ah, right. I heard a woman scream earlier.

THE SURPRISE GUEST

S TILL FIVE YEARS AGO

I opened my closet and took out a couple of dresses I had. Then I laid them down on my bed.

Gosh! It's only Ashton. What's wrong if I choose a mismatched outfit? It's not like he would make a big deal out of it.

I put the dresses back in my closet and pulled out a simple shirt and a black skirt instead. I grabbed a clean robe and headed to the bathroom adjacent to my room. I heard my parents talking to an unfamiliar female voice downstairs.

I knew it was the same woman who I heard scream earlier. Something about her made me feel uneasy. My friends asked me if I hated someone I had not even met. I laughed at them back then but I think I understand them now.

The sound of her chatter annoys me. Her laughter sounds rich and seductive, not even the sound of the shower can drown them. Though I do not want to acknowledge it without Ashton's confirmation, I think I know who the woman is. I know she came with Ashton. I turned on the shower and soaked myself in its warm drizzle, trying to wash away the bad feeling. A woman's image appeared in my head. I felt something lumping in my chest.

Why do I feel pain?

"Tasha?" my mom knocked at the bathroom door. "Dinner will be ready in about ten minutes. Make sure you're ready by then." She did not wait for me to answer. Her footsteps faded and then I heard a door open and closed.

I went down as soon as I had changed clothes. I found all of them in the living room. My dad blocked my view of the person who was seated beside Ashton. Then Ashton saw me.

"Hey, Tasha! I heard you were not feeling well?"

He came to me and attempted to put his hands on my face. I turned my face away and quickly took a step backward.

The confusion on his face made it apparent that he was taken aback by what I did. I looked down as I could not meet his gaze.

"I'm fine," I said coldly and forced a smile.

"Are you sure?" I can still sense the worry in his voice.

"Yes, sure." I forced another smile and then glanced in the direction of the woman. "So, who do we have here?"

Ashton clapped his hand once then walked back to where he was seated and offered his hand to the woman. I saw the delicately manicured hand take it. And then there she is, right in front of me.

The woman is beautiful. I'd say maybe she's exactly Ashton's type.

"Tasha, this is Bianca Mason, my girlfriend. Bianca, this is Natasha Collins. She's like a niece to me."

She held out her right hand to me, offering a handshake. I had no choice but to accept it. Her smooth hands slid slowly into mine.

"Hello, Tasha. I've been looking forward to meeting you."

I chuckled. Even her voice is sweet. Her mouth twitched to one side as she talked, which reminded me of the actress Chloe Grace Moretz.

"H—hi, Bianca." My voice cracked as her name left a bitter taste in my mouth.

I withdrew my hands and shyly kept them to my side. My gaze caught it when Bianca wrapped her arms around Ashton's body.

As if right on cue my mom called us from the dining room. Dinner is ready. I let all of them walk to the dining room first, and I slowly followed. I watched from the back how Ashton treated Bianca as if she were going to break time.

Seriously?

I let out a loud sigh, enough to make them both look my way. I raised my brows and whispered," What did I do?"

Ashton halted. I felt like he would be approaching me, but Bianca stroked his arm with her hands, tagging him away.

I rolled my eyes. I wondered which part caused a sting in my heart: the fact that Ashton was already taken or how he referred to me as his niece.

Why? What's wrong with it? I have always treated him like a family too. Why can't I stop feeling weird?

I winced at the thought. I have not paid attention to it before. I did not care if Ashton looked at me that way.

Though not blood-related, we have always treated him as part of the family. Besides, he is twelve years older, which makes him qualified old enough to be my uncle.

I knew he regularly went out on dates before too. I shrugged at the thought. Though I have never met any of them in person, I have had a nice chat with a few of them online. I pushed the negative thoughts aside.

Maybe I felt odd because Ashton had not introduced any of his past girlfriends to us in person before. I made myself believe that it was the only reason why I felt differently towards Bianca.

Despite the inner prep talk, I still couldn't wait for dinner to be over. I hated how sweet Ashton and Bianca were to each other. I hated that she was also staying with us and was sharing a room with Ashton. And it is so infuriating because I don't even understand myself. The smug look on her face as if she had already marked Ashton as her property disgusts me.

Owned. Possessed. Won.

Stop being so immature, Natasha. I keep on reminding myself. Ashton is 28. At 16, I knew he had probably dated and slept with a lot of women before. But knowing who he was sleeping with at this very moment agitated me. And it's not even my business, to begin with

During dinner, they decided to go to the beach on the coming weekend.

"Uhm. I can't come. I'm sorry." I said without looking up. I kept twisting the fork, just watching the pasta swirl with it.

"Natasha!"

Mom's voice startled me and I slightly dropped the fork on my plate. She threw me a warning look and then pointed at my plate. She might have noticed how I have been playing with my food. I twisted my fork again and reluctantly put some spaghetti strands in my mouth.

I momentarily closed my eyes and forced myself to chew and swallow the dish. When I opened my eyes, I caught Bianca staring at me. I don't know if it is the guilt, but I thought I sensed the suspicions coming from her.

"Why, honey?" My dad's brows furrowed as he waited for me to answer.

"Why what?" I looked around and realized that they were all looking at me.

My dad swallowed. And then he twisted the fork in the air and continued, "This weekend."

"Ah, that. I..Uhm... I am hanging out with my friends." I lifted my hand and scratched my head.

"Then why don't you ask your friends to come?" My mom asked.

I rolled my eyes in frustration.

"Mom, can I just not go?"

Ashton cleared his throat. I knew he would be asking something, so I quickly excused myself and returned to my room. When my mom asked, I told her I needed to attend a group study conference. I sighed when she did not ask anything further.

Once inside my room, I looked at myself in the mirror and hated what I saw.

I am tall and skinny. I do not have any curves. Not to mention that Ashton is 26, and I am only 16.

Wait, what? OMG! Do I like him? This is not right!

NATASHA'S CONFESSION

STILL FROM FIVE YEARS AGO

The week went by quickly. It's now Saturday, and my Mom had it her way like she usually does. She had made me and my friends tag along on the family outing.

Luckily, I almost did not see Ashton or Bianca for the past few days as I was busy with school. While at home, I decided to stay in my room most of the time.

The two of them are also always out. They come back at past midnight and are still sleeping in the morning when it's time for me to leave for school.

My parents thought I was going through some hormonal changes, thus the mood swings. For the most part, I think it could be that too.

However, I find it ironic that they notice my mood swings when Ashton also seems to be undergoing a phase. I understand that he and Bianca are on a vacation together. But he's acting rather strange and irresponsible for his age.

I remembered that steamy scene I witnessed in the living room two days ago. Nobody was home when I went home from school, so I went straight to my room. But when I decided to come down and get some snacks, I saw them making out in the living room.

I almost missed some steps because I felt mortified. They were too busy and into the moment that they did not even notice I came and left.

I shook my head to push the thoughts away, but the sight kept popping into my memory. I climbed to my bed and buried my face in the pillow. I heard my phone beep. My hands searched the phone among the other things I scattered around me.

Vea: Hey, girl! Cams and I are together. We'll be there in a few.

Me: Okay, great! See you in a few.

I realized that having my friends around would be a good thing too. I know they can make things feel a little less awkward. I gathered some of my belongings in a small sling bag that hung across my shoulder.

"Honey, are you done packing your things? Do you need some help?"

I heard her luggage making a screeching sound as she pulled them. She's done packing

"No, mom. I am fine. I am almost done. I will come out in a few minutes."

I checked myself in the mirror for the last time. Then I grabbed my things and walked out of my room. I wore a simple summer dress and was feeling fine.

Well, until I saw how stunning Bianca was in her dress, hugging her curves.

Don't be ridiculous. Do you have to be the first to pull yourself down, Natasha?

I counted the minutes until both of my friends appeared on our driveway.

Dad drove the van while my mom took the passenger seat beside him. The girls and I sat in the second row while Bianca and Ashton chose to be seated at the back.

It took us about two hours to reach the beach, and Bianca started giggling in the first ten minutes.

The trip felt uncomfortable. I even caught my parents exchanging worried glances and clearing their throats.

Camille pulled out the tablet and a pair of wireless earphones from her bag and shared a piece with me. Vea did the same and connected her earphones via Bluetooth to the tablet. We spent the long drive watching some series until we finally reached the beach.

My friends and I changed into our bathing suits as soon as we checked in. Then, as usual, my insecurities kicked in when I saw how Bianca looked incredibly hot in her swimsuit. She looked so hot that Ashton could not even take his eyes off her.

I shook the negative thoughts away. I took a deep breath and exhaled slowly.

All bodies, regardless of shape and size, are beautiful. I am beautiful.

But the sight of both of them killed my mood. Somehow, guilt overtook me because Vea and Camille had never left my side. And as much as I wanted to keep their company, I wanted them to enjoy the place too.

So, sometime in the afternoon, I assured them that it was okay for them to have fun and excused myself as I would like to take a short nap.

I saw Ashton on my way back to the room. I turned around to go back to the beach when I noticed we were heading in the same direction. I knew he called my name but pretended I did not hear him. I quickened my footsteps, but he caught my arm. He tugged so that I could face him.

"Hey, can we talk?" His shoulders moved up and down as he tried to catch his breath. "Do we have a problem or anything? I hope it was just me, but are you mad at me?"

I turned my head towards the sea. "I am not mad at you." My voice trailed off when I added, "You are just busy with her."

I saw the corner of his mouth twitch when I glanced at him.

Ah! That smile would be the death of me.

I kicked my feet on the sand too hard and threw some on Ashton's feet. I heard him chuckle.

"Are you jealous?" He wagged his foot one after the other to dust off the sands.

"What?" My eyes widened as I shushed him. I looked back to where my parents and friends were. "No!" I thought about covering his mouth with my hands but decided against it.

He smiled, gave me a side glance, and then looked up. I noticed how his shoulders moved. His laughter echoed and caught the attention of some passersby.

"No way! You're being ridiculous! Why would I be jealous?" I turned my back on him and headed to the villa.

I heard Ashton's footsteps as he ran after me. I hurried to the door, but Ashton blocked it quickly with his body.

I tried to push him out of the door. "Just please, Ashton. Get out."

He pushed his way back in.

"Oh, I get it. Are you now on your.. you know? Those red days?"

I felt my cheeks blush.

"OMG, No! Just, Ashton. Please?"

Ashton is stronger than me, it was no use pushing him away. I decided to walk in and sit on the bed, frustrated. He bent down, his face a few inches away from mine. His eyes are probing, questioning.

"Hey, Tasha. What's wrong?"

I felt like I was drowning in his eyes. My gaze started to wander from his eyes to his pointed nose. Before I knew it, I was already staring at his red lips. I thought about how soft they would be and how sweet they would taste. I seemed to be hypnotized. The next thing I knew, I was reaching out to kiss his lips.

Ashton quickly turned his way ahead even before our lips touched.

"What the—!!! We can't do that. Why did you—?"

He ran his hands through his hair, confused. I thought I also sensed a trace of disgust in his voice. I stared at the floor, blushing from embarrassment.

Why in the hell did I do that?

"Huh! I know what you're doing. You are deliberately trying to push me away." I heard the frustration in his voice. "You know I would if you did that, don't you? You can't trick me."

"What if that's not the case, Ashton? What if I am starting to like you?" I mustered the courage to ask.

I don't know if he truly understood, but he nodded. He leaned forward to tap my head as he always does, but then he stopped his hand midway.

"If that's true, that feeling will pass." He said in an almost hushed voice.

I doubted if he believed me. I felt ignored. The moment was so embarrassing I could not even look at him.

"I'm not sure what your deal is, maybe you are just pranking me. Whatever! But we?" He gestured his hands back and forth between us, then continued, " We cannot happen."

He let out a sigh. "Look, I gotta go before someone else sees us and gets a wrong impression."

"Do what you want. I don't care." I told him in a flat tone. I thought pain registered in his eyes.

Was I too much?

An awkward silence followed before Ashton decided to take his leave. I remained seated on the bed, not knowing what to do next. Then, I heard footsteps approaching my door. It was Bianca.

"I know you're not kidding. I know you like him" Bianca said, half-smiling. She was about to leave when she turned around. "You're still young. Don't go stealing someone else's man. Look for someone who suits you better."

The side of her mouth twitched as she eyed me from head to toe.

Bitch!

She went on her way before I could even say anything. As much as I hated to admit it, I took her words seriously. She taught me to hate myself. She made me believe that I am not worthy.

That was also the last time that I talked to Ashton. Whenever he came over, I spent days somewhere.

A few months later, I heard Ashton got engaged to Bianca. Then, they eventually married each other.

My parents attended their wedding. I didn't. I intentionally scheduled an out-of-town trip with my friends on those dates. It was ironic. What was supposed to be the most liberating three days of my life turned out to be the most painful.

Then four years into marriage, they got a divorce. Mom said Ashton caught Bianca cheating on him. I did not care. I even thought he deserved it. I know, I still sound bitter about it. But what does he expect? He went for her looks above all else.

Ah, I hated how all my insecurities came back with just a thought of them.

My parents said he bought a property near our home right after the divorce. But he hardly stays there. It means Ashton has been close to where I am for the last two years. But, in all those years, I have not seen or heard anything from him. And I am not a bit concerned.

GET HER TRUST BACK

BACK TO THE PRESENT

It's been weeks since I moved to Ashton's house. I have not seen him that much as I always find a way to not spend time with him. I assumed he knew it too. Ashton has also stopped bothering me to have breakfast with him every morning. But he asked me to take the boxed meal and the coffee that he prepares every day. I'm cool with it. As long as they're ready at the kitchen counter, we will not have any interaction. Whenever he wants to talk to me, I'll say, "thesis", and he will be gone.

At dinner, it's either I eat out with my friends, have dinner at their place, or get home earlier than Ashton and have my dinner ahead of him. Then, I'll lock myself in my room because you know, "thesis".

Before all this, I was too lazy to work on my studies. I guess I should be thankful that since I moved here, I've done so much on it. I know Prof. Jackson, my thesis adviser, would agree.

For the past weeks, I have proven that weekends are the most difficult days to avoid Ashton. He almost always stays at home the whole day.

Tomorrow is Saturday again, and I'm dreading how I am going to spend it without needing to see and talk to him.

What bothers me more is the box meal. I was in a hurry this morning when I remembered about the box meal on my way to the university. Ashton has been calling me on the phone all day and that's the only reason I can think of. He usually sends texts, even if he has to say something important, and I'll leave them seen. The box meal that I forgot to take is the only reason I can think of why he kept bugging me all day.

Ah! Did I offend him? Has he gotten too sensitive because he's older? Ah, why did I forget to take the boxed meal this morning?

He's making me anxious.

I thought about spending the day at the university library or some cafe when I heard a knock on my door. I did not answer. I should have let him believe that I was already sleeping.

"Tasha, I know you're still awake." He paused. "I can see the light from your TV. I won't force you to come and talk now. But ba—I mean Tasha, you can't run away from me forever. Tomorrow, we need to talk."

Crap!

ASHTON'S POV

I know she's still awake, but it's obvious she does not want to talk. So I headed back to my room, took a shower, and prepared to sleep.

It's been five years since that "accidental kiss". Sometimes I cannot help but feel sad at the memory. Tasha had an infatuation with me, and that made her slowly drift away. Sometimes I think maybe that was for the best, but then I hope that she does not have to do that.

She's been blocking me on her social media accounts for the last five years. And while I was itching to send her another request, I knew she would not accept it. So I just contented myself with the photos that Jeremy and Julia sent to me or those they posted on their social media accounts.

The first time I saw her in person weeks ago, I honestly could not believe how much she's grown. She's more beautiful personally than in those photos. She has changed a lot. The sweet teenage girl I used to know, the one whose face lit up when I was close, is gone. For all the time that she was here, Natasha always avoided me. She doesn't even want to see me in the hallway.

And I find it amusing how even though we live together now, I still have to check on social media to know what's happening to her. I honestly thought getting things back to how they used to would be easier if I kept her here with me. I was wrong. Everything feels the same. While I am here to be her guardian, I don't think I am doing the part.

I snorted as I remembered what happened two days ago. I got home unusually late from work one night. After I showered, I decided to hang out by the pool. I guessed it was already past midnight so I did not bother to switch on the lights and just sat on one of the benches, barely illuminated by the lights coming from the porch.

As soon as I sat down, I saw Natasha coming from the kitchen, tiptoeing her way to the poolside. She scanned the surroundings. I froze when she looked in my direction and quietly breathed out a sigh of relief when she did not notice me. I watched her sit down at the poolside, her legs were dangling, and playing in the waters.

I contemplated approaching Natasha but decided to observe her from afar. Her face displayed boredom and irritation. She muttered something to herself but I couldn't hear it. Whatever she said, it might have caused her frustration and anger because she clenched her fists into a tight ball, grunted, and then kicked the water with her right foot. I smiled to myself seeing how she still has a childish side to her.

Ah, she looks cute.

It was at that moment that my phone chimed. Because the surroundings were quiet, the sound seemed to be louder than usual. And it got the both of us startled. I searched in my pocket to turn the alarm off as I watched Natasha hurriedly get up from the side of the pool. She almost tripped when she bent down to gather her slippers.

"Be careful!" I couldn't stop myself from telling her.

Natasha took a short pause and searched for me. I realized she had not seen me when she focused her sight on a place far from where I was before she continued running toward the kitchen. I laughed at that recent memory.

The notification sound from my phone pulled me out of my thoughts. I planned to ignore it, but then it chimed again. I thought it was from Natasha's parents, so I went to check the message. I had to re-read to make sure that I was reading the names right.

They were friend requests from her friends. I smiled. I felt a glimpse of hope. For the past week, I have been trying everything I could to close the gap between us. I want to know anything. Anything at all to make her trust me. Anything to make her talk to me like she used to.

And as much as I hated the feeling, I accepted their requests and quickly browsed her friends' photos. In one of the pictures, I saw Tasha with a guy I had not met. I remember Jeremy told me before that they suspect Tasha has a boyfriend. But she does not want to open up to them. He said the guy seemed nice, so they didn't bother to bug their daughter about him.

I continued browsing the photos. He was hugging Tasha in one of the photos while she was all smiling. In the next one, the guy planted a kiss on her cheek. Natasha was wincing in the photos, but it did not seem like she hated it. In the third photo, both of them are facing each other, their lips are only inches apart.

I don't like what I am seeing. I felt like I needed to punch the guy's face. I felt the urge to protect Natasha. I brushed off any negative thoughts I had in my head and reminded myself how I needed to get close to her friends to get to her.

Right. That should be the plan. And I am pinning all my hopes on it that it would work.

NATASHA'S POV

When Ashton was gone, I continued watching shows on Netflix. A little later, my phone beeped. It was the group chat inbox with my friends.

Camille: Girl, he's not dating anyone!

Vea: We sent him an invite, and he accepted us.

Tim: Sometimes, I wonder why I am even a part of this group chat.

Me: Who exactly are we talking about?

Camille: Your man!

Me: What? Who is my man?

Tim: Why are you talking about me when I am here?

Me: Haha! That is funny, Tim! We both know you are not my man. I believe we have that settled a long time ago.

Tim: Things could change, you know.

Me: No, Tim! Never!

Vea: Seriously, he's hot!

Tim: Wait, who's hot? You are all talking about me, right?

Camille: She's not talking about you, idiot! Though I guess you and Vea have something to talk about in private. Haha.

Tim: I'm sorry I don't follow. I'm out of this group chat. Vea, I'll send you a PM.

Me: Hey, Camille. I think we're alone in this group chat now. So tell me. Who is this hot guy you were talking about?

Camille: ASHTON!

Vea: ASHTON

Tim: Hey, Vea! Answer my PM, now!

Me: Oh! Is he hot? I don't know. I'm not sure. And Vea, stop avoiding Tim. Talk to him now.

Vea: Stop making this about me.

Me: Whatever!

I put my phone in silent mode and placed it on my bedside table. I switched the TV off, then I tucked myself to sleep.

A DAY WITH NATASHA

I have been awake since seven. But I don't want to get out and risk bumping into Ashton. So I decided to stay in my room and work on my thesis. At nine, my stomach began to rumble. What made it worse was the smell coming from the kitchen. I suddenly got excited when I heard Ashton start his motorcycle and drive out of the driveway.

Is Ashton going somewhere? But wasn't he preparing breakfast? Where is he going on his motorcycle? I wonder how long it will take him to return.

At that instant, I decided to dash out of my room and went straight to the kitchen. I can still smell the food Ashton cooked sitting at the counter under the dish cover. I wondered if anyone was coming over because Ashton prepared for more than two people. I assumed it was meant for the driver and the cook.

I hesitated, but the hunger I felt got the better of me. I reached for a plate and got one sandwich. I took a huge bite and savored the taste in my mouth. I laughed at myself when I realized I was acting like a burglar in someone else's home.

I finished making myself coffee when I heard Ashton's motorcycle engine. He must have come back with a car tagging along because I heard it parked outside.

Why is he back so fast? Are these sandwiches for his guests?

I tried finishing the rest of my sandwich in one bite and then grabbed the mug. I was in such a hurry that the coffee mug fell on the floor.

Shit!

I started to panic when I heard voices getting closer to the door. I also realized I did not know where Ashton kept his cleaning tools. Just as the door opened, I grabbed some paper towels and bent down to clean the mess I made on the floor. It was at that moment Ashton entered the kitchen. He probably did not notice me because I was bent down behind the counter. Ashton jumped as soon as he saw me.

"AHH!"

It startled me too when the two women standing next to Ashton screamed right after he did. The situation was too funny, so I tried hard to control my laughter. I continued reaching for and picking out the broken pieces from the floor to divert my attention. Then I looked up.

"Ah!" I realized I cut my index finger, but I was too surprised to react to the pain when I realized who the women were.

Camille? Vea?

"OMG, girl! You scared us!" Vea said in her usual cheerful voice. "What are you doing on the floor?"

"I—uhm—" I winced.

Ashton quickly realized what occurred. He took my hand and pulled me to the sink. Then he turned on the faucet and ran some water on it.

"I- it's—I'm fine." I took my hand from his grasp. Ashton got some paper towels before I did. I knew my friends were watching us, so it felt awkward when he took my hand to dry it. Not to mention he is standing too close to me.

"Why are you girls here?" I turned to my friends. They eyed each other and gave me a teasing smile.

"I invited them over." He pressed on my finger. Then he asked, "The cut is small. Do you need plasters for that?"

"No, thanks. This will do." I meant the paper towel that he wrapped around my finger. I pressed it against my finger to stop it from bleeding.

Ashton excused himself. He carried the mop, a small dustpan, and a broom when he returned.

The situation left me embarrassed. I offered to help but Ashton refused. He told me to bring the food to the table so that we could eat.

Camille volunteered to take it. But before she did, she took the dish cover off. I bit my lower lip and turned my head slowly toward Ashton.

He chuckled and said, "Ah. So you were hungry then rushed here to eat as soon as you heard me leave?"

I shook my head slowly. Vea took some steps toward me and inched her face closer. Then she pointed at the corners of my mouth. Guilty, I immediately took the paper towel and used the corners to wipe my lips.

Ashton laughed. "Silly. You dropped the coffee mug because you wanted to hide quickly in your room when I returned."

"Who's hiding? Me?" I took the plate of sandwiches from Camille and exited the dining room.

"Come on. Let's have breakfast together."

"Where is your phone, by the way?" Camille asked. She pulled out a chair and got her sandwich.

I remembered where our chat left off last night and almost knew the topic they would choose. I put the chatroom on mute when I saw the notifications this morning and have not seen a single message.

"How about Tim? Is he coming over too?"

Ashton cleared his throat. He must have caught the conversation because his brows furrowed. He scratched his head and said, "You can have your female friends come over. They can even spend the night if they want." Then he crossed his arms. "As for your boyfriend, that would be a NO.

He turned around even before I could say anything. He reached for another mug from the cupboard. Then he asked, "Do you want another coffee?"

I can't decide whether to clarify his wrong assumptions about Tim or to tell him I want another coffee.

"Is he jealous?" Vea whispered to me. "Should I put a claim on Tim now?"

"What? No!" Then I realized what she just said. I raised my voice when asked, "Put a claim on who? Timmy?"

The doorbell rang before Vea could give me an answer. I looked at Ashton to see if he was expecting anyone.

"I'll get it," Vea got up from her seat and disappeared.

"Hey, Ashton. I want to ask something," it was Camille. "The no-boyfriend-allowed thing. Does that also apply to Vea and me?"

"Hello, everyone! Good morning!" Tim's voice echoed from the living room

Ashton put down the coffee mug in front of me. It made a thug sound against the table. I looked up at him and noticed that he was tight-lipped.

"I—I didn't—" I waved my hands in front of me in denial.

Vea appeared in the dining area, holding hands with Tim.

"I hope you don't mind if I invited MY boyfriend over." The emphasis did not escape my ear.

I spoke even before Ashton made a response. "Wait, what? YOUR boyfriend? Did I hear you right?" I can hear the surprise in my voice.

Ashton looked at me intently. Then he threw an angry look at Tim. I felt like he was ready to punch him anytime.

Tim approached me and put his arm on my shoulder. "Yes, hon." He took a sip from my coffee and then said. "I like how you acted surprised when it was you who told me she got a zing for me."

Tim knew a long time ago. But I just slipped when I told him that. I turned to both Vea and Camille and they both kept a straight face. I still feigned innocence anyway.

"I don't know what you're talking about." I laughed nervously, turned to Vea, and shook my head.

"Oh, shut up! You, rat!" Vea laughed. I could tell she knew the truth.

"Excuse me, uh, Tim, right?"

Vea slapped Tim on his arm.

"Oh, sir! I'm sorry. Yes, Timothy Clarkson. I am Natasha's friend."

I laughed when I noticed Ashton raised an eyebrow when Tim called him sir. He shook Tim's hand and then he told Tim. "Please go ahead and feel free to make your coffee".

I sensed the sarcasm in his words. Tim understood so he got up and said, "Sorry, Tash. I'll make you a new one."

Me and my friends continued our chatter in front of the bemused Ashton.

I nodded. "So are you guys together? No way!" I turned to Camille. "What do you know about this?"

"She told me on our way here."

"Ah! I hate you!" I told Vea.

"What? Finally realized what you're losing, huh?" Tim said while he poured coffee on a mug. "We can try polyamory, you know? I can have you on Mondays and Tuesdays, Camille, on Wednesdays and Thursdays, then, Vea can have me from Fridays to Sundays," He laughed as he said it.

All of us screamed, "No way.", including Ashton. We all looked at him. He looked annoyed. Then he turned to Vea.

Tim sat down on the chair across from me. Then he pulled the reluctant Vea to sit on his lap.

"Ah! My eyes!" I rubbed my eyes exaggeratedly."I can't take it, you guys. Have some decency, please!"

Tim apologized. Camille scooted to another chair and offered Vea her seat.

"Is this kid your boyfriend and not Tasha's?" Ashton asked Vea.

I gave my friends an apologetic look because I thought Ashton was becoming rude.

Tim answered him. "Tasha? Well, I like her. And we used to—-Aww!" Vea elbowed Tim on his ribs.

Sometimes he can be so dense, he can't read the room.

"Used to what?" Ashton kept on probing.

"Nothing, sir! I was kidding." Tim said, rubbing his ribs. Vea gave him the "shut your mouth" look.

"Yes, Ashton. This kid is my boyfriend." Vea said to Ashton. "Excuse him, but may I ask if you allow him to stay now?"

ASHTON'S POV

I looked at Tasha beside me, then at this boy Tim. They have this connection that I envy. I also noticed he was about to say something when Vea elbowed him. Should I believe her friends? What if this was just a show so I could allow Tim to be with Tasha? And so what if that's the case? Why am I so worked up?

They all looked at me, waiting for an answer. If I say no, Tasha might get angrier at me. But if I said yes, she might wonder why the rule does not apply to her friends. That's easy. I am not these other kids' guardians.

Let's allow this Tim kid to hang around. But I will never let my guard down.

"Okay, all of you can stay, even for the night," I said with finality. "So, what are your plans?"

Tasha gave me a puzzled look. "What do you mean?"

"What? I want to join you. After all, I have nothing to do."

This is the whole point of why I invited her friends. So I can have a reason to spend the day with her.

NATASHA'S POV

My friends all got up and headed towards the living room. I volunteered to help Ashton to clean up.

"Are you sure you want to spend the rest of the day and the night hanging with us?" I asked him. He raised an eyebrow at me.

"Because, you know, we might want to go to the bar later for fun and a few drinks. While you, well... I think that maybe you're too old for those things, and you want to Netflix and chill."

I wiped the table clean. I almost jumped when I heard Ashton's voice right behind me. He seductively whispered near my ears. "Baby, if I want to Netflix and chill, I won't invite your friends over. That way, I can have you all to myself."

I felt my cheeks getting warm.

What the hell?

"Uhm, Ashton. I don't think you need any more help. I'll go ahead and see how my friends are doing."

I almost bumped into the table as I hurriedly made my way out of the kitchen. I heard him chuckle.

"Be careful."

OMG! He's driving me nuts!

NEW PLAYER: DEREK MILLER

ASHTON'S POV

Tasha is right. At 34, going out to a party on a weekend is not my thing anymore. If it's up to me, I'd rather stay home. Or I'd rather spend it on out-of-town trips or engaging in active sports, like trekking, camping, water rafting, and running. I outgrew my partying and drinking on a weekend phase when I was 28.

After lunch, her friends went out to shop for clothes. Tasha returned to her room and mentioned getting part of her thesis done, or else she couldn't have fun tonight. So as much as I wanted to bug her, I let her stay in her room. I do not want to spoil her mood and regret it later. I wanted her to trust me again. So that she can open up to me like she used to.

I thought about her relationship with that Tim kid. I wanted to have that kind of friendship with her. In times when she needed a friend like Tim, I wish Natasha would turn to me.

Or maybe I wanted more? Man! Am I getting insecure with a kid?

"We're back!" Camille's voice echoed in the living room.

Tasha came out of her room when she heard her friends were back. Had she not refused to be with them, I'd think she made her thesis an excuse to avoid talking to me. Sometime later, we all got ready to head out to the club. Unlike Tasha's female friends who chose to wear dresses, she donned a chic tomboy outfit.

Natasha wore a gray hanging sweatshirt. She paired it with black, slim jogger pants and white sneakers. She also set her hair into soft curls and let them down to her waist. I do not know what to wear so I just put on a fitting gray shirt, jeans, and sneakers.

Moments later, we are ready to leave. Her friends decided to sit at the back of the car, leaving the passenger seat to Tasha. I opened the door for her. I smelled shea butter as she docked to get in the car.

Camille requested I play upbeat music to set the mood, which I did. Natasha even turned the volume up and they sang along to it. I regretted the decision to go clubbing with them just in the first ten minutes of the ride. But it's too late for me to back out. I convinced myself the noise at the club could be louder. I would be surrounded by many times more young adults.

Thirty minutes later, we arrived at the club. We chose the couch on the corner. I scooted next to Tasha. She seemed to be uncomfortable by our sudden closeness. I moved away from her a little and acted normally.

I could feel the tension between us and was glad when Tim called me to order drinks from the bar. When we returned, I placed a drink in front of Tasha. She seemed unsure.

"She's got low alcohol tolerance," said Tim. He then replaced the drink I got her with a *pomosa*.

I felt stupid. It was also annoying that Tim knows about Tasha, and I don't. I sat beside Tasha while Tim took her to the other side. Next to him are Vea and Camille. Natasha pulled Tim's left shoulder and whispered something to him. I glanced at Vea and noticed that she wasn't even bothered. Vea caught me looking at her. She smiled.

"Trust us, you do not want to get her wasted," she said.

I nodded and just raised a glass toward her.

"Ah, no. Unless you want to see our names trending on social media." Camille chimed in.

They all laughed. And as if to answer the questions I have in my head, Vea added, "The caption would read something like this: 'A college student got wasted with her friends and stripped naked in a club' Then all four of us would be there in the video, stopping and covering her."

Natasha looked a little annoyed with her friends. "Thank you for talking like I was not here." She told them in between laughs.

Then, teasing her friends, she grabbed the drink and emptied the glass.

"Hey, easy!" I said as I got the glass from her hand.

"One shot won't hurt. It has low alcohol," Natasha said as she winked at me. "Right, Timmy? How much more of this do I need to get completely wasted?"

"We won't know unless you try," Tim answered, then they made a high five.

"No, Tasha. I don't think that would be a good idea."

"We got you. No problem." Camille teased her more.

Natasha turned to Tim and asked him to get her two more glasses of the drink.

Then she looked at me and protested, "Why are you still treating me like a kid?"

Natasha grinned at me. Then she tapped my chest. "Easy, gran." She blushed as if she was embarrassed.

Tim pats Natasha on the head. Then he got up to get her more drinks.

Ugh! This kid annoys me!

Soon enough, I got accustomed to the loud music and the chatter around me. The DJ played a new song. I almost jumped in my seat when Tasha and her friends screamed excitedly. They all got up to dance, but she hesitated. She knew I didn't dance. Not to that kind of music anyway. I sensed that she hesitated because she did not want to leave me.

"Uhm, go on guys, I'll accompany this grumpy grandpa for a while." She said as she sat back next to me. Tasha's friends decided to hit the dance floor.

I snorted and did not hide my distaste when she called me a grumpy grandpa.

Who is she calling a grandpa? I am only 33!

"So, what now? Looks like you're stuck with me." I scooted closer to her.

She didn't move away. Then, she pulled her smartphone from her bag. She took photos of the food and drinks in front of her. I don't understand why young people these days do that. Ah, right. Even people my age still do that. And I don't know why.

"Hey, baby. Do you want another drink? Something non-alcoholic?" I said in an attempt to clear out some air between us.

"Uhm.. yeah, sure." She glanced at me, then went back to her phone.

I went back to the bar and ordered her something fruity. When I returned, I saw a guy in his mid-20s talking to Natasha.

"Hi! I think I've lost my number. Can I have yours?" the guy flashed her a seductive smile.

I found the pickup line lame, but it did make her laugh.

Great! First, there was Tim. Now, this guy.

"Hahaha. I'm sorry, what did you say?" I heard her say. She looked genuinely happy.

I cleared my throat. The guy looked flustered when he looked at me.

"Oh! Hi, Sir! I'm sorry. I did not realize she was here with her... wait. I'm sorry. But are you her older brother or perhaps her uncle?"

Tasha burst out laughing before I could even say anything.

"OMG! You're as funny as you are in your videos. Hahaha."

"You watch my channel?" The guy seemed amused when Natasha kept on nodding her head.

She opened her mouth to say something, but I cut her out. "I am her date—"

"NO! Oh! Please, no. Do not listen to him. He isn't my date. He's an older friend." Natasha gritted her teeth. "My parents are sort of away and they leave me with him. He's a family friend."

She just made me lose my words.

Just then, Camille came back to the table. She went straight to the guy and said, "Hey, you look familiar. I think I've seen you somewhere,"

Natasha nodded at her as if confirming what Camille already knew. Her eyes grow wide. Then she put her hands to cover her slightly parted mouth.

"OMG! You're Derek Miller!" I noticed how even Camille couldn't hide her giggles.

Natasha hushed her. "Yes. It's Derek Miller." Then she looked around.

People turned their heads our way, some girls even took photos and whispered among themselves.

Camille blurted out. "We are fans! Especially her." She wrapped her hands around Natasha's arm." We watch your dance covers on YouTube!"

Derek looked pleased. "Really? Wow! What an honor!"

"Yey! You caught me!" Natasha began fanning her reddened face with her hands.

Natasha likes him. And he's a dancer. And with all the attention from other people around us, I can tell she's quite the celebrity.

Great!

"Wow! I'm glad you, ladies, are watching my videos. I'll take it that you dance too?" He motioned his hands toward Natasha's hip-hop outfit.

"Yeah! I mean, maybe not as good as you do. But yeah!"

From what I remember, Natasha dances pretty well. I used to watch her perform when she was a kid. I've also seen a couple of her dance videos, but I realized that I have never seen her dance in person for a long time.

"Do you know any dances? Or do you remember any of the dance covers I did?" Derek asked her as I was standing awkwardly beside them.

I excused myself and took my seat.

"Uhm... How about the Shape of You by Ed Sheeran," she quickly answered.

"Great! Do you mind if I ask you to dance with me? I am friends with the DJ. I can go and ask him to play it for us," Derek said before he turned to me.

"Sure. But can we do a quick rehearsal first?" Natasha asked.

"Of course. They have a space at the back that we could use." Then Derek turned to me and politely asked,

"Sir, may I?"

Natasha's eyes gleamed with excitement as she waited for my response. "Sure," I said, forcing a smile.

They were gone for about fifteen minutes. I was itching to follow her, but the DJ made an announcement, and the crowd went wild.

Ah! Derek is indeed an online celebrity.

The crowd has made way for the both of them. Tasha danced pretty well. The dance routine was snappy and sexy at the same time. At one point, the guy touched her waist and her thigh. Then towards the end of the routine, I held my breath as I thought they would kiss. But then, they froze midway until the dance song faded.

IF YOU WANT IT, WORK FOR IT

NATASHA'S POV
I can't believe I am dancing with Derek Miller!

I have been his follower for nearly two years now and I have been daydreaming about this moment. I never thought this could be possible. There was never a way for us to meet, let alone dance. Yet, here we are. The crowd cheered and hollered at us from the start until the dance routine ended.

"Woohoo! You go, girl!" Vea said while raising her hands in the air.

"OMG! You and Derek look good together!" Camille hugged me.

"I agree. You look so good that you made the grumpy grandpa even more grumpy." Tim said, pointing in Ashton's direction.

I glanced at Ashton. He's got a grim expression as he holds a bottle of beer.

"You're a great dancer!" Derek said. "I'll invite you sometime to do a dance cover with me on my channel."

"You would? As in seriously? For real?" I am too astonished and too happy. The hug came automatically.

"Oops! Sorry, I was just carried away." I giggled. "I hope you won't change your mind about the dance cover."

"Of course not, unless you won't give me your number?" He said smiling. He then handed me his phone.

"Of course!" I got the phone from his hand and keyed in my number.

"Hey, as much as I wanted to hang around, I still have a shoot tomorrow morning. I also wanted to get out of this club unscathed and in one piece." He gritted his teeth and nodded toward Ashton. "He has been looking at me like he's going to strangle me any moment now."

"Hahaha. You are indeed funny!" I slapped his arm.

Derek escorted me back to the couch before he returned to where his friends were. I sat beside Ashton. He moved a bit closer to me and whispered in my ear.

"I am glad you had fun."

The hair on my neck stood up as he talked close to my ears. My phone beeped. It was a text from Derek. I searched for his name on Facebook and sent him a friend request.

Ashton let out a sigh beside me. Then he got his phone from his pocket. Moments later, I received a friend request from Ashton. I ignored his request. He looked puzzled.

"Why not? I sent you friend requests for the last ten years, and you ignored them."

I don't know how to explain it. That's when Tim approached our table. He looked a little bit drunk. And from the way he smiled, I knew he heard our conversation.

"Grandpa, her social media is only for those who understand fun."

Jerk!

What he said is rude, but I understand why he said that. I even hide most of my posts from my parents. I let out a nervous laugh. Ashton nodded. He motioned for him to give us a moment to talk. Tim got his cue and left.

"Tasha, I am dying to know," he leaned his elbows on the table. Then he shifted from his seat and he looked intently at me.

"I know you're still avoiding me even when we live under the same roof. I used to think that once you get through adolescence, things will return to how they used to be " Ashton ran his hand through his hair. "Somehow, I wish they would."

My breathing became heavy. Ashton reached out for my hand and squeezed it. I felt a wave of electricity, just like when he taught me how to play the guitar five years ago. I looked into his eyes. I thought I saw something in there that was not present before.

Was it a desire? Or can it be love?

I bowed my head and freed my hands from his grasp. But he refused to let go.

"Fine. I won't ask any more questions. But can we stay like this for a while?"

He meant our hands. I am confused, but I know I don't want to let go too.

What the fuck is he doing?

Ashton slumped to the couch and rested his head on my shoulder.

"What are you doing?"

"The grumpy grandpa is sleepy. He needs a nap."

"Why do you have to hold my hand?"

"Because they're soft. Your hands made me feel calm."

He brought my hands to his nose. "And they smell so nice."

I know he is not sleeping. A little later, Derek caught my attention. I supposed he is leaving with his crew. He waved at me and mouthed "I'll call you", putting his 'Y' hand on his ear. Derek's brows were furrowed, and he pointed at Ashton as if asking "What happened to him." I nudged Ashton with my shoulder and waved back to Derek.

"What is wrong with you?" I asked. I gently tried to push his head with my other hand.

"I am sorry. But do you feel harassed?"

"No, it's nothing like that but—"

"What's up with you two?"

Ashton slid his hand across my waist. I thought about moving away, but my friends scooted to sit, pushing me closer to Ashton. Ashton chuckled. Then he leaned in to whisper in my ear.

"I love how your friends randomly do things in my favor."

Tim caught my attention before I could say anything back to Ashton.

"Hey, Tash! So did Derek ask you out?" he winked. Then he put some chips in his mouth.

Ashton let out an annoyed grunt. "Except for Tim."

I ignored Ashton. His hand left my waist.

"I... I uh... Derek said he would call."

"You like him, don't you?" asked Tim. I watched him down the content of the beer in his hand.

"Uhm... I am not sure. I think so, yes. He's fun to talk with. He seems fun to hang around with."

Ashton leaned closer to me and whispered, "I know fun too. But you wouldn't know because you don't want to give it a chance."

My lips almost touched his when I turned around to face him. But thanks to my quick reflex, I moved away as quickly.

"Stop it. It's not funny."

"Are you guys going to kiss?" Camille asked, her voice a bit slurred.

"What? No!" I pushed Ashton away. He chuckled. Then he slid his hand back to mine. I looked at him again.

"Just this, please?"

I snorted. He looked like a kid ready to throw a tantrum.

A couple of drinks later my friends are almost wasted. I saw Camille earlier on my way to the powder room.

She's making out with a random guy. Vea said the guy goes to the same university and is an acquaintance of Camille. I guessed she was not coming home with us. On the other hand, Tim and Vea are also getting a little cozy at the far end of the couch, almost across from us.

"Ugh! This is awkward," I muttered, covering my eyes.

"Are you as wild as your friends?" Ashton teased. "Do you want to join the fun?"

What's up with him? He has been teasing me since this morning.

I shook my head and told him I'd rather go home and sleep.

Ashton looked at his wristwatch. "Are you sure? It's barely midnight." Then his lips twitched. "What are you? A woman in her 40s?"

Ah, right. So he wants to prove he's not that old? But I am tired. I slept so late last night I wanted to doze off and rest. The loud music is also causing me headaches.

I looked at Ashton and wondered where he hid his car key. Then I curved my lips into a naughty smile when I realized he kept them in his left pocket.

I got up and leaned closer to Ashton. I could tell he was surprised, but then he smiled as he rested his hands on my hips. My cheeks touched Ashton's cheek. I whispered, "I remember how you were so disgusted by this."

My hand reached out to his left pocket. I slowly hooked my finger on the ring and took the key out slowly. It's not as easy as I thought it would be. I felt his hand run across my back, while he used the other to tuck my hair behind my ear.

"Because you were 16." His breath fanned my face.

"And now you're 33. I realized you're too old."

I clasped my fist on the key. Ashton must have felt the key had slipped out of his pocket as he tried to get it from my hand. I was seated at the end and I stood up quickly. Ashton looked disappointed and confused.

"I don't know what your deal is. I knew you'd been toying with me since this morning."

Ashton tried to grab my wrist. "I am not doing that."

"Are you saying you like me now?"

A long while passed and Ashton still couldn't answer. I would admit, it pained me a little. But I have taught myself long ago not to expect anything from him.

"You don't know if you like me. And I understand—"

"—It's not that." Ashton swallowed before he continued." Yes, I think I like you now."

"You think?" I shook my head. "Whatever." I held the keys in front of him. "I'm going home."

Vea and Tim also got up. I turned to them and asked them if they were leaving with me. Vea refused. Tim slurred and muttered something about resolving the tension. Vea gathered her purse. I helped her with Tim and asked how they would get home. They said they'd already called Uber.

Ashton walked right behind us. Their Uber was already waiting when we came out of the club. When we were alone, I hesitated if I should give the car keys to the valet or not. Ashton and I both had drinks. While I am sober, I doubt if he would let me drive his car.

Ashton grabbed my wrist and took his keys. "I already called us a ride."

I nodded, then walked over to the designated waiting area. There was a group of guys waiting aside from us. They started whispering among themselves when I walked near them. I got nervous when I thought one of the guys was walking towards us. He suddenly stopped when Ashton casually slid his hand with mine.

Ashton tagged my hand and gently turned me to face him. "Tash, listen—"

"Shh. I know it's the alcohol talking. You'll forget it tomorrow." I dismissed him right then.

"I am sober. I know what I'm saying." He sighed out of desperation. "I like you."

There is sarcasm in my laughter and I allowed Ashton to hear it. "Whatever, Ashton. If you feel the same tomorrow and in the coming days, prove it. Work for it."

"I'll show you." He pressed my hand.

I had doubts, but I did not object when he suddenly pulled me in for a hug.

Will you, Ashton? Will you even remember this tomorrow?

That was my thoughts until our ride arrived.

THE ACCIDENTAL KISS

A SHTON'S POV

Natasha is slowly warming up to me. And I would be lying if I said that I did not like where these things were going. I teased her more while we were in the back passenger seat.

"If you will attempt a kiss as you did five years ago, I certainly won't reject it." Natasha elbowed me. "I mean there's no 26-year-old man in his right mind who would agree to kiss a 16-year-old lady. That's pedophilia."

"Don't push your luck." She put her purse between us.

"But if this gorgeous 23-year-old lady beside me—"

"Exactly. I'm 23, you're 33. I realized no matter how I age, you'd still be 10 years older." She avoided my gaze and turned to reach for her seatbelt.

The driver asked to confirm the destination. Natasha and I both said yes. The driver turned to Natasha and asked her if everything was all right.

"Yes, I am fine." Natasha smiled at the Uber driver. Then she said, "I know him."

I didn't understand at first why she needed to say she knew me. I wondered why the Uber driver looked suspicious of me too. Then it dawned on me. The driver might have misunderstood what I was blabbering about when we got in the car. Maybe he thought I was harassing her.

I turned my gaze to Natasha. I am unsure if the annoyed look is intended for me or the seatbelt that seemed stuck.

"What is wrong with this?" She struggled to pull the strap. I chuckled.

"Pull it a little gently, then let go. Once the strap rolls back, it will be easier to pull it out again." The Uber driver instructed her.

Just as I reached out to help her pull the strap, she pulled it out. She turned to her right to buckle it and our lips accidentally touched. As if on instinct, both of us pulled away at once. I hit my head at the window, but

Natasha didn't notice it.

"Hey! You did that on purpose, didn't you?" She snapped.

I heard the anger in her voice.

"What do you mean? Like I hit my head on purpose?" I winced, rubbing the part of my head that hit the window.

Natasha's expression shifted from puzzled to worried when she saw me wincing. I chuckled when she turned to the driver and politely asked him to be careful. It wasn't the driver's fault. But the driver agreed anyway. The driver looked at me from his rearview mirror and I said sorry.

I have a lot of things to say to Natasha, but I decided I should tell her when we get home. It would be more comfortable to talk if the one driving is Max, my driver. But I don't want to bother him during weekends. The only time I will ever do that is during emergencies.

About ten minutes later, she started to doze off. I scooted closer and let her head rest on my shoulder. I talk to the Uber driver and ask him questions every once in a while. He did the same. It was already one in the morning when we reached home.

I tried to wake Natasha and when she couldn't, I attempted to carry her in my arms.

"W—what's going on?"She was startled when she felt my arm going under her thigh.

Since I'd already bent down and positioned myself to carry her, I continued lifting her out of the car.

"Put me down, please?"

She tapped my shoulder so I stopped walking and put her down. I told her a lame pick-up line, which I regretted as soon as she heard. Natasha laughed. Then she turned around and asked if I was jealous of Derek and if I was copying him.

I scratched my head. "What? No! Why would I be jealous?"

Natasha suppressed another smile. "Try harder, Grandpa."

"Call me Grandpa again and you'll end up in my bed tonight."

She stopped walking, then she asked me to stop teasing her. I noticed she stuttered. She keyed in the pin and hurriedly opened the door. Without saying anything, she barged in and headed to her room.

"Hey, don't tell me you're going into hiding again?" I grabbed her wrist.

"I don't know. That depends on you, grand—"

I moved closer to her and gave her a challenging look. I teased her to continue calling me Grandpa. She moved back until she was leaning on the wall. I cornered her by putting my hands on her sides. Her chest heaved as our lips were about to touch.

"Go on, Tasha. Call me grandpa." I said quite seductively, I sensed the hint of lust in my voice.

She cleared her throat.

"Hey. You're jumping to conclusions. What I meant was, uh..." She scratched her head and then pushed me away.

"Staircase!"

I looked at her, confused. "What?"

"I said I hope you had a grand staircase, no?" She tapped the railings with her hand, then ran straight to her room and closed her door. She left me standing in the hallway, laughing all alone.

"Goodnight, Tasha."

She wanted me to work for it, huh? Certainly. Especially when I have a younger competition. It's already late, but her parents might still be awake overseas. Maybe I should take care of that first. I pulled out my smartphone from my pocket and dialed Jeremy's roaming number as I headed to my room.

NATASHA'S POV

That jerk! Does he think he can have me or a kiss without work?

I checked the time. It's already late, but the event this evening would not allow me to sleep easily. I decided to take a shower and make an overseas call after.

I had just gotten in bed when my phone rang. I reached for it and saw that it was my mom. I answered the call right away.

"Hey, mom! I have just finished the shower. I am supposed to call you but you got me first. How are you and dad?"

"Hi, honey! Your dad and I were fine. How about you?"

I thought she sounded a little bit weird. She seemed to be happy and excited. She even giggled like a teenager.

"Well, I miss you and Dad. But I am doing fine, Mom. University graduation is in two months. Will you be home by then?"

"We miss you too, honey. And we'll find a way to spend some days there, in time for your graduation." There was a pause. I thought I heard her giggling and whispering to Dad.

I rolled my eyes. I requested a video call to satisfy my curiosity but my mother kept canceling. Did she call me while they were in the middle of doing something fishy? It doesn't seem that way. My mother would never do that. But she sounded weird.

"Honey, is there anything else that you wanted to tell us? My mother asked after a while.

"Well, actually there are a lot of things that happened to me just today—"

"Really, honey? Like what?" She cut me off like she was too eager to hear what I was about to say.

"Mom, are you okay? Something feels off." There go the giggles again.

"Don't mind me, honey. I am just thrilled to hear your voice. And your stories. So go on, tell me."

"Well you're not gonna believe this but—"

"Is it about a man? Are you dating a—"

"Mom! Let me finish first."

"I'm sorry, sweetheart. I feel that this has something to do with your love life. And I want you to know that I support you."

"What? No! This has nothing to do with my love life...Maybe it has, but it is still too early to tell." I paused. "Anyway, I went out with my friends earlier and a handsome guy, I mean he was hot. So okay, he approached me and used a funny pickup line. Then I realized who he was. Do you want to make a guess, Mom?"

"Oh... There was a hot guy, huh? So tell me who this hot guy we are talking about is." It was my dad. For some weird reason, he blurted out laughing like my mom.

Are my parents high?

"OMG! Am I on a loudspeaker?" I asked as soon as I realized it.

"Yes, you are. But sweetheart, it's fine. Don't mind me." My dad said in between laughs.

"You are a weird couple," I tucked the sheet to my chest.

"Anyway, the guy was Derek Miller! Do you know that online celebrity I follow on Instagram and YouTube?"

I knew she would recognize it. She caught me many times watching his dances when I should be studying.

"Which online celebrity? Oh yeah! That young dancer was hot and sexy!" I heard my mom giggle again. "So that young boy approached you, huh? You met him in person?"

"Yes! And not just that! We danced to one of his routines!" I felt the excitement I had earlier in the club. "Then he said he wanted to guest on his YouTube channel! Oh, mom. Can you believe it? From watching him almost every day to being on his channel!"

"That's wonderful! I am proud of you honey." I can feel the warmth and pride in my mother's voice.

"Me too, sweetheart. I am proud of you." I heard my dad say, "You have exceeded my expectations."

I got a little confused when my dad started laughing. I felt like he meant something else. Like I did another thing that made him proud.

"Hon, we are happy about what is happening in your life. We also appreciate that finally, you are talking to us again about your personal life. Do not forget that your happiness is also our happiness." They whispered again. Then my mom was back on the phone. " I do not want to ruin the moment, but I want to ask you something."

It could be the distance. But I felt my parents were getting a little too emotional and sentimental. I took a deep breath, then I gave my mom the signal to fire a question away. "Okay, mom. Shoot!"

"Honey, how are things between you and Ashton?"

"What do you mean about things between me and Ashton? Things are just fine, I guess. Why did you ask?"

My answer caused my dad to laugh even more.

"Is Dad okay?" Though I did not understand, my father was laughing his heart out, so I started to laugh along with him.

"I am fine, honey. It might be late over there. Have a good rest, okay? I love you." I imagined him suppressing another laugh.

"I love you, Mom." Then I talked louder so my dad could hear. "I love you too, Dad."

"I am sorry, sweetheart for all the laughter. I am on the phone with Ashton." My dad finally explained.

I got up from bed abruptly when I processed what my dad said.

Whispering, I asked Mom, "Have you been talking to Ashton since you called me? Mom! Those things I told you were supposed to be our secret!"

"I am sorry, honey." My mom's tone was apologetic.

I suddenly remembered why I chose not to share some of my private matters. She tends to overstep her boundaries. I learned about this when I overheard her sharing stories about me before. But I guess the distance made me forget all about that.

"Fine. What else can I do? Bye, mom." Then I shouted again. "Bye, Dad! Love you both."

I heard my dad say bye before I ended the call. Why would Ashton call them at this hour? I shrugged the thoughts off. Ashton and his family are our business partners. Maybe they were discussing some business.

TELLING HER PARENTS

A*SHTON'S POV*
It's still early where Jeremy and Julia were, so I thought about calling them. I thought I would discuss business matters first. Then we can talk about the personal stuff.

Jeremy is only ten years older than me. I was a young 15-year-old then and Jeremy has just started a business. My father is one of their first investors. We met each other at one of those company events.

Despite my young age, I've always had a good eye for business. I must have learned it from my dad. And Jeremy has always liked my business ideas. When I graduated from college, Jeremy took me in as a co-owner. We rebranded the business into A&J Furniture and we've been running the business together since.

"So, how is Tasha?"

Finally, Jeremy mentioned her daughter before I did.

"I'm glad you asked. I have something important to talk to you about."

"Why? Is my daughter giving you a headache?" Jeremy gave me a hearty laugh.

"No. Not really." I paced the room.

Ah! How would I tell him that I wanted to date her daughter?

"Well, it's been weeks, and generally, things are running smoothly between us."

"Haha. It seems like Tasha has warmed up to you, huh?" Jeremy seemed relieved

"Not quite, but I guess we can say that."

"What do you mean?" Jeremy asked. I can sense his getting a little worried.

I reassured him that there was nothing for them to worry about. I updated them about Natasha's routine and studies as I've been doing for weeks. Out of nowhere, Jeremy wondered about how Natasha had been for the past five years.

Natasha did not tell me directly about it. She did not confirm it. But I have always thought that her actions that led to the attempted kiss say it all. I don't want to feel smug about it, but I knew Natasha had developed romantic feelings toward me when she was sixteen.

I knew I was probably partly to blame. I told her something on her sixteenth birthday. I told her I was going to wait for her. I wanted to say that as a joke. I realized how bad the joke was as soon as I said it. I want to tell her how she turned into one fine lady. But I did not clarify it because I thought she did not hear what I said. The music was loud back then and she did not say anything back.

Looking back, I guess she heard them. That one statement made her confused. Maybe because I did not say anything to retract them, I also did not follow through. I remember how frequently her texts were after that. But I got myself busy with Bianca, I paid little attention and gave no meaning to it. Then I went on a vacation and introduced my girlfriend to them.

I told Jeremy what I knew, but filtered the parts he did not need to hear. I chose my words carefully. That's when I heard Julia gasp. I realized I was on a loudspeaker. Then Julia shared something from that timeframe. She said she now understood why her daughter acted that way.

I apologized. They understood. Jeremy also said sorry if their daughter had put me in a difficult situation. I felt a little awkward when I said it was fine. Then Julia became worried for her daughter. She started blaming herself because she felt like she pushed Natasha to spend the past weeks with me. She wondered if it had been uncomfortable for her daughter. That's when I started my confession.

"Where are you getting at? You're making me nervous, Ashton."

I took a deep breath and braced myself for their reaction. It's now, or I will forever hold my silence.

"Well, I have been fighting this for the past weeks. But I think I am developing feelings for your daughter."

There, I said it.

A long, awkward silence followed. Jeremy stuttered when he asked me to clarify what I meant.

"I want to date your daughter."

Another long silence. I heard whispers, from Julia mostly.

"Hello?"

"We're still here. We're just trying to take it all in." Jeremy said, his voice cracking.

I expected the couple to get mad at me and end the phone call. I imagined Jeremy would prohibit me from seeing Tasha and that they'd fly back here ASAP.

God, what would I do if that happened? Should I fight for Tasha? Would she choose me over her parents? Should I go somewhere far and forget about this feeling while we have not started anything?

My thoughts were interrupted by Jeremy.

"This is weird. I never expected that we would talk about my daughter this way." I felt his suppressed anger. "I honestly want to punch you... I could punch you if you're here. I mean, what were you thinking, Ashton? I know Tasha is already an adult. She may date anyone she pleases. But we're friends, and you have a 12-year age gap."

I understood what he meant. Julia also expressed her thoughts. She's mostly worried about her daughter acting immaturely. She asked me what would happen if the relationship didn't go well. It will tarnish the personal relationship between our families and the business partnership.

I have thought about that. But I still proceeded with it anyway. Droplets of sweat began to form on my forehead. I swallowed hard as I waited for Jeremy's decision.

"I know you would protect Tasha as I would. Do you love my daughter, Ashton?" His voice is calmer than before.

"Yes, I do." I gave them a straight answer.

"Thank you for approaching us first. As I said, Natasha is an adult." Jeremy looked at his wife and she nodded.

"The decision is hers." She said, "If she wants to be with you, I guess as parents, we will support her."

I felt relieved. We were still talking when Julia decided to give Natasha a phone call. Julia put her on a loudspeaker.

She asked about the updates in Tasha's life. Tasha informed her mom about her upcoming graduation and other things. She told her everything about 'the hot online celebrity from YouTube'.

Tasha started with how he used a pickup line on her to his invitation to be a guest and do a dance cover with him on his YouTube channel. She even referred to Derek as her budding love life.

They talked for about ten minutes, and she did not mention anything about me. Nothing until Julia finally asked. Then she said, "I guess we're fine."

I felt crushed. Everything Tasha said hurts. It hurt so bad that I almost wished I didn't tell her parents what I said. I can tell how much Jeremy is enjoying all these. His laughter echoed in my ears. Like he's telling me I stand no chance.

"Hahahaha. I am sorry, man. But have you told her?" Jeremy could not hide his happiness.

"Yeah, I did. I told Tasha earlier." My voice was suddenly down. "And that woman was tough. She told me if I work hard to gain her trust."

"So you started with calling her parents?" Jeremy chuckled.

I felt like Jeremy intended to be mean to me. But how can I blame him?

"Yes. I thought about letting you know first."

"Well, what can I say? She's her father's daughter." Jeremy must be feeling smug. "Now, I am relieved. I know Tasha is making it hard for you, like I want her to."

I heard Julia's laughter.

"Right, man. It feels like this is going to be a long chase." I agreed.

"Well, good luck, Ashton. I'd love to say I am for Team Ashton. But really, I am for whoever my daughter chooses." Julia said in a calm voice. I'd say she took all these better than her husband did.

"That sounds fair, Julia. Thank you. This conversation ended better than I expected."

Well, except for that part where Natasha blabbered about Derek. Back on the couch at the club...in the car... and then earlier tonight. I thought we had it. I was confident she still felt the same way about me. What changed?

"We trust you, Ashton, as long as you won't do anything against Tasha's will." I felt the warning in Jeremy's voice. And I understood.

"Of course, Jeremy. And thank you, both of you. I know we all had a long day. I don't want to tire you, so I'll end this call now. Bye." I told them.

"Take good care of my princess." There is a bit of sadness in Jeremy's voice.

"Of course," I reassured them.

Julia also said goodbye before I ended the call. I stared at my phone for a while. Then I headed to the bathroom to shower. A little later, I changed into a sleeveless shirt and sweatpants.

I felt sleepy and tired, but I couldn't sleep. I laughed at myself. For the past week, I felt like a distressed teenager. I still felt down from Tasha and Julia's phone conversation earlier. I decided that I wanted to see her again.

So I left my room and found myself staring at her door. I knocked a few times, but no one answered. I checked for the gap between her door and the floor. The TV was off. She must be sleeping.

I tried to open her door, and I guessed it right. She forgot to lock it again.

For the past weeks, I have been coming to her room to check on her before I go to sleep. Sometimes I only give her a quick peek before I lock her door. The last time though, I wanted to stay longer, so I unintentionally napped on the sofa beside her bed. Tasha was never a light sleeper, and she has never noticed me.

I suddenly felt so tired. I thought about sitting on the sofa again, but I felt lonely. I wanted to snuggle next to Tasha, who was sleeping on her side. I moved to the space by her waist and lay on my stomach across her bed, my feet dangling on the edge.

Hmmm. Tasha feels like my home. Knowing that she was inches from me gave me a relaxing feeling.

"Goodnight, baby," I whispered. I planned on getting up but I was too tired so I gave in to sleep.

A BEAUTIFUL MORNING

I don't know how long I slept when I felt the warm sun against my skin. I grabbed my sheet and buried my face in it. I thought I felt a strong arm move across my waist when I tugged the sheet.

Hmm. I guess I am just dreaming.

"This pillow feels nice and warm," I murmured as I felt the warmth on my back. I slowly turned around and buried my face in what I thought was a pillow.

I hesitated when I thought the pillow felt like an actual human. But I am still too sleepy to open my eyes. I used my hand to feel it and was confused about how the pillow felt a little hard to the touch. Still, in a daze, I decided to just snuggle it tightly.

"Ahh! This feels nice." I heard myself slurring.

Someone made a short "Mmm" sound then I felt being squeezed.

No way!

Gray is the first color I saw when I opened my eyes. My pillowcases are all green and pink. Maybe I am still half-asleep. I poked it with my index finger, then pinched it. I gasped when I realized that a hand caught mine. When I looked up, I saw Ashton. His eyes are still closed, but his lips make a mischievous smile.

"AHHHHHHH!"

I pushed him with my feet, and he fell off the bed.

"What? What happened?" He looked confused.

I grabbed a pillow and hit him with it.

"You, pervert! What are you doing in my room? Why are you sleeping in my bed?"

I screamed. Ashton tried to wrestle me in bed to cover my mouth.

"Damn, baby! Stop screaming! You're hurting my ears, and I did not do anything!" Before I knew it, he was already on top of me, covering my mouth with his hand.

His lips stretched into a smile. "Well, not unless you want us to."

My eyes widened in disbelief. I bit his hands and yelled at him. "Get off me!"

He winced, then he pinned my hands over my head. Then he said, "I swear I'd kiss you if you don't stop screaming."

I closed my mouth fast then I bit my lips.

"Uh-uh. No, baby. That's not helping." He sighed. "Don't do that."

I nodded. He let go of my hands but I don't know why I kept them above me. I think I have also forgotten how to breathe properly. Finding my pace, I steadied my gaze into his face. I noticed how he fixed his lustful eyes on my lips.

Then he rested his fingers on my jawline. We spent the moment just staring at each other. I turned my face away when I could no longer hold his gaze. Ashton began to lower his lips on my cheeks, near the corner of my mouth.

"You're beautiful."

He used his hand to turn my face towards him. Thoughts rushed into my head. I wanted to push him away but I also wanted to experience his kiss. I saw he closed his eyes when he inched his face slowly. I decided to do the same. Gently, he brushed his lips. I anticipated the kiss to get deeper, but nothing happened.

When I opened my eyes, he greeted me with a wide grin. Heat rose to my cheeks when I realized he was teasing me.

"You're such a manipulative psycho!" I said under gritted teeth.

Ashton smiled before he buried his face in my neck.

"Seriously?!"

His speech was a bit slurred when he spoke. "Are you hungry?"

"No."

"Do you need to use the bathroom?"

"No."

"Do you find this uncomfortable?"

I wanted to say yes and no at the same time. I answered him with a sigh.

Ashton slid his body to my side and put me between his arms and legs. "How about this?"

I snorted. "You're holding me too tight."

He loosened the hug and asked again, "Are you still sleepy?"

"Yes! So I hope you would—-"

He used his index finger to hush me.

"Me too. Then let us sleep some more. It's still too early. Let us cuddle and sleep." He buried his face against my neck and started to nuzzle it.

Hmmm. That feels good. I swallowed hard, wondering how he expected me to sleep like that.

"Baby, I love the smell of your skin." Ashton murmured against my neck.

I wore a loose tank top shirt. Ashton began planting small kisses on the exposed skin on my shoulders. With my eyes closed, I tapped him on the shoulder. I murmured, "Sleep." He stopped and rested his hand on my waist.

"You're driving me mad." He got up then he looked at me while his hands were on his waist. I think he wanted to tell me something but he just shook his head. Then he leaned towards me and gave me a peck on my lips.

Ashton bent so quickly that I was not able to turn my head away.

"Hey!" I covered my mouth with the back side of my hand.

"I can't help that. I'm sorry. Go back to sleep, baby."

He walked over to draw the curtains, then he was gone.

I want to scream. But instead, I pulled the sheet above my head. I might be too tired. My heart was racing, but it found its pace when Ashton left. I didn't know how I fell asleep. But I didn't wake up until two hours later.

I am a little hungry. I searched for my phone and saw that it was nine in the morning. I smelled coffee brewing from the kitchen. I contemplated whether I should get myself a cup of coffee or not. The coffee smells so good I can almost taste it. It got the better of me. So I tied my long hair into a messy bun, and I headed downstairs.

Ashton was busy pouring a cup for him. He was a bit startled when he turned around to see me, that he accidentally spilled hot coffee on his hand.

"Fuck, it's hot!" He placed the cup down on the counter.

I chuckled. "Sorry," I said grinning.

I grabbed a table napkin and helped him wipe the coffee from his hand. I told him I smelled the coffee from my room and wanted to get one for myself. I moved away to get a cup from the cupboard.

"How's your sleep?" He grabbed me by my waist and hugged me from behind. Then he pulled me in to plant a kiss on the side of my nape.

"Uhm. Good." I pushed him away. His kiss tickled me. It sent goosebumps down my arms. "Please, stop doing that."

"I'm sorry." Ashton might be a little embarrassed, he hesitated when he got the cup from my hand, and he headed towards the coffee maker. He put it on a saucer before he handed it to me.

"Be careful. It's hot."

I laughed. I blew at the coffee before I took a sip from it. Ashton walked towards the refrigerator. Then he asked, "Are you hungry?"

I nodded my head. He asked me if I could wait. He didn't say, but I think he just woke up too. I told him it's fine. I grabbed a granola bar and told him I'd do my homework while I waited. I was about to leave when he asked me what my thesis was about. I gave him a summary of it, though I am not really sure he understood.

"Is your adviser a male or a female?" he turned to me before he put the bacon on the pan."You do consultations in private, right?"

I do not understand why he was asking that.

"Yeah. Hey, I'm heading upstairs. Thank you for this." I referred to the coffee. "And Prof. Jackson, she is harmless. I mean if that's why you're asking."

"Oh! You have a female adviser then. Okay. I'll bring you your breakfast in a while."

I watched the color rise to his face. "You don't have to. I'll just come down when—-"

"Please, let me do it for you." The look in his eyes is pleading.

"All right then."

Is he serious? Is this him working his way to have me?

I made my way back to my bedroom. Then I got myself busy running statistical analyses on my laptop.

UNEXPECTED CONNECTION AND SURPRISES

I went back to my room to do my thesis. A couple of minutes later, my phone beeped. It was a text from Derek.

Derek: Hey, Tasha. This is Derek. The guy from YouTube? ;) Good morning! I wonder if you're already awake.

Me: Hello, Derek! I saved your number when you texted last night. Good morning to you too.

Derek: I hope I didn't wake you. I have been up since five this morning. We had a busy schedule.

I texted a reply and heard Ashton knock on my door.

"Hey, Tasha? Can I come in? Your breakfast is here."

Wow! Where has the bickering gone?

I opened the door for him. On a tray are bacon, eggs, and pancakes. There are also two glasses of juice and a mug of coffee. I gave him a puzzled look.

"I don't know if you want another cup of coffee or some juice. So, here. Where can I put these?"

I cleared my study table and put my laptop on the bed. My phone beeped again, and I saw Ashton glance at it.

"Are your friends coming to pick up their things?"

"Uhm, no. I haven't heard from them since last night. I guess they're still in bed." I dragged the stool from my dresser.

"Ah. Mind if I ask who is texting?"

I bit my lips. Why do I feel like I am cheating? I pushed the thoughts in my head. Just then, the phone rang.

"Do you need some privacy?" Ashton asked.

I thought for a while before I said no. I had nothing to hide from him. It's up to him if he wants to leave or not. I stuck the earphones in my ears and answered the call without waiting for Ashton's response.

"Hello, Derek!"

Ashton's brows furrowed, forming a crease on the space between his nose bridge. I put the phone on the table and helped Ashton with the food.

"Ah... That voice, they're music to my ears."

Ashton rolled his eyes. He does not hear the conversation between me and Derek, but I guess I am blushing from what he said. I ignored Ashton and focused on what Derek was saying at the other end of the line.

"You're such a smooth talker." I laughed as I sliced a piece of pancake.

"So, why did you call?"

"Because I thought it would take you forever to respond. Haha."

"Sorry. I'm having breakfast. How about you? Have you eaten?"

Ashton started to scratch his head. Then he scoots over trying to listen to our conversation.

"Yeah. I have."

There was a short pause before Derek spoke again. "Hey, are you free next weekend?"

I glanced at the post-its on my table before I answered."No. I am afraid I am not free next weekend. Why?"

Ashton must have figured out what Derek asked because he started to clear his throat.

"Got a long line of dates in waiting, ha?" Derek chuckled.

Ashton pushed my plate towards me and motioned for me to it. I drove it away and walked over to my bed.

"I wish that's the case, but no. I am working on my thesis." I looked at the ceiling, wondering what Derek might be thinking. "You might be thinking I am boring now, huh?" I asked.

"No way! Do you know what they say? Intelligence is the new sexy." He made his voice a little husky.

I laughed. "Ah, then does that make you a sapiosexual?"

Derek laughed at the other end. I heard other people, probably his friends, teasing and asking him about the phone call. On the other hand, Ashton glared at me. I am not sure, but he seems unfamiliar with the word.

"So, back to the topic," Derek's voice on the phone broke the stare between me and Ashton. "I wonder when you will be free? I am asking because first, I want to ask you out on a date. Second, I want to schedule our dance collab. So?"

"Well... my defense is in three weeks. But I am unsure if I will have free time after that." I looked at Ashton who was busy with his food.

"Are your parents strict?" Derek asked. He sensed the hesitation. Maybe he's not convinced by the reason I gave him.

"My parents are actually out of the country." I glanced at Ashton. "So I can, pretty much, do whatever and go wherever I decide to."

Ashton threw me a challenging look.

"Cool. Nice. But how about the grumpy guardian from last night?"

Derek made me laugh so hard. "Grumpy who?" Oh, yeah, him? It's fine."

Ashton pointed at himself as if asking if we were talking about him.

I walked to the balcony and ignored Ashton.

"I don't like him. He's intimidating." I heard Derek say from the other end.

I laughed even more. "Hahahahaha. That is hilarious. But no. He is not intimidating." I looked at Ashton. He stopped eating. He got up, ready to follow me to the balcony. But I was quick to slide the door closed.

I was startled when Ashton suddenly drew the curtain and stared against the glasses.

"He's just old. Way too old. But not intimidating."

I couldn't focus on what Derek said because Ashton got my attention. He's mouthing "Old? Me?" From the other side of the glass door. I laughed when I realized he'd been lip-reading me.

"Anyway, the schedule for the dance collab, let's work it out. I can't let that opportunity pass." Ashton shook his head. "I mean you're Derek Miller. Other girls would kill to be on your dance cover. Haha."

I walked closer to Ashton and talked slowly for him to read my lips properly.

"As for the date, we'll see."

Ashton looked annoyed. He pulled the curtain and it blocked my view. I smiled.

"I hope no guardians on the date?" Derek asked.

"Let's hope." I chuckled.

"Okay. Good luck with your thesis. I'm just a text or a phone call away when you need me."

"I know. Bye, Derek. I am looking forward to having a collaboration with you."

"Yeah, bye. Stay gorgeous."

I blushed. Maybe my cheeks were still red when I went back to the room.

"Look at her. She's blushing." Ashton teased me.

"I can't control it. Sorry." I fanned my face with my hands.

"And you are smiling like an idiot too." The tone of his voice told me he was annoyed. "I am a bit hurt, you know. All these efforts, but with just one call from that kid, you're willing to date him."

Ashton smiled. I cannot tell if he's serious or not.

"When did you ask me on a date?" I asked. "And the last time I checked, we're not even exclusively dating.

"We're not together, are we?

Yes. I needed clarification.

Ashton smiled from ear to ear.

"Ah. You're right. We're not." He moved the chair for me to sit on. Then he asked, "Does that mean I can still date other women too?"

"It's up to you. But let me ask you this," I held him by his shoulder, "Is it me who begged for us to be together? Is it me who promised to do what I can to have you?"

As if acknowledging defeat, Ashton bowed his head. Then he nodded.

"Date as many women as you want. But then, if you do that, you can't have me." I tapped his shoulder. And with confidence, I asked, "Are we clear?"

Ashton tilted his head. Then he asked, "How old are you again? Sometimes I feel like you're older than me."

"I'm old enough to decide who I want to be with." I sliced my pancake and put it in my mouth.

Ashton is getting pissed. It feels like we're going back to bickering any moment now. He crossed his arms on his chest. "Why don't you just decide to date him then?"

"Why are you pissed? I don't need to explain myself."

I have no plans on backing down. I held his gaze. I didn't intend to, but I twitched my lips when he was the first to look away.

"I am not pissed. Don't get mad, okay? Let us not fight." He reached for my hands.

"What?" At this point, I must admit that I am feigning my anger.

"Have you been in a relationship before?" Ashton suddenly asked.

Why is he suddenly asking me about my previous relationships?

"Tasha?"

I stared at the floor. "I'm not sure if they can be considered dating."

"What do you mean?" Ashton asked, confused.

"I went out with other guys on a few dates. But they're all flings. Just casual dates. Perhaps with a little making out."

Ashton looked surprised.

"What? I am an adult. What is wrong with that? Do you feel I am unworthy now?"

Ashton shook his head. He said he didn't care and it didn't matter if I dated other guys before him. Then he added, "You will be mine. But when that time comes, you will be stuck with me...for good."

"What if I choose Derek?" I raised my eyebrow, too eager to hear his opinion.

"I am worried. I am scared to lose you. But I don't want to be selfish. I don't want to deprive you of your happiness." He sighed. Then he touched my chin. "I don't want you to choose me because you thought you had no other options. I am worried that by the time we're together, someone will come along and you'll decide to leave me."

His answer confused me at first. But then, I remembered. Bianca cheated on him, thus their divorce. He might be afraid that my lack of dating experience would make me curious about other guys and cheat on him later on.

"That's sweet... and thoughtful."

I said it almost to myself. But Ashton must have caught it. He smiled. I put my hand up to his face. He seemed pleased. Then I surprised him with a peck on his cheeks.

"You deserved that."

Ashton smiled. I was pleased to see his reaction. But I wanted to regret it when he pulled me into his lap and held me on my waist so I would sit still.

"Making out with a fling is not new to you, huh?" The corner of Ashton's lips raised in a half smile.

"Does that count as making out to you? That's a peck." I answered.

I reached out for my coffee and took a sip. I regretted the decision as soon as I felt my heart beating crazily against my chest. Coffee can't calm my nerves.

"Answer my question. Because I think I deserve more. Do you make out with all of your flings?"

"It depends—"

"Just answer with a yes or no. If it's with me?"

I can tell that Ashton is losing his patience. His right hand is already at my nape.

"Uh, I guess, yes—"

Without a warning, he pulled me in for a kiss.

ASHTON AND NATASHA: THE FIRST KISS

Ashton took me aback. Ashton pressed his lips to mine. They were soft and warm. I felt his tongue brushing my lips, then he moved slightly away.

Now only our foreheads touch. I bit my lips and rested my hands on his shoulders. He placed his right hand on my lap while the other cupped my face.

"Sometimes, I wish you were not born 10 years late. But then again, I wonder how our paths would have crossed if that would be the case." He took a deep breath. "Would you be my neighbor? A classmate from high school? A colleague at work?"

He tucked my hair behind my ear. "If we were born in about the same year, will I treasure you as much as I do now?" He grabbed my hand and brought it to his lips. "In the end, I can only be thankful that no matter how late, our paths have crossed. And I wish to spend the remaining days of my life with you."

Ashton left me dumbfounded with his confession. I licked my lower lip with my tongue. In an instant, Ashton pressed his lips against mine. I put my arms around his neck and let him deepen the kiss. I pushed his chest and broke from the kiss when his needs started to grow underneath me.

Panting for more air, I told him to stop. He already got more than he deserved.

"Tease", his eyes burning with desire and needs.

"I am not teasing you. You have crossed the line."

Ashton nodded. Then as if to himself, he muttered something about reaching the limit. My reaction must have been apparent on my face because he suddenly said, "With your flings."

That changed my mood quickly.

"Ah. So that kiss is about that then? Are you testing the limit?" I crossed my arms. Then I asked. "Why? Are you considering now if you should settle for a fling?" I raised my chin.

I hate how he reacted. I felt... offended. It's like he now saw me as easy. I felt mad at myself because his look made me feel just that. Now I want to blame myself. It's not that I had a lot of flings. I probably had about five. And that's in the course of those six years.

Why did I kiss him back? What's wrong with kissing him back?

I like what I did. But I don't particularly appreciate how he thinks of me now. I can't help but wonder why it seems okay for men to have casual, consensual flings, but when women do the same, the act becomes... immoral... unacceptable... dirty.

Or is it just me? Do I feel guilty? Why do I feel so guilty about it?

Ashton lifted his hand and reached for mine but I refused his touch.

"No, no. Of course not. I didn't mean it to sound that way."

I knew he realized his mistakes when he buried his face in his hands. Ashton cleared his throat before he spoke again.

"Forgive me, but I'm curious. So may I ask one more thing?"

I nodded my head telling him to proceed with the question.

"Tasha, are you going around without a bra?"

Ashton is asking the weirdest of questions. First, he asked about my flings. Now he is questioning my choice to wear or not wear a bra. I squinted my eyes, still trying to figure him out.

"Yes."

Ashton gasped. Then he nodded as if to let me know he understood my choice.

"I mean no."

I sighed out of desperation.

Where did that question even come from?

"What do you mean?" Ashton leaned closer.

I pushed him away.

"Why do you even want to know that?" I started cleaning and putting the plates in the tray. "I am wearing breast lifts. Now get out."

I handed him the tray and Ashton accepted them but put them down again on the table. But by doing that, I caught how he glimpsed at my chest. I crossed my arms again.

"I am sorry. I am just curious. I don't think I have seen a breast lift before." His smile teased, but he acted unsure. He pulled me closer and he ran his hand across my back.

Ah! That's how he found out. Was I too deep in the kiss I didn't notice when he rubbed my back earlier?

"Ashton, stop feeling me. Just google it." I took the tray and put it in his hands again.

"How about giving me a sneak peek?" He winked his eyes at me.

"How about no way?" I pushed him towards the door. "Thank you for breakfast...and the kiss. Now, get out."

"Ah! I hate this." He looked at the ceiling as if in protest.

"And I am starting to hate you. Move. Out. Now."

I tried to close the door when he stopped it. He leaned on the door frame, still holding the tray.

"So how was our first kiss?"

Oh! Now, this jerk wants to boost his ego, huh?

A smile played across my lips. "It was horrible because my lips barely touched yours. You were so disgusted, you even pushed me away!"

Ashton didn't get it at first. But when he did, he found my answer amusing. Then his face became serious.

"I am sorry about that, baby. But can we move on from that awkward part? That's so five years ago." His eyes pleaded.

I agreed.

"Do you mean the kiss I had after that horrible kiss?"

"Aha," he winked at me. "But don't get cute. I don't want to hear about last night in the car. That does not count. It was accidental."

"Okay. So what do you want to know?"

"I mean our first sensual kiss."

So he wants to boost his ego. Let me ruin it for him.

"What do you mean? What's so special about it? Do you think you are the first guy I French kissed?" I smiled at Ashton.

"Ah, Tasha! You're going to be the end of me!" I heard him say before he turned around to walk away.

ASHTON'S POV

Natasha did not say anything when I asked her about her previous relationships. Why did I assume she has zero experience with the opposite sex? Why was I so curious? And the bra! Why would I care whether she wears one or not? Uh, I sounded like an old man. Now I feel so stupid and ashamed of her and myself for asking those questions earlier.

But Natasha kissed well! Damn that young woman! I know she's an adult. I know it's normal to explore and have fun. But I couldn't help but wonder how many men have tasted those lips. Ugh! God! Why am I so jealous now?

I put the plates on the sink with more than enough force that they clinked at each other.

Other than Derek, how many younger competitions are out there?

Right now, I want to take back what I told Natasha. I wanted her to forget about dating and casual flings with other guys.

Shit! I am an idiot. I am so screwed!

BIANCA MASON IS BACK!

Three months have quickly passed since I moved to Ashton's house. My mom told me they knew Ashton was pursuing me. I worried about how they would react, but they took the situation well. Their commitment to support my decision also seems to have favored Ashton.

It boosted his confidence enough to express his affection toward me more openly.

It's been three weeks since I met Derek and we exchanged messages on social media. But our conversations had always been friendly. We have scheduled to meet several times, but something always comes up so we haven't met since that night at the club. He told me he counted the days until my defense was done, like a kid waiting for Christmas.

I am now in my room studying for the last exam at the university. I felt pressured by my thesis defense but I've done everything I needed two days ago. All I have to do is present and defend it tomorrow.

It's past 9 in the evening. Ashton isn't home yet. He usually knocks on my door at around 9, with a cup of coffee. He used to be against it at first. He said I shouldn't drink coffee at night. But no matter what he said, he knew I'd make my coffee anyway. So every night, Ashton serves me my last cup of coffee.

Then he would stay and read a book to emails or check some documents until I finished school work. We talk about what happened to us that day between our tasks.

Sometimes he'll only spend about thirty minutes in the room and leave early. Other times, like on the weekends, he stays until midnight, when I sleep. I still caught him sleeping on the sofa or at the foot of my bed. And I warned him against it. I asked him to respect my privacy. So each time he leaves the room, I lock the door.

I glanced at my phone again to check the time. I wondered what was taking him so long. I decided to text him.

Me: Hey, are you still in the office?

Ashton: Hey, yeah. I'm still here. I am still reviewing and signing some urgent documents. Sorry. I didn't realize the time. I can't make you your coffee. But do you want a Starbucks instead?

Me: No. Just come home safe.

Ashton: Ah, finally. You've learned to miss me. Maybe I should do this more often. Heh.

Me: Whatever.

Ashton: And I miss you too.

I realized that I love this side of Ashton. He's sweet and caring. He's always looking out for me. In the past months, I saw how he treated me well. While I, on the other hand, had always been a tease, just like what he always told me.

I have also been cranky these past few days. I have even shouted at him once. But he did not get mad. Instead, he left and gave me some time to think. He even texted me to ask if he could come to see me. And when I said he could, he got a red velvet cake and coffee ready for me.

I feel embarrassed by my immaturity in times like that. But I guessed that's the advantage of our age gap for me. The thought bothered me so I sent him another text.

Me: Am I not being fair to you?

Ashton: What do you mean? Hey, I am going home. Let's talk about that when I get home, okay? I have something to discuss with you as well.

Me: Okay. Take care, and tell Max to drive safely. See you later.

I put the phone down. I have been studying for the last three hours. I should take a break. I went down to the living room and waited there for Ashton. Sometime later, I heard his car pull up in the driveway. Then I heard him by the door. I guessed he was talking on his phone.

I opened the door, and he looked surprised to see me. He ended the call abruptly, which I find weird. I know I cut him mid-sentence, and he did not even say goodbye to the person he was talking to. I don't know what came to me, but I ran to him and hugged him. While he looked pleased, he also moved away rather quickly. I also thought he smelt like a cigarette. I didn't know he smoked. I have not seen him smoke.

"Why? What is wrong?" I asked him worriedly.

"Let me just take a quick bath. You can wait for me in your room, okay?"

"Oh! All right. Do you want some coffee? Maybe it is my turn to make you one?"

"No, babe. Thank you. See you in a while."

Babe. I have asked Ashton not to call me that before. And he reluctantly obliged. Since then, I noticed that when he's done something wrong, or if he wants to ask me a favor, he calls me babe almost automatically.

I watched him climb the stairs before I went to the kitchen to get snacks for myself. Then I went back to my room. Though Ashton's voice was a little muffled, I knew he was on the phone again when I passed his room.

Over an hour has passed, and Ashton has not come to my room. I hesitated on whether I should check on him because all the time I was here, I had gone to his room only a few times. But the worry got the better of me so I checked on him. I knocked, but he didn't answer. I tried the doorknob and was surprised to know that it wasn't locked.

When I entered his room, Ashton was already lying on his stomach, his arms spreading widely on his side. He appeared to fall asleep right after showering because he was still in his bathrobe. I also noticed how tired his face looked. I then turned towards the door and took my leave.

I went back to my room and prepared for bed. Then I grabbed my phone. There are only a couple of minutes left before midnight. I browsed my Instagram, checked my messages, and saw some of the photos posted by my friends.

I saw a photo posted by my classmate about four hours ago. She had her thesis defense this morning and went to dine with her family to celebrate. I double-clicked the photo and was about to leave a comment when something caught my eye.

Sitting behind my classmate from another table, there was Ashton. He went dining with another woman. My hands trembled as I tried to zoom in and look at the woman.

OMG! Am I seeing things? She's back? Bianca's back? They dined together and Ashton did not even mention it to me?

NOWHERE TO GO

My friend posted the photo four hours ago. That means Ashton and Bianca were probably together when I texted him. Why did Ashton say he was in the office working with urgent documents? He lied. I know we're not officially together.

But Ashton lied. They were together at that restaurant. He was with his former wife!

I cannot think clearly. I wanted us to talk but not while I was emotional. I don't want this to end up in a fight. And how would I ask him about her? Do I have the right to blame him? Do I have any right to even ask him about this? I cannot face him now. I needed to cool down. I needed to spend the night and a few more days somewhere else.

I packed all the things I needed for tomorrow. I thought about getting the suitcase but figured carrying it would make noise. I got my laptop bag and put my lecture notes and laptop inside. Then I tossed some clothes and toiletries in a duffle bag. My vision got a bit blurred as I cried the whole time. I made my way out of the house in between sobs.

Once outside, I tried ringing my friends. Unfortunately for me, none of them answered my call. They haven't even seen my texts.

I can still see Ashton's house from the distance I have walked. But I do not want to return to his house. I sobbed, overwhelmed by helplessness. I just sat there on the pavement and cried. I do not know how long I was crying when I heard a motorcycle pass by me. Then it screeched from a distance. I got a little scared when it turned around and stopped where I was. I got up and planned to run away. But when the rider removed the helmet, I recognized him.

"Derek?" Suddenly, I burst into a hard, childlike, and ugly cry.

"Hey! What are you doing here alone, with those bags, at this hour?" He seemed worried when he got off his motorcycle. He sat beside me and reached out to pat my head. He then used his hands to wipe the tears from my eyes.

"How did you know it was me?" I asked him in between sobs. I opened my purse and got some tissues.

"I didn't. Not until you got up. I just felt that you needed some help." He got the pack of tissues in my hands and wiped my tears. "What is wrong?"

"I don't want to sound too forward, but I needed a place to stay for the night. Can you take me in?" I dried my tears using the handkerchief and wiped some snot that was coming out from my nose.

"Are you sure about that? Do you want to stay the night with a stranger?" Derek tilted his head.

I realized what he meant. I thought about it for a moment. Then without filtering my thoughts, I said "I have an exam and a thesis defense tomorrow. And I am so exhausted." I started crying hard like a child again.

Derek tried hard not to laugh. I probably look funny. "Then Ashton lied to me. He said he was in the office. But he was really with his ex-wife. Why does this hurt so badly?"

Derek furrowed his brows and wrinkled his nose. He's got no clue about what I am blabbering about. "Hey, are you drunk? Stop crying." He said as he pulled me close.

"No. I was not even drunk." My voice sounds muffled. I can't make sense of what I was saying.

"Okay, Let's go." Then he laughed. "Your tears and your snot are all mixed up. They're not pleasing to my eyes." He wrinkled his nose as he said that as if he was disgusted by the sight of me. "Come on, let's take you home."

"No, no. Not home. I don't want to go home. Take me somewhere else, please." I put my hands together, as if in prayer.

"Fine. I will not take you home." Derek hesitated then said, "I am living with my girl best friend. Maybe you can share a room with her for tonight.

I am worried, anxious, and relieved, and sad all at the same time. The feeling was so overwhelming that I laughed and cried at once.

"Now you're losing your shit. Come on, wipe your tears before someone else sees us. People might think I am harassing you."

Derek reached for the extra helmet on the case attached to his motorcycle and put it on me. Then he put his helmet back on.

He asked for the duffle bag I held in my right hand and put it in front of him. Then he took my hand and assisted me as I mounted behind his motorcycle.

"Are you ready?" He reached for my arms and wrapped them around his waist so I could grab the handle of my duffle bag. "Hang on tight." He said, and then we sped away.

Moments later, we arrived at an apartment complex. I turned away when Derek keyed in his pin. But the door sprung open and revealed a younger-looking Asian girl. She looked happy and excited but I noticed how her smile faded quickly when she saw me.

I recognized the pain on her face when she looked at me. I know that painful look. I saw that look in the mirror that night when Ashton introduced Bianca to our family. I was that way too when I learned about their engagement and wedding. It's probably the look I had when I saw their picture eating together.

I am positive, this woman likes Derek more than just as a friend. And she could have been waiting for him to arrive for hours. I also think this is the first time Derek took a girl home.

I might have seen myself in Derek's best friend, I suddenly burst into tears and hugged her.

"Uhm, okay. Here we go crying." Derek removed his shoes from the door and put on his sleeper before he entered the house. He carried the duffel bag with him. I removed my boots too. The woman handed me a pair of slippers, and we followed Derek inside. He stood by the sofa as he scratched his head with his hand. Then he clasps his hands.

"Natasha, this is Lindsay Park. She is my best friend. I've known her almost all my life. She's also the official photographer of my team. She's Korean, but she grew up here." Then Derek approached me and put his arm over my shoulder. "Lindsay, this is Natasha, a new friend."

Derek explained what he knew to Lindsay. I realized she was very transparent as her emotions registered on her face. She seemed worried about me by the time Derek finished talking.

Lindsay's face lit up a little before she took my hand and guided me toward her room. Derek grabbed my duffle bag before I reached it and followed us into Lindsay's room. When Lindsay and I were alone, she guided me to sit on the chair. Her room is so tidy. I guessed right away how the both of us are alike.

"Are you all right?" I felt the sincerity in her words.

It took a long while before I could answer.

"It's okay if you don't want to discuss it now. "She went to her closet and grabbed a fresh towel. Then she gave it to me. "I am sorry there is only one bed for us to share. But it is huge enough for us to sleep comfortably. If you need to change, the bathroom is outside. It's the door to the right."

I understood what she meant. She asked me subtly to change first before I headed to her bed. She seemed like she was scared to offend me. I searched for some sleeping clothes, and I said to her, "Don't worry about me. I am not offended. No outside clothes on the bed? I get you. We're the same."

She smiled and admitted she was scared to offend me. I opened my duffle bag. I don't know how I managed to fold my clothes and organize my toiletries neatly when I cried hard earlier.

"You're right. We're the same." I heard Lindsay say while watching me lay my things neatly on the bed.

It was about two in the morning when I returned to the room. I have an exam at 9 AM. I know it's weird, but I don't want Ashton to worry when he wakes up. I typed a message for him but I feel so exhausted that I fell asleep as soon as I lay on the bed.

NATASHA LEFT ME

My job is already tiring as it is. But what exhausted me most today was a personal problem that popped up in the office mid-afternoon. To say that I had a long day is an understatement. I didn't even notice how much of the day had gone.

As soon as I went home, I wanted to rest. I had also been enduring a headache since the afternoon. I wanted to, so I lay down in my bed right after I came out of the shower. I am so tired that I dream about getting up many times but wake up only to realize I am still in bed. I even dreamed of Tasha coming to my room.

At about three in the morning, I decided to get up. I thought about checking on Tasha but decided against it. She has learned the habit of locking her doors now. If I wanted to see her, I would have to knock. I don't want to disturb her sleep. She has a busy day ahead of her. Maybe I'll go later. I realized I missed her last night and badly wanted to cuddle her.

When my alarm rang around five in the morning, I got up and went to her room. I gently knocked, but she did not answer. I turned the knob and it opened. Natasha's bed was empty and already made up.

I thought that she might be in the bathroom. I walked over to the door of her bath, but it was silent. "Tasha, baby? Are you in there?" I knocked at the door three times, but there was no answer. I turned the knob slowly and opened the door a little.

She wasn't there. I am starting to feel nervous. But I keep myself calm. I thought of other places in the house where she would probably be. The kitchen? Maybe she got thirsty and got herself something to drink. The poolside? I noticed she has a hobby of hanging out in the pool to calm herself when tired or anxious. I lay on the bed and waited for her for a while.

Five minutes felt too long. A yawn escaped from my mouth as I sat up from her bed. I realized that something was different among the things on her study table. It looked too clean. The notes that Tasha usually stacks at the corner of the table, her laptop, and even her purse are gone. Natasha also has a habit of hanging the clothes she'll wear the next day on the handle of her closet's door. But nothing is hanging on it.

Has she already gone to school? Why would she leave for school this early?

I know her exam won't start until 9.

I followed my instinct and moved towards her closet. Some of her things fell out on the floor when I opened them. I am not sure, but apart from the fact that her clothes are not properly folded and stacked, it also looks like some clothes are missing.

The duffle bag! I gave her that duffle bag. It usually sits in the corner of her closet. It's gone! Tasha is also too organized to let her things get disorganized. It's as if she left in a hurry. Was there an emergency that I didn't know of? Did something happen to her parents? If that's the case, I know the first thing she'll do is wake me up. Think, Ashton. Think! Where is Tasha now?

I went back to my room and grabbed my phone. She did not leave me a message. I dialed her number. It was ringing at first, but then she canceled the call. I texted and asked her where she was, but she did not respond.

Why did she cancel my call?

I paced back and forth in her room, dialed her number over and over, and racked my brains out. I tried many times to reach her but she's now out of reach. I rang one of her friend's numbers. It was still too early in the morning, and they were not answering.

It's still too early to leave for the office, but I need to find Tasha. I walked to my closet and got ready to go. Then my phone rang. I reached for my phone quickly to check if it was Tasha calling.

It's Vea!

"Hi, Vea! Thank goodness you answered!" I felt my heart skip under my chest. I brushed my beard with my hand and smacked my lips before I spoke again. "Are you with Tasha?"

I heard Vea yawn. "Sorry about that. Good morning, Ashton. Tasha isn't with me." She mumbled words I couldn't understand and heard Tim's sleepy voice. He asked Vea who she was speaking with.

"Ashton's on the phone." I heard her answer briefly. Vea cleared her throat. Then I listened to their conversation on the other end.

"Honey, did Tasha call you last night around midnight?" I overheard Tim ask her.

"What?" Vea said.

I know he was still talking to Tim so I did not answer. Then she apologized and asked if she could put me on hold. I heard scratches and taps before she went back to talk to me. "Still there?"

"Yeah. So did I hear that right? Was Tasha calling Tim last night?"

"Ah— yeah. It seems that she called both of us around midnight. But we both slept early and put our phones on silent, we didn't hear her call." I can now sense the worry in Vea's voice.

Tim started to curse in the background. I guessed he tried to call Tasha too because he's repeatedly asking her to answer. I can feel Tim's suppressed anger when he snatched the phone from Vea.

"What happened, Ashton? Did you fight? Did she run away?"

I gritted my teeth to hold the irritation I felt from the tone of his voice. question. "Look, man. I appreciate your concern. I have no idea what happened or what is running through Tasha's mind. All I know is that she was gone when I woke up this morning." I took a deep breath before I continued. "I understand how you feel. But I'd rather you let me know when she contacted you. I am sorry for ruining your morning too."

Vea got her phone back from Tim and she apologized to me. She told me she'd check their other friends, and that she'd inform me once she knew where Tasha was. I put my phone down and sent another text to Tasha.

Me: Please, baby. Talk to me. Tell me what happened. We are worried about you.

I stared at the screen and waited for her name to pop up. Minutes have passed and nothing. It's already past six and I am ready to leave. I went down to the kitchen. I was hungry, but I couldn't bring myself to eat. I sat on the stool by the counter, just staring at my phone. I got up and decided to have my cup of coffee in the office. I went outside and saw Max already waiting in the car. The thirty-hour drive to the office felt longer than it was.

For three months, Max and Tasha also developed a bond. I asked my driver if Tasha told him anything about a trip, or going away after her thesis defense since it fell on a Friday. I thought maybe she mentioned it to me but it just slipped my mind. Max said Tasha did not say anything like that.

Amanda, my secretary, wasn't at her desk yet when I arrived. I sat on my desk, looked over some documents, and signed those that I wasn't able to finish last night. But the thought of Tasha missing got me distracted. I decided to ring her cell again. This time, my call went through. But instead of her voice, I heard the voice of a man.

"Hey, sorry she can't answer your call. She's in the bath. Just try to call her again later—" The call got disconnected even before I spoke.

If Tim was with Vea, then who was that guy? Did they spend the night together? Was Tasha kidnapped? But if she was, the kidnappers would be the first to call. And they won't ask me to call her back.

All sorts of thoughts keep running through my head. She's safe. She seems safe. That's all that should matter now. But who in the hell was that guy?

I slammed my hand on the table. It startled Amanda who had just arrived at her desk. She looked at the pile of documents that I had already signed and glanced at the watch on her wrist. It's only 7:30.

"You came early, Mr. Greene. Is everything all right?"

I thought for a second. If I told her Natasha went missing, the news would spread like wildfire in the office. If the news reached Julia and Jaime, it may cause unnecessary panic. I shook my head and decided to keep it under wraps for now. Then I told her to ask the board if the nine o'clock meeting may be moved to ten-thirty.

She came just ten minutes later and told me that the meeting had been moved. A little past eight, I left her with a few instructions before I went to the parking lot. I found Max already waiting for me when I got there.

Tasha's university is only fifteen minutes away from the office. At eight-thirty, Max pulled over and parked near the entrance of the College of Business Building. Tasha attends her classes at least ten minutes before they start. I have enough time to check on her before her exam starts.

Fifteen minutes have already passed. I stepped out of the car so I could have a better look at the people who were coming in. I thought I smelled vanilla in the air when a motorcycle passed me by. My gaze followed the motorcycle. It came to a halt in front of the building. The back rider was a woman. She was getting off when somebody called my name.

"Hey, Ashton!"

I turned around and saw Camille. She pulled out the earphones from her ear and came running toward me.

"I'm sorry I wasn't able to take your call earlier. Tasha kept calling last night too. Is everything all right?" She said in between catching her breath.

I sensed the worry in her voice.

"Have you heard from Tasha? We even saw each other last night. But when I checked on her this morning, she wasn't in her room. She's also not returning my calls or answering my texts."

Except for that time when a man answered the call.

"No, I have not heard from her either. I'm sorry."

I knew Camille saw something when she opened her mouth and gasped. I followed her gaze. All I saw was the back of the motorcycle, speeding away. Puzzled, I looked back at her.

"What's wrong?"

"Huh? Nothing! I just thought I knew that guy on the motorcycle" She scratched her head, adjusted her beanie, and waved goodbye. "Hey, I've got exams to take. I'll ring you when I see Tasha, okay?"

I knew there was something she saw. But I nodded at her. Camille did not even wait for my response. She hurriedly made her way to the entrance of the building. I lingered around the entrance until a little past 9, but I saw no signs of Tasha.

Only a few students are now coming in. It's unlikely for Tasha to skip an exam like this. Her thesis defense is also scheduled for later this afternoon. I turned to Max when he cleared his throat.

"Mr. Greene, Amanda texted. He told me to remind you about the board meeting."

"You didn't see her Max?" I got in the car and waited for Max to get in too.

Max looked at me for a moment. "Well, sir. I thought I saw her."

"What? Where? Why didn't you tell me?"

"I wasn't sure. I mean, I saw a girl that looked like her. She got off the motorcycle but when I turned to call you, she was gone. So I didn't see her face."

That was her! That's why I smelled her scent in the air the moment that motorcycle passed by me.

And Camille, I am sure she saw her too! Then the realization hit me.

F*ck! The guy who was driving the motorcycle was the one who answered the call earlier.

I glanced at my watch and saw that I didn't have much time to spare. I buried my face in my hands in mixed frustration and anger. I texted Tasha again before I instructed Max to take me back to the office.

I BROKE HER TRUST... AGAIN!

*A*SHTON'S POV

My day drags on slowly. I lived it as if I were on autopilot. I signed papers, read documents and reports, and met people. The board meeting ended and I did not even understand half of it. I went to the toilet in my office and washed my face with water. I need to hold it together. It's already mid-day but I have not received any text from Tasha.

I tried to call her earlier but she turned her phone off. I glanced at my wristwatch and counted the time I had to spend in the office. That was the last meeting. I only have more papers I need to sign. Unless another issue comes along, then I can call the day off.

Natasha's defense must be over now. I wanted to get out of here badly so I could go and see her. But I have remaining work that I cannot put on hold. I browsed my social media account, and there! Natasha has a recent post on her Instagram account. It was a black-and-white photo of her, wearing a halter top.

She has her back to the camera, while her face is turned to her right where the text "Don't bother me" was written. The photo was set against a black background.

Someone named Lindsay Park took the photo. On the second slide is a photo of a page torn from a book. The entire page was blackened leaving out scattered words that looked random until someone read them. Natasha calls them blackout poetry.

Her Instagram page has a lot of that. I took a closer look at the second photo and the poem says: I am not into guys who only think about sex and run crotch-first toward every girl.

It's a cryptic post. Somehow, I feel like the post is intended for me. I wondered about Lindsay Park. I have never met or heard her name before. The photo was posted only a few minutes ago. Where is Natasha now and why is she hanging with Lindsay Park?

Amanda spoke on the intercom and pulled me out of my thoughts.

"Mr. Greene?"

"Yes, Amanda?" I brushed my hand in my hair and adjusted my sleeves.

"Alex Murphy is on line 2. He says he can't reach you."

Alex is my close friend who works as a Private Investigator. He might be calling me when I was trying to contact Tasha.

"Okay, thank you." I picked up the receiver, pressed a button, and heard his voice.

"Hey, man! I want to tell you that I have successfully secured a copy of a sample and sent it to the laboratory for DNA testing."

"Thank you. So when can I have the result?"

"In about two to three days, man. I'll ring you when it's done. Call me again when you need me."

"Okay, I will. Thank you again."

I thought about my meeting with Bianca, and then it hit me. Tasha knew about the meeting I had with Bianca. I have no idea how she knew, but that's the only thing I can think of. I looked back at her post and read the caption. There, there. She said it right there.

The caption reads: He has never actually said that he loves you. He sees you as a challenge to be worn over or a trophy to be collected and owned. While he always comes to you and says "I'll make you mine" and still chooses another.

I thought about all the moments I had shared with her and realized that Natasha was right. I have never, not once, told her I love her. This post is everything about how I made her feel. I leaned back on my chair and buried my face in my hands.

But how did she know about Bianca? Max and Alex were the only people who knew about the meeting. Natasha does not know Alex and Max wouldn't tell her that unless I instructed. Was it Bianca? Did she intentionally tell Natasha to create this mess?

Ah, that woman! I swear I would strangle her!

NATASHA'S POV

I woke up with swollen eyes and a puffy face. I went to the kitchen and found Lindsay. She has prepared breakfast for us.

"Good morning! I don't know what you are going through, but a hug always makes me feel better..."

She offered me a hug and I hugged her back.

"Hello. Good morning!"

I felt a little embarrassed because of the situation. I offered to help her but she refused. She asked me to wait at the table. I looked at the food in front of me. There were egg rolls, sausages, spam, pancakes, fruits and vegetables, and rice. Lindsay also pointed me to the cereal in the cupboard and told me to feel free to use the milk in the fridge. Then she walked toward me and handed me an empty mug.

"The coffee is right there." She pointed at the counter behind me.

I did not notice last night, but the unit was small. The living area is just a few steps from the kitchen and the sink. The space between the kitchen and the living room is the small dining table, enough to accommodate four people.

"Thank you, Lindsay!" I noticed the dark circle around her eyes and I instantly felt guilty about it. "I'm sorry if you didn't get much sleep because of my sobbing and the constant ringing of my phone early in the morning."

Lindsay shook her head. She said she understood. She seemed a little shy so I told her it was okay to ask.

"Is it about your boyfriend?" she laughed nervously as if trying to gauge my reaction.

"Well, the truth is I don't know." Lindsay took the apron off and hung it on the back of a chair.

Then she pulled the chair beside me and sat on it. When she was settled, she nodded, asking me to go on. "I don't know where I stand in his life. Am I just a fling? Or am I his lover? I really can't tell."

Lindsay nodded. Then as if in a daze, she stared at Derek's closed door before she said, "I think I get you. And it's driving you crazy because you still want to stay by his side." She paused, took a sip from her coffee, and then continued. "I wanted to be the person he needs, though he does not see you how you want him to."

I knew it. She has feelings for Derek. Ah! I'll talk to that jerk! If love does not happen to me, I should let it happen to someone else. An idea crossed my mind. But it went away on its own when Derek's door opened. He took the seat in front of me.

"Good morning, gorgeous!"

I almost cringed. Then I looked at Lindsay. Her back was on us as she went to prepare coffee for Derek. She placed the coffee in front of him, who was still smiling at me like an idiot. To clear up any misunderstanding, I got up and excused myself. It's about time to have my bath.

While I was in the shower, I heard that my phone was continuously ringing. I left it on the dining table. Its battery is running out and I forgot to bring my charger. I was supposed to borrow a charger from Lindsay, but I forgot about it while we were talking. Then at some point, the ringing stopped. The battery might have died. I heard Derek's muffled voice, but it didn't seem like he was talking to me so I just ignored it.

I remember that when I woke up this morning, there were missed calls and texts from Ashton and my friends. I knew I texted Ashton before I slept. Maybe he wants to ask where I am. But I did not open his texts because I was not ready to have a conversation with him yet. As for my friends, maybe Ashton contacted them to ask about me. I could meet and explain to them the situation later at the university.

I was right. My phone was dead when I came out of the shower. I don't know who left it, but there's already a charger beside it. I plugged it in and I checked the messages. I opened the text from my adviser first.

Professor Jackson informed me that my defense was moved to eleven in the morning because there was a problem with the schedule of one of the panelists. She asked me if I was amenable to the said changes.

While I was sure that the exam wouldn't last for more than an hour, I needed to look for someone who would sit for me as my scribe. The girls still have classes until 12 and I do not know if I can trust Tim as these things bore him.

I was seated at the edge of the sofa, my hands on my face when Lindsay entered the room.

"Hey..."

I looked up at her and she quickly sensed my worry.

"What's wrong, hon? Tell me."

"My defense was moved to eleven. I'm okay to present. But I need a scribe I can trust." I got up and gathered my things for school. "Though I can do it, I need someone to jot down the notes and the comments from my panelists and adviser. That way, I can focus on my presentation."

She smiled warmly. "I can do that. Do they allow outsiders as scribes?"

My face lit up. I smiled and hugged her. "Really? Seriously? Thank you! I'll snatch you from Derek and make you my best friend for the day. Haha!"

"Oh, dear! I'll be your best friend anytime. Haha. I can also take photos of your defense if you want."

"I would love to. So I can have something to send to my parents."

"Okay, I'll be there at ten-thirty."

A little later, Derek knocked on the room. He offered to give me a ride to school. When we reached the College of Business, I saw Ashton's car parked near the entrance. Camille was talking to him while I was getting off Derek's motorcycle. I hurriedly ran to the building when I heard Camille's voice behind me.

"Hey! I already saw you!

I turned around to face her. I know I am blushing because I feel that my cheeks are a little hot.

"Hey, Cams! I am sorry but I have an exam to catch. My defense was moved to eleven too. So I got to go."

"What? I cannot be your scribe. I don't think Vea can too. Who will sit as your scribe?"

"Don't worry about that. I already got that covered. See you at lunch, I'll introduce her to you."

"Introduce her?"

"My scribe. She's great, you guys will love her. By the way, please do not mention anything to Ashton. I am not ready to talk to him yet."

Camille seemed puzzled, but she nodded. Then we headed our separate ways. It was a little hard to focus on my exam after everything I went through the night before. Though I am confident I will pass, I do not expect to get the highest mark.

A little past ten, I received a text from Lindsay saying she was already in the building. I met her at the front before we proceeded to the defense room. She helped me set up what I needed and then sat at the front just as the panelists and my adviser arrived.

The defense lasted for more than an hour and a half. I felt so drained and exhausted when it ended. Lindsay did well as a scribe too. She took all the important points and suggestions from the panelists and I was glad it went well. I only have minor revisions to do this weekend.

I asked her if she was free for the rest of the day and invited her to have lunch with me and my friends. Lindsay agreed. When we reached the cafeteria, Tim was the first to see me. He almost ran to hug me and said, "There you are! You got us all worried!"

Vea followed Tim and hugged me too. "What happened? We're sorry we missed your call last night. Where did you spend the night?"

"I think I know where", Camille chimed in. Her singsong way of speaking was teasing. "I saw her get off some hunk's motorcycle this morning."

My eyes widened as I automatically looked at Lindsay. "Okay. I'm sorry if I got you all worried. Anyway, please, meet my new friend, Lindsay Park. My defense was rescheduled earlier, as I have mentioned to Camille." I glanced at Camille who was smiling from cheek to cheek.

"I am glad she volunteered to be my guide." Lindsay bowed and smiled warmly at my friends who were doing the same. "She is Derek Miller's best friend."

We all walked toward an empty table. They all gasped when they realized what I just said. Vea was the first to react.

"Oh! So you spent a night at Derek's? OMG! So did you—-"
I cut her off.

"Yes, I was at Derek's and I shared a room with our friend Lindsay here, who, in my opinion, looks good together with Derek." I gave my friends the cut-the-crap look and hinted about Lindsay's feelings toward Derek. I assumed they all understood when Lindsay's cheeks suddenly turned pink.

"Lindsay, these are my friends, Vea and Tim, they are together. And this is Camille."

They all shake their hands.

"I have been with the girls since the third grade. As for Tim, we met him here at the university."

"So, you speak English? Right?" Tim asked nonchalantly.

Vea smacked Tim's arms. "Forgive him. He can be slow-witted sometimes." Vea apologized to Lindsay. Lindsay just shrugged it off.

"Haha. Yes, Tim. I do speak English." She said in a perfect American accent.

"Oh, sorry! That was embarrassing." Tim said. He clasped his hands together in front of Lindsay and asked for forgiveness

"It's all right. I get that a lot all the time." Lindsay appeared more embarrassed than Tim.

Before the situation got any more awkward, I asked them to grab some food.

Over lunch, I told my friends about a photo of Ashton and Bianca having dinner together. I told them about Ashton's text and when our friend posted the photo on social media. The girls were as annoyed as I was when I first saw it. And as expected, only Tim took Ashton's side.

"It's just a photo of two old friends dining together. I am not taking Ashton's side, but I don't see anything wrong with it." Tim explained.

"How about the text? Why would he lie about working at the office?" Vea countered.

"Are you sure the photo was posted when you received Ashton's text? Their meeting might have happened before you texted him." Tim said despite the disagreeing look from me and my friends.

Lindsay seemed to understand Tim's point of view too. But then she also said that Ashton didn't have to lie. A little later, Vea and Tim are voicing out their differing opinions. I stopped them before they started to fight just because of my situation.

"So how did you end up at their house?" Camille asked me.

I noticed how Lindsay leaned a little closer toward me.

"Derek found me on the road." I laughed at the memory. "To be honest, I got scared at first when his motorcycle stopped in front of me. I thought someone was going to kidnap me or something."

They all laughed when I told them how I cried and laughed with Derek. Lindsay also told them how I looked when I arrived at their unit.

"So, what is your plan?" Camille said after a while.

"I don't know yet. I am still not ready to talk to Ashton. Like, seriously. I cannot spend the weekend with him."

"He was so worried when I called him this morning," Vea recalled. "Ashton and Tim even screamed at each other over the phone."

Tim nodded. Then he turned to me. "You could have, at least, told him not to worry about you."

"I did. I texted him before I went to sleep." I told them. I opened my purse to get my phone. I was going to show my friends my text, but when I went to see it, "Oh, no!"

"What?" They are all looking at me.

I realized I did not send the text. I must have dozed off before I could send them. Then I saw the three dots beside Ashton's name. He's typing a message. It would be too awkward to send the text now. I turned off my phone again and put it back in my purse. I told my friends about it and they do not know whether to laugh or cry at how the situation has turned out.

"If you continue to drag this on, the situation might go out of hand," Tim said.

"I know. I know that. It's just that I am not ready to talk." I didn't realize I had raised my voice until Tim reminded me to calm down.

Vea took a bite from her food and then faced me. "If that's the case, I am sorry. But I don't think you can stay with us."

We all understood what Vea meant. Well, again, except for Tim.

"We were the first people Ashton contacted when he realized she was gone," Vea told him patiently.

"And if he knows where she is, do you think Ashton would sit and wait?"

"Maybe I'll just book a room in a hotel or something", I couldn't hide the uncertainty in my voice.

Lindsay shook her head. "Well, I know you have the money to spend, but that's not necessary. You can still stay with us. I am sure Derek wouldn't mind."

"Hey, aren't you and Derek planning to do a dance cover together?" Tim asked as he pushed his empty plate away from him. "Why don't you do it this weekend? It will also help you put your mind to something else."

We all looked at Tim as if he said something sensible for the first time.

I looked at Lindsay. Her face lit up in agreement. "Yeah! I agree. I think we can do that. Do you still have classes this afternoon?"

"None. I have also taken all of my exams. I only have revisions to do. Thanks to you, you made it easy."

She clapped her hands, then she continued. "I think we can shoot the teaser photos this afternoon. Then tonight, you and Derek can work on the routines, and practice them. Then by Sunday, maybe we can shoot the teaser and the video for the dance. Is that fast enough for you?" Her eyes beamed with excitement.

"Would that be fine with Derek?"

"Oh, he's been looking forward to having you on the channel. Even some of his fans were." She raised her hand and gestured that I shouldn't worry.

"What do you mean his fans are excited?" I looked at my friends and realized they were as surprised as I was.

"Derek posted a video from that night at the bar," Lindsay said. That's actually where I first saw you. Lindsay looked a little shy when she said that.

We all went to Derek's channel to check the video. It's true. No wonder why Derek has been asking me for it. Most of his fans are clamoring to have me on his channel.

"How about his crew?" I asked Lindsay.

"They usually do what Derek says." Then she laughed. "Your friends can visit us at the studio on Sunday too.

"We are your friends too," Camille said. She gave Lindsay a quick hug, which she fondly returned.

Now I can also feel the excitement as she does. Thoughts about the dance cover suddenly filled my mind, making me forget Ashton momentarily.

Soon I drowned my worries in my friends' endless banter and waves of laughter.

FIX YOU

Lindsay and I decided to head back to their apartment after lunch. I was stunned to learn that she rides a motorcycle too. I guess that explained her outfit. I thought the look of surprise was evident on my face. She shook her head while laughing at me.

"I can teach you to ride if you want."

"Haha. We'll see. I don't even know how to ride a bicycle."

Her eyes widened, and I felt slightly embarrassed. She then handed me a spare helmet and we went on our way. As soon as we reached the apartment, she began to prepare her equipment. She suggested we take a test shot to make me feel comfortable in front of the camera during the shoot with Derek later.

Posing bareback was my idea. But the way it was executed was all hers. She guided me with the pose, where to look, and what emotion she wanted to see. I loved the result that I posted to my Instagram account right away. Moments later, I received a text from Ashton.

Ashton: Hey... I miss you.

I thought hard about whether I would reply or not.

God! I miss him!

My longing for him got the better of me. I decided to send him a text too. Ashton said he wanted us to talk and sort out our misunderstandings. I agreed. He's right. But I told him I needed to spend a few days by myself. He said it was okay with him but requested not to let another five years go by. Somehow his remarks have made me laugh.

I turned my phone off after the conversation I had with Ashton. Lindsay and I did more test shots until Derek arrived around four in the afternoon. Then we began shooting for the teaser photos.

ASHTON'S POV

Finally, I received a text from Tasha. It was nothing much, but at least I knew she was safe.

Ah! I forgot to ask him where she stayed and about the guy who answered my call earlier.

I called Amanda to my office and asked her to spearhead setting up Tasha's workstation. I should have done it sooner but it took me a long time before I could tame the 'rebel' in her. I thought she could use either of her parents' offices. But then, since Jeremy asked me to have her daughter Executive Assistant for a while, I prefer to be in the same room with her. After all, more than enough space is in this office for both of us.

Jeremy asked me to teach her daughter about the nitty-gritty of the company's operation, thus the assistant post. Soon she will be assigned to lead one of the departments and working with me would be a great training ground for her.

There was nothing much to do after I had all the meetings. I still have some documents I need to read and sign, but I didn't mind when people started coming in and out of the office and the noise they made while setting up Tasha's workstation.

Before we headed home, I asked Amanda to sort out some files that Tasha could work on by Monday. I checked my phone and automatically browsed Tasha's social media account. Tasha reshared in her story a post from Lindsay Park. I clicked the tag and it brought me to the photographer's page.

THE CAPTION READS:

I am proud of this girl. I taught her how to drive a motorcycle. And now she has acquired a new skill. She's now an expert model. *laugh-cry emoji* She's a lovely subject though!

Lindsay took the photo from a lower angle. Tasha wore a denim jacket with the upper buttons opened, over a fitted black tee. Her black pants were a tight hat highlighting the length of her legs. Black leather boots completed her outfit. Her legs are slightly spread, one stepping on the motor's pedal, and the other on the floor. Her hair was tied in a messy bun, and her hand supported her head which was slightly tilted to her left. Her lips were partly open, her gaze talked to the camera's lens.

I've never seen her this alluring! She looked like someone else in the photo, she made me miss her more. I have to say Lindsay is a good photographer too to be able to bring out that side of Tasha.

I checked more of Lindsay's posts and there: Lindsay Park, Freelance Graphic Artist, and Official Photographer of Derek Miller's Dance Crew.

That led me to check Derek's account. I saw that he has also posted new photos. It took me a while to realize that he was with Tasha in those photos, which seem to be teasers for his fans.

He wrote the words FIX YOU and told the fans that the photos are quite raw. He also said, "I rarely do this kind of dance because it requires chemistry between partners. This will be the first in the channel. This is Tasha's first time to be featured in a dance cover. Thus, I am looking forward to our many firsts together."

The first photo was of Derek, bending forward with arms stretched. One of his legs was bent forward, and the other was stretched out behind him. He was half-naked and only wore denim pants. His toned muscles and ripped abs are on full display.

Tasha laid down on Derek's back. She wore a black midriff top and skinny denim pants. Her hands were outstretched; clasping with Derek's. Her back was slightly arched, and her bum rested on Derek's lower back. She bent one of her legs and stretched the other to match Derek's form.

In the second photo, Tasha was in mid-air. Tasha is looking toward her right, away from the camera. Her upper body faced the camera as she gracefully spread her arms, while her lower body faced the same direction as her head. She stretched one of her legs in front of her while the other was bent. Derek wrapped an arm around her waist, leaning toward Tasha's opposite direction. It's as if he caught Tasha in mid-flight.

Both photos were magnificent. The lights highlighted the best features of their bodies. I read some of the comments:

"Derek will do a contemporary dance!"

"Does anyone know that lucky girl he will dance with? She's gorgeous!"

"OMG! She's that woman from the club. Check Derek's YouTube channel. He shared a clip of them dancing before."

"They are doing Fix You by Coldplay! Oh, I love their chemistry!"

"Derek, you are breaking my heart! Please tell me this stunning lady is not your girlfriend!"

"Her name is Natasha Collins. Check out her IG, she's adorable."

There are more comments that I didn't bother to read when I realized one thing. The guy from earlier was Derek! Tasha is staying at Derek's!

My chest throbbed in pain. It's as if someone has cut me open to squeeze my heart. I read the rest of Derek's posts and it says a new video will be released by Monday. So they'd spend the weekend together too.

I looked at the photo again. Natasha exuded confidence. The kind she never had in front of me. For all the months we spent together, she always seemed shy and intimidated in front of me. Even during that 'bickering stage', she mostly acted as if she walked on thin ice. And whenever we get intimate, she tends to tense up and move away.

But in these photos, she seemed relaxed, at ease, and comfortable, but sensual at the same time.

Although I am not a dancer, I know contemporary dances are intimate. It involves a lot of hugging, touching of body parts, and lifting. And the song Fix You by Coldplay? I have sung that song a lot of times. I know what the lyrics convey. Did they personally choose that?

I am confused.

Did she leave because of Bianca? Or was it because she just wanted to be with Derek? Why do I feel like I am losing her?

DEREK AND LINDSAY: A BACKSTORY

NATASHA'S POV

I have learned that Lindsay and Derek are renting a space across their apartment complex and have turned it into a dance and photography studio. The space was huge and was surrounded by large mirrors. Lindsay said he held dance classes every night from Monday to Saturday. I got a bit worried and asked about the courses for that night and tomorrow. Lindsay shrugged her shoulders and asked me not to worry about it.

Lindsay began setting up her equipment, and some of Derek's crew helped her. I saw Derek leaning against a table in the corner, his hands in his pockets. He got his eyes fixed on Lindsay. I decided to go and approach him.

"I like her. She's a genuine person." I told him as I leaned against the space beside him.

"Aha. I am lucky to have Lindsay around." He glanced at me before he returned his gaze to Lindsay.

"So, how did you guys meet? Lindsay seems to be even younger than me." I looked at Lindsay. I have wanted to ask her which university she attends, but Lindsay is so bubbly, that the topic kept jumping from one to another and I kept losing the chance to ask.

Derek chuckled, "Hah! Lindsay? She's 26 like me."

"What?! No way! I thought I was older than her!" I looked at him, searching for any sign to indicate he was joking.

"She's Asian, that's why," Derek said.

That makes sense. I love watching Korean and Chinese series. It always amazes me when I search the cast and learn about their age.

"Have you seen her studio?" He pointed to the room next to his.

I shook my head. I told him I went to the dance studio and waited while she got her equipment.

"Her studio is bigger than mine. She kept all her photography and equipment in one room. Then, she turned the other part into a classroom." Derek used his hands to gesture how Lindsay parted her studio.

"Oh, Lindsay teaches photography?" I experienced Lindsay's talent firsthand. I know how capable she is.

Derek proudly nodded his head. "She obtained her degree from UCLA," he tapped my arm then pointed at Lindsay, "then decided to work as a freelance graphic designer and teach photography in a studio next to mine."

That has surely piqued my interest. "So, tell me your story." I crossed my arms on my chest and nudged Derek with my elbow.

"Well, Lindsay, she was the new kid in middle school." He brushed his chin with his hand before he continued. "And because she's new and different, other kids are always coming to bully her. Although she's not petite, her facial features make her look weak."

He glanced at me. I nodded at him, urging him to continue.

"She used to always be on her own. And it, kind of, hurts to see her that way. His parents are rich. I used to come to their house to mow the lawn or help run some errands. You know, extra money too." He put his palm on his chest when he said, "Her parents are like her. They are also kind and warm."

I looked at Lindsay and watched how she treated others. I realized how in two days, I grew so fond of her. Then I imagined the kind of parents she has.

"That afternoon, I found Lindsay alone on their porch, crying her eyes out. She kept saying she wanted to go back and live in

Korea." A smile played across his lips. Then he pointed his index finger at me.

"The sight of you crying on that pavement last night kinda reminds me of how Lindsay used to cry back then."

I laughed at the memory of me crying on that pavement. My chest throbbed, but I ignored it and focused on the conversation with Derek. "So how did you and Lindsay end up living in an apartment together?"

He looked at Lindsay but it seemed like he was looking past her as he reminisced about their past.

"She wanted to pursue a photography career and move here." He took his hands out of his pockets and crossed his arms. "And I can't leave her on her own, you know. I felt like I should be around to defend her from her bullies. So I, kind of, follow her here."

His left foot moved as if he was kicking an invisible stone. Then he stopped. Derek looked at me. His eyes were also smiling. "And now, we're here. She became a freelance photographer and graphics artist, and I created a dance crew and worked as a freelance web developer on the side."

I smiled and rolled my eyes. "Is it just me, or all the guys I become close with are idiots?"

He furrowed his brows. "Huh?"

"I mean, look at her! She might look weak on the outside, but that girl is tough! Who are you to kid that she needs you to protect her?" I stand there with one of my hands on my waist and the other motioning toward Lindsay.

He scratched the back of his head. Then he put his hands back into his pockets.

"Did she ask you to come here with her?"

He shook his head while laughing. "Eh... no? She's persistent in trying things on her own."

"So it was you who begged her to tag you along?" I let out a loud laugh. I caught Lindsay's attention. I waved at her, and she waved back. She told us to wait just a little longer.

Derek blushed. Then he answered, "I guess you can say that. I even talked to Mr. and Mrs. Park about it."

"Haha! So it was you who didn't know how to live without her!" I glanced at Derek and saw how the color rose to his cheeks. "Do you like her?"

He did not answer, but the smile on his lips somewhat gave him away.

"You like her!" I said in a louder voice.

Derek pulled me closer and tried to cover my mouth. "Shhh! Shhh!"

I tried to conceal my laughter too late. We've already gotten the attention of his crew. But because they had no idea what was going on. They started to tease us.

"I told you to keep it down," Derek whispered after a while. Now he's the one laughing at me because I am so affected by the teasing from his crew.

"Why did I turn out this way? You like Lindsay." I poked Derek on his side.

"I do not!" He caught my hand.

"Yes, you do," I said, much quieter this time.

"Well, she's caring and easy to get along with, so she, kind of, grows on me you know?" Finally, he admitted his feelings, though indirectly.

"Did you make an effort to tell her you like her?" I followed him when he walked away.

"Are you not done yet?" Derek laughed, and then he bit his lips. "Nah. I don't want to scare Lindsay away." He put his hands on the back of his neck before he continued. "I mean, do you know how conservative most Asian families are? Yet she trusted me so much that she was willing to live with me under one roof. I don't want to ruin that trust."

"Idiot."

His jaws dropped. Then he smiled. "What did you just call me?" He locked his arm around my neck and playfully flicked his knuckles on my head.

I laughed as I tried to escape from his grasp. "She agreed to live with you because she likes you too."

Derek seemed doubtful. I followed his gaze when he looked at Lindsay. I felt guilty instantly when I recognized the pain registered in her eyes.

"You think so?" Derek pouted his lips, then he tilted his head.

Without looking back at him I said, "I know so."

"So how about you and your 'guardian'?" He made quoting gestures with his hands.

"Ashton? Ashton and I have some background stories like you and Lindsay."

"I knew it. Ashton has put that "this girl is mine" vibe on me there in the club. You know I tend to do that too whenever other guys approach Lindsay and try to hit on her.

Just then, Lindsay approached us. With his back to Lindsay, Derek stepped closer to me and whispered, "I wasn't talking too loud, right?"

I ignored him.

"Hey, you guys seem already comfortable with each other. We're ready to shoot when you are." Lindsay said.

I walked toward her and linked my arm to her arm. On the other hand, a crew approached Derek and offered him some donuts.

"Uh-huh. Talking about personal stuff. You know, the person I like... the person he—"

I didn't finish what I was going to say because Derek suddenly stuffed some donuts in my mouth. I laughed and hit Derek on his arm.

"What are you doing?" Lindsay asked Derek. She walked over to get some wipes from her purse and returned to wipe my mouth with them.

"She loves donuts, don't you?" Derek gave me a warning look.

I shook my head and was about to speak again, but Derek offered me some donuts again just in time when I opened my mouth. I laughed and asked him to stop doing it. But because my mouth was stuffed with the donut, the words came out gibberish.

All three of us ended up laughing.

"What did you say? Do you want more?" Derek stepped closer toward me. I waved my hand and said no. I zipped my lips too and promised I wouldn't talk. I was thankful when Lindsay stepped in to stop him.

A crew approached me and gave me a bottle of water. When I finished drinking, I noticed that the camera caught what happened. My jaw dropped as I pointed to the camera and they all laughed.

"That was embarrassing." I looked at Derek and Lindsay.

But both Derek and Lindsay said I look cute. Derek talked to someone named Lisa, who turned out to be a video editor. He gave her some instructions and told her to include them in the teaser.

Soon, the meeting started. Derek said he started choosing songs and the dance the night I agreed to do it with him. He chose the song Fix You by Coldplay and decided on a contemporary dance.

Then he glanced at Lindsay and me. We both made an okay sign with our hands. Lindsay whispered to me and said that Derek had already worked on the steps. He had also thought about alternative steps and routines, in case I could not do what he wanted.

The hairs on my arms stood when we started shooting. Derek looked at me and smiled. He put his hands on my shoulders and said, "Relax, we can pull it off."

Minutes later, I got comfortable doing dance poses with Derek. One of the crew suggested that Derek slightly bend over and stretch his arms and one of his legs outwards. Then they made me lie on his back.

For the next five minutes or so, all we can hear is the sound of Lindsay's camera shutter and the clapping of hands from time to time.

The crew suggested another dance move shot. Derek called one of her female crews to demonstrate it to me. It took us several shots before Lindsay said she was satisfied with the photos.

After the shooting, the three of us went to browse the photos that Lindsay took. I truly admire her talent. All the pictures came out good, especially where she made me lie on Derek's back. The light cast shadows on our body highlighting the patterns created by our outstretched muscles and the ribs on our sides.

Derek suddenly bent over behind Lindsay to the point that their faces were touching. Then his arms reached out to the keyboard, enclosing her. I saw her blush while I caught a glimpse of Derek's mischievous smile.

Ah! These two were finally coming around.

Derek chose two raw photos. "These are good. They did not need much editing." Then he posted the photo on his Instagram account. Minutes later, his fans went crazy for it.

Derek's and Lindsay's faces are almost glued together while they read the online comments. I decided to leave them, grabbed the coffee they had given me earlier, and went over to the table where the snacks were served.

FIRST DAY AT THE OFFICE

ASHTON'S POV

I spent my whole Saturday at the office and stayed until ten. Then I went straight to drink at a bar until past midnight. It was already noon when I woke up on Sunday. Maybe I drank way too much alcohol last night that I woke up with a massive headache. My voice was coarse, and my mouth felt dry. There is a tinge of bitter taste when I swallow.

The house felt warm, bright, and colorful for the past two months that Tasha was here. Last night, it was just different. It was too silent, cold, and empty.

Tasha shared a 30-second reel of her and Derek fooling around during their rehearsals yesterday. The post was mostly about Derek making fun of and pulling a prank on Tasha. She looked happy with Derek. She laughed aloud and was comfortable around him. Somehow, I agree with most of the comments on the reel. They have chemistry. Their connection seems natural and authentic.

I feel like I am losing her and I cried myself to sleep at about four this morning. God! It has only been two days, but I miss her! I reached for my phone and sent her a text.

Me: I miss you. Come home tonight.

When she did not respond, I logged on to Instagram. This time, Tasha shared in her story a reel from Derek. This time she played a prank on Derek. The time of their posting and the content looked scripted. I understand marketing and publicity stunts.

Apart from the prank, her story also showed them riding the motorcycle late last night. The rest are videos and photos of Tasha and Derek together. They casually hugged and whispered, having fun with the rest of the group, and eating together.

I cursed when I saw the overlooking view of city lights in the background. I realized Natasha and I were hanging out in the same area last night. They were at Joe's, I was at The Shack Bar & Grill. We were just in the same block!

NATASHA'S POV

These guys are fun to work with. Saying that I had a fun weekend would be an understatement. This was also my first time hanging out with quite a large group. I have experienced many firsts just in one weekend. I rode a motorcycle, did photoshoots, and hung out with other people who were not Vea, Camille, or Tim.

Derek and Lindsay have also taught me to loosen up. We did the project while having fun. And once we completed the shoot, I felt that all the bruises and the body pains I got for the past two days were all worth it.

The crew sometimes adjusted and changed the routines if they felt that I was not comfortable with it. During the last part of the shoot, I hesitated in one of the routines, so I slipped from Derek's grip. And while his reflexes are quick to hold on to me, I still ended up hurting my bottom. And no matter how I assured them that I was fine, after the shoot, Derek and Lindsay brought me to the hospital, so that they could have my lower back scanned.

Vea and Camille came to the studio on Sunday. We all hung out together and did some TikTok dances in between breaks. Like me, both of them love to dance too. They were as excited as I was when Derek invited us to his dance class. He said if we finished 10 sessions, he would officially accept us as dance crew members. I love the idea. It feels like I have something more to look forward to at night or during weekends.

I have also become closer to Lindsay. Even my friends were comfortable having her and Derek around. A smile came across my face when I thought about the budding romance between Lindsay and Derek. I felt used because he made Lindsay admit her feelings by making her jealous of me. But at least Derek's plan worked. They are now starting to acknowledge and become more honest about their feelings toward each other.

When we returned to the apartment, I showered and packed my things for tomorrow. Then I went to bed. I forgot about having to work at the office when I ran away from home. I forgot to bring any clothes that suit the office working environment. I am glad that Lindsay and I are almost the same height and that she lent me one of her clothes. She also agreed to accompany me to shop for more clothes tomorrow after the office.

The last two days were enjoyable. I was glad I agreed to it. The dance video was done by the afternoon. Maybe because it's still the weekend and my mind is still in vacation mode, I feel lazy. This morning, I thought about revising. But since they are only minor revisions and I have until Wednesday to submit the final draft, I decided to spend the day resting. Maybe it was because I was tired, I slept around nine in the evening and woke up early the next morning.

Derek offered to give me a ride to the office. He said he has some official business in the same building anyway. I heard from Lindsay that Derek is a Software Engineer. However, he works freelance because he does not want to be bound by the rules and conditions of the office environment. I assumed his meeting might have something to do with that other job.

When we arrived at the parking lot, Derek said he was early for his appointment. Derek seemed confused when he noticed that the guards and the other people who saw us either stopped or nodded to greet me. Derek held my wrist and tried to stop me from walking.

Then he asked me to confirm if J. Collins, the person the building was named after, was in any way related to me. I laughed at his reaction when I told him J. Collins was my father.

"W- wait, what?" I walked toward the elevator ahead of him. Like the guards, a few people in the elevator greeted me when they recognized me.

Derek leaned closer and whispered, "Your family owns this building?"

I hushed him and he understood. Then he said, "I'll take it back."

"Take what back?" I asked him.

"The dance class discount. You don't need a discount." I laughed at him.

Derek is supposed to meet someone on the twelfth floor. Since he was still early for his appointment, Derek asked if he could see the office where I work. I didn't see anything wrong with it so I invited him to the 16th floor.

Once in the office, I learned from Amanda that my workstation was actually inside Ashton's office. Nervousness slowly crept into my system and I wanted to back out right away. But Derek gave me a look as if telling me that I should heed the same advice I gave him about Lindsay: I should sort things out with Ashton.

I gave Derek a short tour and a summary of what my family business is all about. When Derek was about to leave, I told him how anxious I was about meeting Ashton after two days. He hugged me warmly to assure me that things would be all right. He asked about the minor injury from the routine as we broke from the hug.

It was at that moment when Ashton came in.

ASHTON'S POV

I came in earlier than usual in the office today. I missed Tasha so much that I wanted to see her right away. When I reached my office, I saw Amanda was already working on her computer. She looked up at me and gave me a warm smile.

"Good morning, Mr. Greene." I nodded at her. "Ms. Collins also came in rather early. She's already at her workstation with her friend."

"Thank you, Amanda."

I was hoping to see either Camille or Vea. But when I opened the door to my office, I saw her standing there with Derek. Both of them were startled when I opened the door. I noticed that Derek's hand was on Natasha's waist, and her hand was on his arm.

They both took a step away from each other. I stood there, looking at both of them. Natasha's cheeks are blushing, and so are Derek's. I wondered about what they were doing just before I walked in. Hugging? Kissing?

"H—hi! I mean, good morning, Mr. Greene!" Derek broke the awkward silence. He smiled politely, but I felt like he was mocking me. I nodded towards him and mouthed a very dry "morning". Then I headed to my desk.

The two of them whispered and I heard parts of their conversation. Derek asked Natasha if she was still in pain. Natasha said no. She just complained about being tired of trying to match Derek's stamina. Derek chuckled.

He told her she would eventually get used to it if they did it more often. Before Derek headed out, he asked Natasha to give him a call and keep him informed about the result and reminded Natasha about meeting again on Wednesday.

Result of what? And why do they have to meet again on Wednesday? What was that conversation about?

The tension remained in the air the moment we were alone. Tasha went to her station, pulled out one of the folders on her table, and started working. I guessed Amanda had already given her instructions.

I stole glances in her direction for the past 30 minutes and noticed that she seemed uncomfortable. I saw her stretch her arms, crack her neck, twist her shoulders, and snap her elbows.

When Tasha went out to talk to Amanda, I noticed how she touched her waist when she got up and sat slowly on her chair when she returned. She winced a little as she took her seat.

The last part of Tasha's conversation with Derek echoed in my head.

'I couldn't match your stamina'.

'You'll get better if we do it regularly'.

"Shit!"

I threw the folder at the table, and it made a loud thud. The sound startled Tasha. I got up from my seat abruptly and went out of my room.

THE HEATED ARGUMENT

NATASHA'S POV

N "Shit!"

I nearly jumped from my seat when he shouted, followed by a loud thud. Ashton got up abruptly and walked out of the room.

What is wrong with him? He kept saying he missed me, yet he did not even talk to me.

I slowly shifted from my seat, as my lower back still hurt from the fall. I made a mental note to get the scat's result this afternoon. Moments later, Amanda's head poked out the door.

"Dear, Ashton wants you in the meeting on the sixth floor, NOW!" How she said 'now' gave me the idea that he was still in a foul mood. "They are in the Budget and Accounting Conference Room. You can bring this with you."

Amanda handed me a folder containing the agenda of the meeting and some financial reports of the company.

"Thank you, Amanda."

I put on my blazer and grabbed my tablet. Then I headed out to the conference room.

ASHTON'S POV

The board members got into another heated argument just as Tasha emerged from the door. Everyone suddenly stopped talking and looked toward her. She hesitated when she saw the empty seat beside me. I motioned for her to take it and help her sit. Her scent wafted through my nose. I resisted the urge to hug her.

God, I miss her!

I knew most of the company's officials wanted to grill her. She's bound to lead one of the units, sooner or later, and there were people in this meeting room, who believed it wasn't fair just because she was Jeremy's daughter. One of them is Jacob Thompson, a man in his mid-50s and the VP for Finance.

He threw a question at Tasha the moment she took her seat.

"So, Ms. Collins. How shall we solve our problems regarding the lack of a physical storage facility for the company's increasing documents?" he smirked. He aimed to humiliate Tasha.

"Good morning to you too, Mr. Thompson," she said with a confident smile, garnering laughter from some of the people in the room. "Other companies have shifted to a paperless transaction. I don't understand why we're not doing the same."

"Can you please elaborate?"

"Well, one of the things I noticed when I worked as an administrative staff a year ago is that we print out a copy of every document for every unit to file." She looked at me before she continued. "I suggest that instead of doing that, we should just maintain centralized storage or library of hard copies and—"

Jacob cut her in mid-sentence. Tasha still looked composed, her hand resting calmly in front of her.

"Say we establish your so-called centralized storage in the room adjacent to the CEO's office on the twentieth floor, and we from Finance from the 12th floor wanted to access the file. Does it mean we have to go all the way up to have a hand on it? That's a waste of time and doesn't sound so efficient." His face showed a feeling of triumph.

"As I was saying, the centralized storage may be placed, like you said, in a room adjacent to the CEO's office. However, each unit can also keep electronic or soft copies of the documents accessible through a database."

The younger attendees of the meeting nodded their heads in agreement, while the older ones seemed perplexed at the idea.

"I have been telling this to my fa—I mean to Mr. Collins. I don't know why the company still has no database if the company is planning to expand. If this is a problem because our IT unit cannot handle the job, we can outsource it. We can hire freelance professionals to do the job for us."

"So who would manage the database?" Jacob pressed on.

"The same administrative personnel in every department receive, log, and distribute the files. Instead of using a record book, they enter the same information in the database. The documents will be scanned instead of photocopied. And only the electronic copy will be saved and filed in the database." Tasha lengthy explained.

She then talked about efficiency in editing drafts by taking advantage of the technology instead of printing drafts for the comments of each department head.

Jacob cut her again, but he spoke in a calmer voice. His face doesn't show as much pride as he did a while ago. But his comment remains sarcastic. "So how do we do it? Do we go around carrying flash drives with sticky notes for comments?"

Tasha kept smiling, but I could sense that she was also getting annoyed with the sarcasm from Jacob. "I believe you all have your email addresses?"

She looked at me and pointed at my laptop. "May I?"

I was searching for DNA and DNA samples, and I guessed she saw that before I closed the tab and logged out of my account. She gave me a questioning look. I feigned ignorance. I pushed the laptop towards her, and she logged on to her account. Then she showed them an app.

Natasha lengthily explained how the company could make use of the app to reduce paper use and conveniently quicken the company's working process.

The room fell silent. I scanned the people in attendance and waited for a response.

"Are there any more questions for Ms. Collins?" I asked. No one answered.

"Everything that Ms. Collins has said is true and correct. But let us not grill her. She's here to observe and participate and she's right. An IT professional could address your questions better."

The VP for Communications, Paul Hawkins, thanked and smiled at Natasha. Then he briefly explained and elaborated further on everything that Natasha had said. They have discussed that and the IT Head just met with an IT Consultant.

Just then, Keith Morgan, the Head of the IT Department entered the room, together with the said IT Consultant. My bad mood returned when I learned who it turned out to be.

"Good morning, Mr. Greene," the IT Consultant's smile widened when he turned to Natasha, "Ms. Collins."

Natasha whispered, "Seriously?"

What's this? Natasha doesn't know?

The IT Consultant introduced himself to everyone else. "I am Derek Miller, a Freelance IT Consultant."

Keith handed us Derek's portfolio. Then he apologized to Natasha because he didn't have a copy for her. Natasha just smiled and pulled her chair closer to me. A mix of curiosity and excitement filled her eyes. I moved the folder to my right, further from her.

"Ah!"

Natasha pinched my side. I got everyone's attention but Natasha acted like she did not do anything and casually snatched Derek's portfolio from my hands. She gave me no choice but to share the file with her.

Natasha kept her voice low, but I could hear all the "oh!" and "wow" coming out of her mouth as she read Derek's accomplishments. I sighed because the portfolio was impressive. I glanced at Derek. I feel even more pissed now that I realize how he seemed to have no flaws—he is smart, good-looking, a graceful dancer, funny, dependable, and most of all, young.

If I do not set aside my personal feelings, I will not hire Derek. After all, the need is not urgent. I can ask them to find someone else. But I would also make a fool of myself if I did that. Even the Head of IT believes that Derek is the best fit for the job, among those he screened.

After the meeting, Natasha and Derek stayed behind in the meeting room. I let the others go first and decided to wait for Natasha by the elevator. The elevator going down came first and Derek went in. When Derek left, only Natasha and I were left waiting. The awkward silence is back again.

Natasha seemed in a daze, even when we boarded the elevator. She positioned herself in front of the buttons but did not push the floor we were going to. When I moved to press the buttons, she only stepped back a little as she was seemingly lost in her thoughts. I called Tasha's name many times, but she was staring blankly in front of her.

"Hey, baby?" I tapped her shoulder.

Natasha jolted. It's as if she just realized she got in the elevator. She stepped forward to push the button but realized the number 16 already had a light on. She turned to me, still looking confused. "I'm sorry. What? Are you talking to me?"

"Are you... coming home tonight?" I never thought I would feel scared to ask her that.

"Maybe?" I'm not sure she understood my question.

The elevator door opened, and we walked straight into the office. My heart sank when I thought that maybe she was hesitating to come home because of her situation with Derek.

"So how are you and Derek?"

She looked at me, puzzled. "What? What do you mean? We just saw him."

I put the laptop on my desk. I thought it was weird how Natasha's eyes were following my movement.

"You stayed at Derek's, right?"

Her eyes moved back to my face when I spoke.

"Huh? Yes. Why?"

I knew it. I felt the familiar pain in my chest.

"So are you guys dating, sleeping together, or something?"

Her gaze went blank. Then her jaws dropped when she finally understood what I meant. She furrowed her brows. She answered me in a low voice but I could feel her anger with every word she uttered.

"Did you seriously just ask me if I slept with Derek?" She fanned her face as she walked back and forth. Then she pointed her finger at me. "Did you mean to sleep together? In one bed? Having se—?" She did not even finish her sentence.

Tears started to roll down her eyes. I don't know whether to approach her or not. I feel so stupid at the moment. I know she's crying because she's angry. Natasha let out a deep sigh before she continued.

"Yes, I stayed at Derek's. But we did not sleep in the same bed. Hell, we did not even share the same room. All the time I was there, I was in a separate room with Lindsay, her best friend." Now she came closer to me as she angrily pointed her index finger at my chest. "And please, do not make this about me. It was you who kept secrets from me. You had dinner with your former wife and lied about being in the office. It was—"

I grabbed her hand and pulled her in for a kiss. I felt my cheeks wet from the tears falling from her eyes. She pushed me away. She tried to slap me, but I caught her hand and hugged her tight. She resisted. I wrapped my arms tightly around her waist.

Natasha buried her face in my chest. I felt the tears falling from my eyes too. I gently stroke her back. She relaxes slowly. I held her until my shirt got soaked with her tears. I felt so ashamed of myself. It took me a long time before I finally spoke. I cupped Tasha's face with my hands.

"I'm sorry, babe. That was stupid. I am stupid. I don't want us to fight. I only want you to come home, please?" I cupped her face with my hands.

Natasha held my hands, which were holding both sides of her face. She avoided my gaze. I wiped her tears with my thumb. "Please, come home?"

I kissed her nose. Then I gave her a peck on her lips, but she tried to move away. I put our foreheads together as I asked her to forgive me.

"I'm sorry. Come home tonight and let's settle this, okay? I will tell you everything you need to know, okay? I miss you. I feel like I am losing myself if I can't have you back."

We were interrupted by a knock on the door. Then an innocent-looking Asian woman, about the same height as Tasha, appeared on it.

NEW BEGINNINGS

NATASHA'S POV

Amanda apologized to us. I told her it was fine and invited Lindsay in. I introduced her to Ashton and emphasized that I was with her too during the past weekend. Lindsay said both she and Derek felt concerned and guilty about the injury that I sustained during the dance routine, so she already took the result of my scan from the hospital.

Ashton asked Lindsay to hand her the result. His face was a mix of guilt and worry when he realized I got hurt during the rehearsals. He asked me to sit, then called Amanda to bring us something to eat. Lindsay refused. She said she only went to hand me the result and would return after office hours to pick me up again for our 'date'.

My scan turned out to be good. I did not hurt or break any bone but I am experiencing muscle pain. The doctor prescribed medications that should be taken only when the pain worsened. I guessed Ashton was still feeling a little embarrassed. He hinted that I can take the rest of the day off.

"Are you seriously giving me a rest on my first day at work?" I asked to clarify.

Ashton scratched his head. He also thought it seemed inappropriate, especially when we both knew how I was treated at the meeting earlier. I told him I was fine to work. Ashton said that he had a working lunch to attend to. He said he wanted me to come but might have noticed that Lindsay brought me lunch.

Lindsay apologized for not asking first, but Ashton told her it was all right. Ashton said he was thankful that Lindsay came. He said he was worried I wouldn't eat lunch, then went to his table to prepare things he'd need.

I cleared the round table at the corner of the room and helped Lindsay take out the lunch she brought us. There were three sets of everything. I knew the third one wasn't for Ashton, so I assumed Derek would be coming too. Maybe he's still talking with the IT Department Head.

Amanda knocked. She told Ashton she would spend her lunch with the other staff. Then she said, "Ms. Collins, your friend who was here this morning is here again. Shall I let him in?"

"Derek!" Lindsay and I said in unison.

Ashton furrowed his brows. But before he could answer, the door flew open and revealed Derek.

"Hello again, Mr. Greene." Derek did not even wait for him to respond. He turned to us and asked, "Are we ready to eat?"

Ashton looked at me asking. I just shrugged my shoulders. When I did not answer, he talked to Derek directly. "Excuse me, Mr. Miller. But what are you doing here in my office?"

Derek has already pulled out a chair. He looked at me confusedly, "His office? I thought your family owned the building?"

I pointed to the name on Ashton's desk. "Yes, this is his office. And yes, Ashton is family."

I don't think Derek understood, but he turned to Ashton and grinned. "Ah, right. Ashton is your uncle."

Lindsay puts her palm on her face and subtly asks Derek to stop. He refused to stop as he was purposely edging Ashton.

"I am not—" a phone call interrupted Ashton. He answered the phone and ended it quickly. Then he asked Derek again. "Why are you here? The meeting has long been over, Mr. Miller."

"I am here because my would-be girlfriend invited me to have lunch with our common friend." Derek vaguely answered, still grinning.

Ashton gathered his coat, then in an irritated tone, he turned to me. "You said—"

"It was me. I am the would-be girlfriend. No, I mean—what?"

"It's not me, Ashton. Aren't we dat—"

Ashton, Lindsay, and I spoke at the same time. Ashton appeared puzzled, then he smirked when the situation sunk in. Lindsay suddenly looked mortified when she realized what she just said. She started to fan her face with her hands. While I left my mouth opened as I turned to Derek in disbelief.

"Ooops! I was hoping to hit just one bird with a stone. I didn't mean to hit all three." He said before putting a kimbap in his mouth.

Ashton's phone beeped again.

"I believe you have to go, Mr. Greene. You can thank me later." Derek casually said.

Ashton kept his face serious when he nodded at Derek. Then he reminded me that we needed to talk later before he left. Derek took two more bites. He smiled when he noticed that Lindsay's cheeks were still red. Then he surprised her with a kiss on the cheeks and excused himself. He said he had to meet someone, then he left.

Derek closed the door behind him, Lindsay and I tried our best not to squeal. Later, Amanda came in to tell me about the instructions Ashton had left for me. He wouldn't be back for the rest of the afternoon.

Since Lindsay works freelance and has to stay in a nearby cafe to do her work anyway, I asked her if she wanted to stay for a while and do her job in the office. She agreed. It would be practical too so we can leave together earlier, without her having to go back and forth.

Ashton had left me tons to do and I was just grateful that Amanda was patient to teach me everything I needed to do. Lindsay remained at the round table, where she quietly did her job.

We take breaks and have some talk during breaks, then we head back to our respective tasks again. We didn't even notice the passing of time until Amanda knocked on the door and asked if she could leave.

Lindsay and I decided to have dinner first, then shop for office clothes. Then she took me to a famous Korean cosmetic line and chose skin care products. I was surprised to learn how much one uses solely for the face. Lindsay also gave me some skin care tips and taught me to wear light makeup, like she did mine that morning.

We got tired from all the walking that we did. After shopping, we visited the massage spa. Kimberly, the receptionist, greeted us.

"Hello, Ms.Collins! We're glad to have you back." She made a few clicks on her computer.

"Hi, Kim! Just call me Natasha, please." I smiled at her politely.

"Sure, Natasha. So is Mrs. Collins with you today?"

"Nope. She's overseas with my dad. I'm here with my friend, Lindsay Park."

"Hello, Ms. Park! I'm glad to meet you."

Lindsay reached out to shake Kim's hand "I'm happy to meet you too."

"So will you use Mrs. Collins' card?" I never got my membership card because I always went to the spa with my mom anyway. Kimberly asked as she probably typed my mom's name on her computer.

"Ah, no. We will use this." I showed him Ashton's membership card.

She gasped and put her hands in her mouth. "You're Mr. Greene's girlfriend?"

I don't know if she was disappointed or envious, but her facial expression did change. Then she composed herself. "I'm sorry. I mean he called us a while back. He told us his girlfriend and her friend were coming to use his card. Oh my God! You got a good catch right there!" She glanced at her computer and typed a few things. "I'm sorry. Excuse my mouth. Helen and Martha will attend to you. Please wait for a moment."

Lindsay and I went to the lounge and waited for our turns.

"Wow! She looks envious of you." Lindsay giggled. I smiled and shushed her. I took out the phone from my bag and dialed Ashton's number.

"So, I heard you got a girlfriend, huh?"

"Hah. Are you mad? I almost said you are my wife. But then I remember that it depends on how I will behave tonight."

I looked at Lindsay. I could tell from the way she smiled how flushed I looked.

"So, is the spa your last stop?" Ashton asked after a while.

"Yeah." I looked at Lindsay before I continued. "We were too tired. I think we're gonna sleep anytime."

Ashton asked if we had dinner or if I wanted him to prepare dinner at home. I told him that Lindsay and I ate before we went shopping. Ashton said he informed the spa about my lower back, but I should remind them again. I laughed at how he was trying to show me his affection.

"OK, thanks! I—Uhm. Bye!"

"I'm sorry, babe. Were you saying something?"

I can tell that he's teasing from the sound of his voice.

"Nothing. I said bye." I said shyly.

"I love you," Ashton said quickly, fearing I might end the call and wouldn't hear it.

This was the first time he told me that directly and caught me off guard. My face got a little warmer. I tried to hide my face from Lindsay.

"You what?" I whispered, wanting to make sure I heard him right.

"I wanted to say it later in person, but I can't help myself. So I'm saying it now." I heard him chuckle. Then after a long pause, he said, "I love you, Natasha Collins. And I understand if you're still shy to admit you love me too.

"Uh-uh. Okay. Thanks. Bye!"

I heard Ashton laugh before I ended the call. I felt my heart thudding loudly inside my chest. It is cliché, I know. But I cannot describe just how much I am feeling right now. I was confused, worried, nervous, satisfied, and happy that I didn't know whether I wanted to laugh or cry.

Did I hear him right? Did he say he loves me?

I convinced myself that maybe he was working me up so I could forgive him later. Soon, the therapists came to attend to us. They led us to a secluded room with dimmed lights. Soothing music surrounded the room. I felt so tired. My mind wanders as I listen to the song that hypnotizes my thoughts. The therapist's hands were so good too that I fell asleep with just a few strokes. I felt so relieved after. Ashton came to pick us up. We dropped Lindsay at their apartment first before we went home.

From when he came to pick us up to when we set foot inside the house, Ashton has been so caring and thoughtful.

I crossed my arms on my chest and faced him. "So what's this? The calm before the storm?"

"Heh. You can say that. But first, I want this."

He pulled me in for a kiss but I pulled away before he deepened it.

"Um, I think I should take a quick shower first."

He sighed. His eyes burned with desire, and his voice sounded a little husky when he said, "Yeah, baby. You are right."

I laughed because right after he said that he pulled me in again for another kiss. His hands stroked my thigh and cupped my butt cheeks. I felt my cheeks get a little warmer again.

"Ashton. I said I need to shower."

A naughty smile appeared on his lips. "You are good at ruining these moments. All right then." He released me from his hug and said, "Go, have a quick bath. I know you feel sticky with all that oil in your body."

I turned left when he leaned in and whispered, "I forbid you to make any more excuses later."

Ashton had a mischievous smile on his lips when I looked at him. It caused my heart to beat wildly and my breath heavy. I went to the bathroom to shower. I sang along to the music from my phone as I lavishly enjoyed the bathing products I bought with Lindsay earlier. I laughed at myself because I felt like a child using her things for the first time. I looked at all the products in front of me. I realized why I hadn't thought of using them sooner.

When I got out of the bath, I almost jumped when I saw Ashton sitting on my bed. I hesitated if I would come out or get back inside the bathroom. I didn't bother to take the bathrobe when I went in. The only thing that covered my body now was a tiny white towel that I wrapped around me.

"I'm sorry if I startled you." Ashton raised his brows as if teasing me.

"I didn't hear you come." I tried to hide a part of myself behind the bathroom wall.

"Because you're listening to a song while in the shower." He smiled.

Shit! What were the songs I was listening to when he came?

I tried to ignore him and asked him to hand me the clothes lying on my bed, right next to where he was sitting.

"Why don't you come over here and get them?" He lay down on the bed.

I blushed. "Ashton!"

He laughed. Then he got up and gathered my clothes for me. He picked my underwear, held it up, and then said, "How long do you think this little thing will last on your body?"

My jaw dropped. He's made up his mind on this. I grabbed my underwear and the rest of my clothes from him. "Are you planning on getting me laid so you can get away with what you've done?" I gave him a challenging look.

His face became a little worried. "Sorry, baby. You're right. We need to talk."

I went back to the bathroom and changed. When I returned, I found Ashton lying on the bed, his back leaning against the headboard. He studied me well and shook his head. I wore a tank top and silky shorts way above my knees.

"Babe, are you planning to torture me with that so you can get the truth out of my mouth?"

"What? Oh, this? No!"

My god! Of all the times I ran out of clothes to wear, why does it happen now?

"I wear this too when I sleep."

"Liar! I have never seen you wearing that before. Did you buy many like that one?"

"I am not lying. This isn't new, I just ran out of my "normal clothes"." I made a quotation gesture with my hands. "I only bought office clothes and cosmetic products earlier. I wear clothes like this too. You can ask my parents or my friends if you want to."

"Has Tim seen you wearing something like that?" I sensed a little annoyance in his voice.

"What? Of course not!"

That was a lie. Tim has seen me wearing one of these, but only for a brief moment.

"And Derek? Did you wear one of those when you slept over at his place?"

He's jealous, I can feel that.

"No, I did not."

That was another lie. Since I came here, Ashton has been teaching me to do my laundry. I started running out of my "normal clothes" on Thursday last week because I had no time to wash them. I let out a sigh of relief and felt guilty at the same time when Ashton believed what I said.

"Okay, tonight is the night of truth for the both of us right?" He said with his eyes probing. "Not just for me?"

"Why does it have to include me? You were the one who lied, remember?" I hate to admit it, but that came out too defensive.

"Natasha!" He said as if he was about to lose his patience.

"All right, chill! I'll tell the truth too, okay?" I raised my hands in the air. Then I asked him, "What are the rules?"

"Let us start with our recent issue with Bianca and me. Let us settle that first." He sighed. "Then tell me why you turned to Derek that night—-"

I cut him. "I didn't just turn to him!"

He put his index finger across his mouth and shushed me. "You can explain that later."

"Fine! And then?"

"Then, we will take turns asking and answering questions about things bothering us."

I felt that the back of my shirt was getting soaked with water. I thought my hair needed more drying.

"Okay. Give me more time to dry my hair. They are dripping and wetting the back of my shirt."

"Go ahead and get here fast so that we can talk." He murmured huskily, "Then let us make you wet and drip somewhere else once we're done."

"Ashton!"

I am not that naive. I understood what he meant. My face got so warm I wanted to disappear in front of him. I ran back to the bathroom to save myself from further embarrassment.

Ugh! Why does he always do that?

MOMENT OF TRUTH

Looks like I can't dodge Ashton's sexual urges tonight! I grabbed the towel and squeezed the ends of my hair with it. Then I grabbed the blow dryer. I absentmindedly watched my hair dance with the wind coming from it. Ashton's husky voice and his mischievous smile played inside my head. I stared at myself in the mirror and watched the color rise to my cheeks.

My hair had already been dried but I stood in front of the mirror. I thought of how I could divert Ashton's attention to something else. Once I gathered enough courage, I got out of the bathroom. Ashton remained on the bed, his brows furrowed as he was busy reading something that seemed to be important from his phone. I sat by the study table. He did not notice me.

Really? I've wasted a couple of minutes thinking of a way to put his mind away from dirty thoughts then, he just ignored me like this?

My cheeks warmed up again. But this time, because I felt ashamed of my thoughts. I cleared my throat. Finally, he put his phone down and looked at me. He raised the corner of his mouth. His smile reached his eyes when he asked, "Why are you sitting there?" Then he patted the space next to him with his hand.

"I am just keeping a safe distance from you. Else we would not get done."

"Hah! You have a point. So?" He crossed his arms on his chest.

I mimicked his actions. "I am ready when you are."

He clapped his hands and rubbed them together. Then he cleared his throat.

"So last Thursday, I received a phone call from Bianca. Listen, babe...it's the first phone call in four years."

I nodded at him, telling him to continue.

"She asked me if I could meet her at that restaurant," he said.

"Aha. Go on."

"I agreed because she and I were done, anyway. So in my mind, there wasn't anything wrong with that."

I guessed he sensed my disapproval when I chuckled and rolled my eyes.

"Okay, I admit it was wrong because I didn't tell you." he raised his hands as he talked.

"Exactly. So?" I signaled him to go on with his story.

"At the restaurant, she does not seem to be at ease. So I figured out that maybe, there could be some problem. And when I asked her..."

Ashton looked at me as if taunting me.

"What, Ashton? Stop with your hanging sentences. Just tell me!"

"Babe, please? Please do not get mad at what I am about to say. Please do not walk out on me and listen to everything. Promise me."

"Okay. I promise. Now, tell me!"

"She told me we have a son."

I can't resist letting out a loud gasp as I put my hands on my mouth.

"A....son?" My chest throbbed at his confession.

Did he say a son? With Bianca?

The crease between his brows sunk when he continued, "She said our son is sick with a rare condition, so she needed the money."

I tried to open my mouth, only to close them again afterward. I have a lot going on, but the proper words wouldn't come to me. I placed my hand gently on my lap. I took a deep breath and said, "Do you believe her? Is she even telling the truth?"

Ashton shook his head. "I almost believed her. But I remember that a few years ago, I heard she and Brian, the guy she cheated with, were financially struggling."

His phone beeped. He picked it up and tapped on the screen before he continued. "Our common friend said that Brian is a gambler and could be a drug user as well."

"So do you think she's using her child to extort money from you?"

He snapped his finger, then he pointed at me. "Clever girl."

"Is that the reason why you were searching about DNA earlier?"

"Yes. The day you left, I asked Alex, my friend, who also works as a private investigator, to look for something that can be sent to the lab for DNA testing." He touched his chin. "He has also checked about the child's medical history, and found out that he's perfectly healthy."

I gasped. "So she was just really using her child to take money from you."

"Yes. But I have to confirm whether the child is mine or not. That way she can't use the child against me."

I rubbed the side of my head, and then I asked him. "How long until you have the DNA results?"

He raised his phone. "I received an email from Alex today."

I slightly leaned forward. "And? Is he your son?"

"I know that child was conceived by the time Bianca and I were still together but were no longer having sex." He slightly tilted his head, trying to gauge my reaction. "The result of the DNA test has just confirmed that."

I let go of the breath I didn't know I was holding. I folded my arms in front of my chest. Ashton raised his brows. I know he knew something was coming. "So, is that everything that happened that day?"

He licked his lips. "Would you please elaborate?"

I got up from where I was sitting and slowly rubbed my hands. "Ashton, tell me. Why did you lie about being in the office while having dinner with her?"

He shook his head and then he chuckled. "Woah! I was not lying about that."

I stared at him. "Are you sure?" I picked up my phone, logged on to Instagram, and showed him the photo of him and Bianca dining together.

He made a clicking sound with his tongue. "Ah. So this photo is the culprit."

"Well?"

"Baby, I was in the office when I received your text. That dinner lasted for only about fifteen minutes or so. I did not even get to finish my food." He shifted to his position and his face slightly showed a worried expression. "I went to the office after that to do my work."

I know there is still more to him than meets Bianca. I bit my lower lip, took a deep breath, then asked him. "Then why did you smell weird that day?"

I knew my instinct was correct when he averted his gaze.

"Ashton?"

"Yes?" He looked at me, but his eyes avoided my gaze.

"I'm asking you."

"Uhm. What do you mean weird, babe?" He ran his hand through his hair.

I could tell he wanted to hide something. I debated whether I should continue probing him, I just let it slide. I took another deep breath and said softly, "When I kissed your cheek that night, you smell like a cigarette and some other woman's perfume. I also noticed how quickly you moved away from me."

He scratched the back of his head. Then he raised his hands, as if in surrender. "Okay. It was her perfume. That night, we sort of...kissed."

"Right." My chest constricted as if someone just squeezed my heart. It made the corner of my eyes water a little. I blinked, trying so hard not to cry. I walked back and forth to the room, my mind was racing. From the corner of my eyes, I can see Ashton studying me. When he was about to get up to approach me, I put my hands in front of me signaling him to stop. "Don't."

He nodded his head and sat right back to bed. "Hey, babe. Listen. It's not like what you think, okay? She kissed me. I was stunned. I've kissed those lips a hundred times, so." He looked frustrated.

I cleared my throat but could still hear my voice crach=k when I said, "So you kissed her back?

"Yes—no. No, I did not."

I put my hand on my waist and the other on my mouth. Then I turned away from him. I walked towards the closed door that led to the balcony and stood there. Ashton walked towards me and hugged me from my back.

"I'm sorry, baby. But believe me, the kiss was brief, and I was the one who pulled out first." I tried to remove his hands, but he tightened his grip on my waist. He rested his chin above my shoulder. "I mean her kiss felt familiar, but those lips. They are not yours."

I chuckled. "So each time she approaches to kiss you, you'll just kiss her back? Is that it, Ashton?"

He kissed the side of my head. "No, baby. That's why I left her without even finishing my food. I don't want her anymore. I don't have any feelings left for her."

"Are you sure nothing else happened aside from the kiss?"

He raised his right hand. "None, I swear!"

"Then, why were you so tired that night?"

He turned me slowly so that I was facing him. Then he pulled me closer to him. "Baby, I was tired. I have kept you company while you stay late doing your thesis for the past weeks."

Is he blaming me now?

He lifted my chin and planted a soft kiss in my mouth. "Then, sometimes I would join you in bed to sleep. And believe me, it's hard to fall asleep when I have this beauty right next to me. Each night was torture."

I can see the burning desire in his eyes as he claimed my mouth again. His kiss was soft and warm. Our foreheads touched when he stopped.

"I'm sorry if I doubted you." I buried my face in his chest and inhaled his masculine scent. I leaned on them and said, "That night, I believed you were working late in your office. I thought about how tired you were for the past week. I was even sorry that I lashed out at you many times I was stressing over my thesis."

I looked up at him. "Before you went home, I planned on talking about us." I bowed my head so that my forehead was touching his chest. "I tried to put aside my negative thoughts when you came home and you acted a little off that night."

I lifted my face again and met his gaze. "Even when you didn't turn to join me after you said you would just have a shower, I was more worried than mad that's why I came to your room to check on you."

I touched his face and felt his stubble in the palm of my hand. "I saw you dead tired. I was so guilty because I thought it was my fault. So I decided to go to my room and let you sleep."

Ashton lowered his head to kiss the tip of my nose. "I was planning to sleep then but decided to check my social media for a while. That's when I saw the post which has your photo."

I stepped back and sat on the edge of the bed. "Then my thoughts just seemed to spiral from there – You talking on the phone by the door and ending it without even saying goodbye to whoever you are talking to…”

“Alex.”

“What?”

“The person I was talking to. That was Alex.”

“Ah. Anyway, you end that phone call, the shock on your face, and that weird smell. I thought all those have something to do with the photo I saw.”

“So you called Derek to come and fetch you?” Ashton stood right there, in front of me. One of his hands was in his pocket while the other scratched the side of his face.

“No! My emotions were everywhere that night. I don't even know how I packed all the things I needed. I cried even until I was walking outside.” I touched the side of my head as I recall what happened that day. “I remember calling Vea, Camille, and Tim. But they were not answering.”

I got up and walked towards my study table and leaned against it. “I don't know how long I was crying beside that road when a motorcycle screeched from a distance. I was scared when it turned around and stopped. I was ready to run. But when the rider took off his helmet, I saw it was Derek.”

Ashton folded his arm on his chest, and then he chuckled.

“Cute.” The sarcasm was obvious. “Like a perfect knight ready to save his damsel in distress”. Then he waved his hand before he bowed down as if paying some courtesy.

I shook my head and rolled my eyes. Ashton returned to sit on the bed, resting his elbows on his lap.

“He's more like a jerk who teased and made fun of how miserable his friend was before he offered help.” I laughed at the memory from that night. “He laughed at me because he thought I was drunk. He said I was speaking incoherently.”

Ashton stretched out his arms and asked me to come and sit on his lap. He put his hand on my waist and kissed me on my lips. "Baby, I'm sorry if I turned you into an emotional wreck that night. I was hurt the moment I realized you left. And when I eventually learned that you were staying with him, I felt like I was breaking into tiny pieces."

I cupped his face with my hands. "I've already said how that one ended. He took me to his home, where Lindsay also lives."

"How about those intimate Instagram posts?"

I pinched his nose. "I know you knew what those meant. Those are just strategies for the clicks." Ashton furrowed his brows. "Every time you click their page and get lured to visit Derek's official website, you help make him rich."

I tilted my head to the side and squinted my eyes. "One more thing, Derek is off-limits. You witnessed it earlier, right?"

Ashton looked at me. Then he brought my hand to his lips and kissed it. "That dance video shoot. Was it something you and Derek scheduled a long time ago? I mean did you originally plan that to be on that weekend?"

"Uhm...no. It was Tim who suggested doing the dance video last weekend." Ashton rolled his eyes at the mention of Tim's name. "We were in the cafeteria, and I was planning where I could stay and what to do to get my mind off you. Lindsay was with us at that time too. So Tim suggested scheduling the said dance video."

Ashton laughed and pinched my cheek. "Ah. So you saw your friends last Friday, and none of them told me where you were."

I laughed at how cute his reaction was. "Well, that's why they are my friends and not yours."

He bit his lower lip, then he stared at me. It was becoming a little awkward because I didn't know if he was going to kiss me again, or if he was going to say something. I slapped him on his shoulder. "What? Stop staring!"

"Tim suggested that you spend the weekend with Derek, huh?" He scratched his head then he said, "And Tim?"

"What about Tim, did you have any romantic feelings for him in the past?"

I let out a confused laugh. "How should I answer that? Hmmm. Well, Tim and I got along really well. besides you," I paused and said, "Besides you and before Derek, he was the only guy I feel like I can talk to about anything in my life." I tilted my head to the side again while squinting my eyes.

"Although Tim did not know about you until I came to live here in your house."

"And why do you hide things about me from Tim?" Ashton probed.

"It's not that I am hiding things about you from him. It's more like for too long, it seems like an unspoken rule for the girls to not talk about you or any guys whenever Tim is around. Though the four of us are friends, there are still things that we don't tell Tim."

"And?"

"And originally, Tim was my friend first and I only tagged him along when meeting the girls." Aston nodded. "I don't know if the girls are talking about you when I am not with them, but the point is there was no chance for Tim to know things about you because we just don't talk about other guys when Tim is present."

He scratched his chin with his hand. "How did you meet Tim?"

"You sure have a lot of questions about Tim. Do you want to marry him?" I put my hand on my waist.

"Ah. So you're teasing me instead of answering my queries?"

I laughed. "We used to be groupmates in one of my classes during my freshman year. I was the only one in the group not smitten by his charms." Ashton smiled, probably from the realization that I did not like Tim the way he was thinking.

"Sometimes I feel like Tim is one of the girls." We both laughed. "I mean, you know. When he's around, I am just...me."

"How about Tim, does he have any romantic feelings for you? Or in the past, did he love you romantically?"

I chuckled. "I cannot answer that. Do you want us to dial Tim's number and ask him?" Ashton widened his eyes at me. "I think Tim sees me as one of the boys too. He taught me basketball so he can have someone to play with when he's hanging out with us."

"You play basketball?" Ashton seemed impressed.

"Yeah. But only a little. Tim has someone to play with when hanging out with us." I brushed my hand on Ashton's hair. "He taught me some jiu-jitsu too. He tried to teach the three of us, but Camille and Vea are not as interested in learning as I am."

There was a long pause. I began to think that our conversation was over. Then suddenly, he brushed his thumb over my lips. "Who was your first kiss?"

"A guy I went out with from high school." I casually answered. I don't know why Ashton suddenly wanted to ask me that. "So are we done talking now?"

"Uhm... Let me think." He paused for a while, and then asked, "Are there any other guys I should be worrying about?"

He pulled me in and gave me soft kisses on my shoulder.

"No. I can't think of anyone so drawn into me as this old man." I giggled. "And you?"

"None too." He squeezed me.

"Liar! Were all the girls around you blind, Mr. Greene?"

"All of them can try to catch my attention. But my gaze will always be held by the young lady." Ashton planted another kiss on my lips.

"Hmmm. You are not pulling away? This is new."

"Well, let's just say you have eased my mind from worrying."

"Did I? Hmm. Hey, let me ask you one more thing."

"Yeah?"

"Your conservative, tomboy outfits. Did I cause you to change into that?"

"Well, partly yes. But mostly, I guess it's because I just prefer to dress that way."

I got up from his lap. He moved closer to the headboard and arranged the pillows beside him. Then he reached for my hand and gently pulled me next to him.

"What do you mean?" He pulled me into a hug and kissed my neck.

"Ashton, you are distracting me." I laughed. I showed him the goosebumps on my arms. He laughed as he brushed his hands to feel them.

He leaned in and whispered in my ears. "Are you now dripping somewhere else?" Then he bit my earlobe.

I gasped. The hair on my neck and my arms raised again. He laughed against the skin of my neck.

"Hey, stop. Let me finish talking first."

"Okay. But you're not getting away this time. I have waited long enough for this." The lust was evident in his eyes.

"Hmmm.. maybe?"

"Okay. So explain."

"It was Bianca."

"What do you mean?"

"That day at the resort after you left me in the room, she came to talk to me. She told me things that made me insecure about my skin and body. She flaunted her assets and hit right back at my insecurities." Without knowing, I raised the collar of my top to cover my breast. Ashton saw what I did.

"Hey, come here." He moved so fast, and the next thing I knew, I was lying under him. His elbows were propped on the sides of my head. Then he kissed me slowly. His hands roamed to the side of my waist and stopped there.

"Are you sure you are not going to stop me?"

"Will you let me stop you?"I don't know what was happening in my body but I noticed I couldn't catch my breath.

Ashton shook his head. He cupped one of my breasts and it made me gasp. He taunted me with a smile. "First of all, they are not small. Second, they fit perfectly in my hands. And lastly, I love them."

Ashton buried his face in my neck as I offered him myself.

STATUS: IN A RELATIONSHIP

I woke up feeling sore and a little disoriented. I didn't realize I was in Ashton's room. Ashton wrapped his arm around my waist and buried his face at my nape

"Hey, little bunny! Good morning!" I turned around to face him.

Ashton kept his eyes half-shut. He gave me a mischievous smile before he asked, "What did you call me?"

I recognized the tone of his voice. I knew it was too late to take back what I said, so I ignored it. "Nothing. I said let's have breakfast. I am starving."

"That's not what I heard." He got on top of me. "Why don't we see what this bunny can do?"

"Oh no, Ashton. We can't." I pushed my hand against his chest. "I am.. a little bit... sore.."

"Does it hurt?" He looked genuinely worried.

I felt embarrassed when I nodded. Scenes from the previous night flooded my thoughts. I pushed Ashton aside, snatched the blanket from him, and pulled it to my head.

Ashton started to laugh. "What are you doing? Natasha?"

He tugged at the blanket, but I held on to it tight. I poked my head out of the blanket, Ashton started rolling me in and hugged me.

He locked his arms and legs around me and said, "I do not want to go to the office and just want to stay in bed with you a whole day."

Then he planted a kiss on my lips. When he let go of my lips, I moved closer and buried my face in his neck. We stayed that way for a while until the alarm turned on again. Ashton got out of bed and proceeded to the bathroom. I got up too and decided to make up the bed.

I returned to my room to tidy myself and readied for work. Then I went to the kitchen to prepare some breakfast. I made coffee and waffles for us. Ashton came behind me and wrapped me in a warm embrace. He's already dressed for the office.

"Hmmm. The smell of the coffee, these waffles, and you in my kitchen: what a beautiful morning to wake up to!" He kissed the back of my neck and smelled my hair.

"Ah, your graduation is in a few weeks. Then, your parents might be back for good." I heard the sadness in his voice. "I want to keep you here," Ashton said as he rested his chin on my shoulder. "Would it be selfish if I ask you to stay, and live here with me, even after your parents returned?"

I realized we hadn't told my parents about this yet. I put the sausages on a plate. Then I turned around to face him. I wrapped my arms around his neck. "I wanted to stay here with you too." And I gave him a quick kiss on his lips, "For the rest of my life."

He lowered his lips to meet mine and devoured me with his warm kisses. He pressed himself to me. I felt his growing needs between us. I pulled away from his hug "I'm sorry, bunny. I am feeling sore."

I blushed when his laughter echoed in the room. Ashton kept on stealing kisses from me until we finished eating. I headed to my room to shower and prepare for work. Ashton called me, his smile was teasing.

"Hey, are you sure you don't want to shower together?"

"No, thanks! Ashton, you are one insatiable bunny!"

He frowned. "Hey! I have slept with you for almost three weeks. I restrained myself from touching you." Then he winked, "I honestly believe I deserve some rewards."

"Well thank you for behaving like a gentleman. As for the rewards, let me think about it." I moved closer to him and kissed him on his cheeks. "Now let's prepare for work, else we will be late."

An hour later, we held hands as we walked from the parking lot to Ashton's office. Everyone had their eyes on us. We heard a few congratulations from people we both know. Others were disgusted or unimpressed with the display of affection. Not too long after I got settled at my workstation, my messenger kept beeping non-stop. I first checked the ones sent by my mom.

Mom: Hi, honey! How are you? I hope good things are happening to you lately.

Me: Hey, mom! Yeah. There have been a lot of good things.

Me: First, my defense was done and the dance cover I was telling you before was shot last weekend.

Lindsay also took some photos while presenting my thesis, and I sent them to my mother. I also sent her the link to the video released on Derek's website last night.

Me: I have not seen that video yet. But I sent you the link.

Julia: Anything else, dear? I have heard some good news from your boss in the office. When are you planning to tell me, honey?

Julia's teasing sounded along with her laughter. I glanced at Ashton who was busy with his phone too.

Me: Well, Mom, Ashton, and I... we, sort of, started to be together last night.

Julia: Hon, I hope you don't mind me asking. But is Ashton your first boyfriend?

Me: Yeah, mom! I don't remember introducing someone before.

Julia: Your dad and I thought you were with Tim. We even told Ashton that when he asked us before.

Julia: We thought you just wanted to have some privacy, and since Tim was a good guy, we did not bother you to open up to us.

Ah! That explains why he kept asking about my relationship with Tim last night.

I didn't notice I was laughing until Ashton cleared his throat. I ignored him and turned my back on him. Then I sent my last text to my mom.

Me: Hey, Mom I got to go. The boss you left here is looking grumpy. Maybe he wants me to get to work ASAP!

Julia: Okay, hon. I miss you. See you in three weeks?

Me: I miss you too, Mom. I miss Dad too. Say hi to Dad for me. I love you both.

Then I put my phone on silent mode. I put it down on the table before I turned my computer on. The phone buzzed, and I knew the messages were probably from the group chat.

I picked it up again while waiting for my computer to start up.

Vea: What is going on?

Camille: He changed his status on Facebook!

Vea: Tell me it's with you!

Tim: I am gonna kick his ass if he's in a relationship with someone else!

Camille: Did you guys talk? He's not with Bianca again?

Tim: Are you putting this conversation at the seen zone?

I laughed at their lack of patience when my phone started ringing. Tim's photo appeared on the screen. I was about to answer it when Ashton grabbed it from me.

"Hey, you kid. My girlfriend is at work. Stop bothering her."

I couldn't help but laugh at Ashton for what he did.

"What? We are at work." He gave me back my phone.

"At work, huh? Then why do you have flared nostrils?" I laughed at him again. "Were you jealous of Tim just then?"

"What? No, I am not jealous!" He fixed his tie and then walked over to his table.

"Yeah, says the big guy right here." I raised my phone to him. "Hey, I might be laughing now, but I do not like what you did."

I got up from my seat and walked towards him. "You can't just grab my phone to answer calls for me, okay? That's not cool."

His eyes couldn't meet mine. I can tell that he was slightly embarrassed. He placed his hand on the back of his neck, while the other rested on his hips. "You're right. I am sorry."

"Do you know Cupid and Psyche?" I went back to my table and grabbed the documents I had yesterday.

I saw Ashton shake his head. I walked over to his table carrying the documents and placed them in front of him.

"It's a story from the Greek Mythology book I've read before. Do you know the moral of their story?"

Ashton glanced at the documents, then he set them aside. "No. Tell me."

"Love cannot live where there is no trust. Let us not forget that." I pushed the documents in front of him. "These were the documents I finished yesterday. Amanda has already seen them. Let's do our job now, shall we?"

Ashton scratched the back of his head. He mentioned something about me bossing him around, but he couldn't complain. Because technically, I am the boss. I laughed at him as I walked back to my desk.

Before I put my phone away, my phone vibrated. Ashton asked me to check it and then he winked at me. He posted a photo of our hands intertwined on Instagram and tagged me on it. He captioned it, "Officially taken."

As expected, my phone's notification fired up. I rolled my eyes and decided to put it on silent mode before I put it in my drawer.

"Officially taken? Are you sure about that?" I looked at Ashton. I knew I couldn't contain my happiness when I heard my voice was an octave higher. It made him laugh. Then we both put ourselves to work.

OFFICE BANTER

It was about lunchtime when a petite woman entered the door. The woman wore a sexy, provocative outfit and walked hurriedly as a genuinely worried Amanda followed.

"I am sorry, Mr. Greene. I tried to stop her, but she insisted on entering your office."

I did not need to take a second look to know who the woman was. It's Bianca. I know she did not notice me as she went directly toward Ashton. She tried to plant a kiss on his lips, but Ashton moved away. The kiss landed on his cheek.

Ashton got up from his seat and wiped his cheek with his hand. He glanced at me as he wiped the kiss with his hand. I waited for Bianca to follow Ashton's gaze, but she did not. I crossed my arms as I watched the scene happening before me.

I looked at Amanda and she gave me an apologetic look. I forced a smile at her. "It's okay, Amanda. I will handle this."

Ashton broke the awkward silence. Then he moved to his desk to retrieve a white envelope from his drawer. He handed it to Bianca, who seemed to be overly excited.

"Oh, sweetheart! I know you can't resist our child."

She opened the envelope, which I guess was the DNA test result. She confirmed my suspicion when she slapped her hand on the table and threw the papers at Ashton.

"What is this, Ashton? Where is the money for our child?"

"Why don't you look at what the paper says?"

Bianca picked up the sheet of paper on the table. It only took her a few seconds to realize what she was holding.

"F*ck you, Ashton! You did a fucking DNA on our son?"

"Your son, Bianca. The paper you are holding says that. Now, please leave!"

Instead of leaving, she wrapped herself around Ashton and they both struggled because Ashton kept resisting. At some point, it felt too awkward to watch, I wondered if I should interfere or leave the room.

I decided to leave them quietly when I heard Bianca speak. My curiosity got the better of me, so I sat down again and even crossed my legs. Ashton chuckled, obviously amused by my reaction. I don't know if Bianca didn't realize I was there or if she was faking it. Because Ashton kept on glancing my way, and she had not, even once, looked at me.

"I am sorry, sweetheart. I did this because I want you back. I'll do everything for you to take me back."

Bianca's arms were still wrapped around Ashton, her back on me. I made a sad face and shook my head. I glanced at my watch and without a sound coming from my mouth, I asked Ashton to make Bianca leave. Ashton nodded and he mouthed a 'sorry' to me.

"Please, Bianca. Just leave. I have no need for you in my life." He tried to break free from her hug.

But it only made Bianca even more persistent. She tried to kiss him again, obviously rubbing her body against Ashton's. Although Ashton tried to stop and push her away, I could see he was also doing his best not to hurt her.

I understood that he isn't the abusive type. Ashton does not want to hurt her. I do admire that in him. But he's over six feet tall while Bianca is only a little over five feet. A little force would be enough to put her in her place.

My eyes widened when I saw Bianca try to unbuckle Ashton's belt.

That's it!

I smacked the table with my hands and it startled Bianca. I got up abruptly from my seat, walked up to her, and gave her face a loud slap. Everything happened in an instant, even Ashton was stunned.

And while Bianca is wearing a high-heeled stiletto, I am still taller than her. She couldn't just fight back. A moment passed and Bianca was still standing in front of me, her left hand brushing her left face. Her eyes began to water, but she couldn't even speak.

After a while, Bianca gained her composure. She held her head high and smiled at me.

"Hello, I didn't see you there. I assume you are Ashton's new bitch?"

I did not have time to think. I raised my hand and my palm landed on her cheek.

Ashton rushed to my side. I guess he wanted to shield me against Bianca, in case she would retaliate.

"The only bitch here is you." I pushed Ashton aside and slapped her face again, much louder this time. Ashton hugged my waist to stop me.

I took a deep breath to compose myself. Then in a calmer voice, I told her, "If I were you, I'd watch my words and actions because you are stepping on my property, Bianca. Leave before I get you arrested."

Ashton whispered in my ear, asking me to calm down. Meanwhile, Bianca's face was suddenly drained with color when she heard Ashton say my name.

"Tasha? Is that...is that you?" He looked at how Ashton hugged my waist. "You and Ashton—-are you...?"

Ashton turned to Bianca. He put his arm across my back and let his hand rest on my waist. "Leave, Bianca. Please, stay away from us.

We're done the moment you cheated. I won't have you back, don't bother us again."

Bianca refused to be defeated. She scanned me from head to foot. "What did you see in this walking stick that I do not have?!"

Ashton warned me. I gritted my teeth and under my breath, I told him I wouldn't let it pass. I took a deep breath before I turned to Bianca and said, "Well, honey. I guess he's choosing me because my brain is bigger than my boobs."

Oh, why am I not surprised that she can't even grasp what I said?

I raised my eyebrow at her as Ashton chuckled beside me. I elbowed him. I walked to the door and opened it and gestured for Bianca to leave. But instead, she clung to Ashton and raised her head.

"Amanda, please call security!" I turned to Ashton's secretary who promptly obliged.

Ashton has ordered Amanda to inform security that Bianca is banned from the office. Amanda was on her way to hand them Bianca's picture when she appeared in front of her, demanding to see Ashton.

The security arrived in front of Ashton's office, waiting for Amanda's call. Soon, two security personnel came into Ashton's office to escort Bianca out. Ashton called one of the men and instructed them to restrict Bianca from coming near the building.

Once we were alone, Ashton reached for my hand.

"Does your hand hurt?"

My palm was indeed red from slapping Bianca's face. Ashton tried to embrace me, but I moved away. I pinched my nose with my hand and disgustingly pushed Ashton away.

"Her smell is all over you. Go away!"

"What? Are you now mad at me too?"

Ashton laughed. It seems he enjoyed what happened a while ago and how I am reacting to him now.

"She's so tiny. All you have to do is push her a little, but you were not even making a move." I slapped Ashton on his chest. "Tell me, did you enjoy that kind of proximity with her? If I was not here, Ashton, what would you do?"

"I wanted to use force on her. But I don't want to scare you. I am sorry, babe."

Ashton tried to hug me again but I stopped him. He sniffed himself and then he laughed.

"Do I smell like Bianca? Strange! Because I can only smell shea butter and vanilla."

I rolled my eyes at him. "Oh, shut up!"

I heard him call Max on the phone. Later, Amanda came in with our lunch, and ate together at the pantry. I can tell that Amanda was a bit uncomfortable at the constant playful banter between me and Ashton. After all, for the past few days, she was used to seeing Ashton and me acting coldly toward each other.

Sometime later after lunch, Max came in with a paper bag in his hand. Ashton got it from him. Before he went to the toilet, I laughed as I turned to Max.

"Max, will you inform me if he ever asks you to bring him a fresh set of clothing again?"

Max looked at Ashton, and then they both laughed.

"Sure, Ms. Collins!"

"Just Tasha, Max. You and Amanda always forget that."

"All right, Tasha. I'll report him to you if he does that again."

Ashton stood by the toilet's door and crossed his arms over his chest. "I wonder what happened to Cupid and Psyche this morning."

"Heh! Shut up! Go on and change!"

Our laughter chimed in and can be heard even outside Ashton's office.

A NIGHT OF FUN AND LAUGHTER

Two weeks went quickly. It's Friday night and the weather is a little hot. Ashton is in his study room, he said he needed to discuss some documents with my dad. Ashton asked me to wait for him by the pool. He has a nice, modest pool at the back of his house. And I have long wanted to swim in it since I got here.

Ashton usually hangs out at the pool every Friday night or Saturday morning. I knew it from those times when I was still avoiding him. I decided to sit by the pool and dangled my feet in the water. I watched the blue light from the edges as it was illuminated in the water.

"Are you ready to go for a swim?'

I might have been so lost in my thoughts that I did not notice Ashton had returned. He stood beside me and I realized he had changed into his board shorts.

"Sorry to startle you." His lips twitched. Then he sat beside me and we spent the next minutes in silence.

I am turning 24 tomorrow. This is the first time I will celebrate my birthday far from my parents. I sighed. I seldom see my friends too. Camille and Vea enrolled with me in Derek's dance class, so we hung out twice a week.

But our meetings have been limited to that since we all began to be occupied with our personal lives. I wondered if this is what they call adulting.

"You know you can always ask them to come over," Ashton said out of nowhere.

"What, can you read my mind now?" I let out a short, quick laugh.

"Your face is not difficult to read." He said as he leaned in closer to plant a kiss on my temple.

I must have been so lost in my thoughts that I didn't even pay attention to him. Maybe he had been studying my expressions for quite a while.

"So, if I invite them, all of them can come over...including Tim and Derek?"

He sighed. "Yes, including them."

I got up to get the phone I left on the nearby table. I opened my messenger and thought about asking my friends if they were available tomorrow. Just then, the doorbell rang. I looked at the time on my phone. It's only a little past seven.

Ashton mentioned earlier that he ordered takeout for dinner. It must be the delivery guy.

I got confused when Ashton smiled. Then he held up the remote in his hand, and pressed a button, and loud, party music filled the air.

"What are you doing?" Ashton started to move awkwardly and shyly to the music.

"What? I am dancing," I followed him to the side of his house, leading to where the front door is, "Let's have a pool party." Ashton danced as he walked.

"Stop it. You're going to embarrass yourself." I laughed at his dance moves."And a pool party? With just the two of us? Or are you gonna invite the delivery man over?"

Ashton stopped dancing. He walked ahead of me and stopped at the corner, where he could already see the front door.

"Come over here and do the invite." He urged me.

I heard a lot of people's voices.

"Are those my friends by the door?" I stopped, wondering if Ashton was playing a prank or not.

"Don't keep them waiting, babe." Ashton took a few steps toward me and held my hand.

I rushed to the front lawn and was stunned when they all greeted me with "Happy Birthday" in chorus.

I jumped into Ashton's arms and gave him a quick hug.

"Thank you, babe!"

Then I ran to my friends and they gave me a group hug. All my closest friends are here – Tim, Vea, Camille, Lindsay, Derek, and some of my friends in the dance class. I noticed that some carried party decorations, while the others brought various food items and lots and lots of drinks.

I invited and led them all to the poolside. Ashton went ahead of us. He said he needed to arrange the table for the food and drinks my friends brought.

"Why are you guys here? My birthday is tomorrow." I asked in between sobs.

Camille hugged and kissed me on my cheeks. "Well, we thought you might have other plans with Ashton, tomorrow. So here we are!"

I was surprised the second time we arrived at the poolside and saw Ashton with a bouquet in his hand. I punched him in the arms. Everything was planned! I was so happy that I cried.

"Happy birthday, babe."

He kissed me on the lips. They all cheered. Then Vea came over, now, holding a red velvet cake. They all sang Happy Birthday to me. I was about to blow out the candle when Tim smashed a separate paper plate full of icing on my face.

I should have known Tim was going to do that. But he got me. I was so surprised, all my friends started to laugh. Well, except for Ashton.

"Timmmmmmmyyyyyyy!!!! I hate yooooouuuu!" I picked up the paper plate that fell on the ground and chased Tim with it.

ASHTON'S POV

Tasha has not seen her friends for quite a while. Vea contacted me yesterday and said they were planning a surprise for her. I agreed to their plan. I asked Tasha to wait by the pool as I went to my study to talk to her friends, who were on their way here.

I joined her by the pool. Soon, the doorbell rang. Tasha initially thought it was the delivery guy. I told her I ordered pizza for dinner. She was puzzled that instead of meeting the delivery guy, I turned the music and started dancing... if you can even call it that. Tasha felt even more embarrassed than I was, just watching me dance.

It didn't take her long to realize that her friends had come over for a pre-birthday celebration with us. Tears began welling in her eyes when she returned with her friends. I excused myself and surprised her again with a bouquet. She punched my arm. I kissed her. Then Vea approached us with a cake. We all sang to her, everything went perfectly as planned.

Not until Tim appeared holding a paper plate full of icing on it and went behind Tasha. Tasha bent a little to blow out her candle. I knew what was coming. I tried to warn her, but it went too fast. Tim has already smashed her face with icing.

Tasha looked annoyed at first, but then she wiped the icing from her face, bent down to pick up the paper plate from the ground, and ran after Tim. She chased her across the garden and to the front lawn. I could hear both of them screaming until they reached the poolside, laughing and wiping the icing from their faces.

"Hey! Chill, Ashton." Vea handed me a bottle of beer. "Those two arc like siblings. They always play a prank on each other. I know you'll get a hang of it too."

I looked at her friends. Camille and Lindsay are arranging the food at the corner. Derek is following Lindsay around and doing whatever she tells him to do. I laughed at myself how I was so jealous of him being with Tasha.

Some of her friends have also finished adding party decorations by the pool. I looked at Vea. She laughed watching Tim and Tasha struggling to get up from the ground.

"Do you want to bet?" She nudged me with her elbow.

I shrugged my shoulders, game to whatever she wanted to bet about.

"Before this night ends, Tasha will play a prank on Tim." She took a sip from her beer. "Tasha does not want to lose, especially to a guy. I guess you have proven that a lot of times."

I knew that very well. I remember the first morning she was here and how I planned to trick her into eating her breakfast. To this day, Natasha still believes that she won that one. I don't want to know how she would react if she learned how I planned everything.

I got lost in the thought that I didn't notice Tasha approaching me. I was not able to catch her hand so she put some icing on my nose. She giggled, and then she kissed my lips.

"Thank you so much for this, Ashton. I am happy."

I handed her a wet tissue and helped her remove the remaining icing off her face.

"Thank your friends. The whole thing was their idea."

Tasha went over to Vea and hugged her. Lindsay and Camille ran over to them and joined them in a hug. Derek followed Lindsay and put his hand on her waist. He held a bottle in his other hand, which he raised when he saw me. I raised my bottle as well.

"Ahh. I missed you, girls! I am thankful for all of these."

Natasha searched for Tim, who was busy talking to some guy by the pool. Then she whispered, "Can you girls do me a favor?"

"Sure, anything for the birthday girl," Lindsay responded.

"No matter what happens, do not let Tim in the kitchen."

Vea winked at me. I let out a chuckle. I wonder what Tasha will do this time.

"I think it's pay time for Tim, huh?" Camille giggled with Tasha.

Natasha asked me to join her in the kitchen. Once we were there, he asked for my help with the watermelon. I still don't understand what we were doing but she got a whole slice. And then one by one, she made the whole from the seeds a bit bigger. It looked like the seeds were popping out from the holes.

I don't know where she got the tweezers, but Natasha chose the biggest strawberry, cut it in half, and then asked me to remove all the seeds on the skin. It took me quite a long time to get it done. Then Tasha cut the strawberry further into halves.

"What are we doing exactly, and why are we doing it?"

"It's childish, but we're doing this because I don't want to lose to Tim."

It's weird and I am still confused, but I love seeing her happy. Natasha set aside the fruits that were cut specifically for Tim. Then I watch her prepare the other fruits and put them in different containers. Natasha smiled the whole time. Then she put more watermelon and the strawberries in a separate container and the fruits she made for Tim on top of it. She ensured the watermelon and the berries with holes were visible and on top.

"Give this to Tim, while I give these to the others. He would not suspect you to play a prank on him."

"Okay...?"

When we got out, I saw her friends looking at us. Vea took out her phone and winked at Tasha. Camille helped Tasha to distribute the salad plates to everyone, except for Tim, who seemed oblivious to what was about to happen.

That's when I approached Tim. I still do not understand what's going on. I started to think that maybe Tasha was also pulling a prank on me.

"Hey, Tim! Have some salad."

Tim looked at me, startled. But he took the container from my hand anyway.

"Wow! Thanks, maa-—wahhhhh. What the fuck is that?" He throws the container away, and some fruits fall on the ground. "Jesus Christ!"

Tim began to scratch his face, his arms, and his torso. At some point, I thought he was about to vomit. I still don't know what is happening, but he looked funny. He wiggled until he was lying on the pavement. Tasha and the girls were laughing. And just like me, the other guests do not have a clue, but we're all laughing too. Vea approached Tim and helped him get up.

"Oh, hon. Tell me you know nothing of this!" He said while giving his girlfriend a dagger look.

Vea shook her head. "It wasn't me. I was with Camille and Lindsay."

Tim rolled his eyes. He realized that Vea was recording so he snatched the phone from her.

"Fuck, it's Tasha! I know it's her. I can't get the image of the clustered holes in my head!" Tim scratched his head and then turned to me. "Your girlfriend is a bully! Ah, and you are an accomplice!"

Tasha laughed uncontrollably while holding her stomach. She couldn't even utter "sorry" to Tim because she laughed so hard.

"Care to explain what happened?"

"Tim has trypophobia. He hates seeing clustered holes. He says it makes his skin crawl." She explained in between laughter.

I finally realized Tim's reaction and everything we did in the kitchen. "You are such a bad girl."

I am starting to see this whole Tasha and Tim relationship in a funny and wholesome way. They reminded me of how me and my younger sister used to be. Later, we were all full from the food we ate. The guests are now in different groups, talking and having fun.

From time to time, Tasha walks up to them to join them and ask if they have all they need. Soon, some of her guests left, and only Tim, Vea, Camille, and her date Mark, Derek, Lindsay, Tasha, and I were in the pool. Her friends were all staying for the night, Tasha's request. But if it's up to me, I would rather have her alone, now in my bed.

At around 11 PM, the guys finished the drinks and the girls decided to have ice cream. I can hear them talking about their graduation next week. They were setting a date to shop for clothes and sharing some details about their after-party the next day.

At past midnight, all the others started to pair up, I moved closer to Tasha too. I think Tasha looked sexy in her one-piece swimsuit. I held my breath and pushed the carnal thoughts away when I saw how she innocently licked the ice cream cone that she was holding.

Tasha is truly a grown-up woman now. She has changed a lot, but she still has the innocence and charm of the young girl I used to know. She still cracks me up and drives me crazy at times, but she has matured too.

I sighed remembering her 16th birthday, which happened seven years ago today. Tasha looked stunning that day, I will not forget how her face lit up when he saw me arrive. And if I had been honest with myself, I think I mirrored that happiness and excitement when I saw her.

I came late to her party, still dealing with an inner conflict. I thought about confessing my feelings casually. I almost did. But I am not sure she heard it. I wanted to tell her about it clearly, but then I looked at all the people surrounding us that day and realized why I shouldn't.

But what if I told her that night? What if I talked to her parents and asked for their permission then? What would they say? How about my parents? That was the phase in my life when they thought I was being irresponsible and was giving them a constant headache. How would my confession affect our family and business ties then?

How about now? I am sure my parents have heard the rumors about my relationship with Natasha. But since they have not asked me about it yet, maybe they treated them just that—rumors. But what if they learned the truth? Will I make the same decision I did back then?

I remember leaving Natasha's party without telling her. I went and I left. After casually telling her I'd wait for her, I left. That night, I went to a bar and met Bianca. And I regretted everything that happened since.

ASHTON'S ROMANTIC SIDE

I decided to rest on the bench, a little further from where my friends were. Ashton said that he used to watch me by the poolside from this spot. He was right when he said it would be hard to notice someone sitting by this bench when the lights are out. This spot is partly hidden from the poolside because of the plants surrounding the pool.

I looked at all the decorations and replayed the events that took place earlier. Though I spent my birthday away from my parents I had a video call with earlier, I can say that this was one of the best birthdays I had. My heart is filled with gratitude just watching my friends who have started to talk in pairs. I sat on the bench and enjoyed eating the cone of ice cream.

Soon, I felt Ashton sitting quietly beside me. I glanced at him, and he smiled. The picture of him holding the bouquet earlier tonight took me back to my debut five ago. In some ways, Ashton still looks as rugged as he was that night. His long and wavy hair was gone, but he still had the beard that covered his face. Somehow, he looked more neat than he was on that day.

I heard him groan.

"Stop what you are doing. You're making me—"

Ashton did not continue what he was saying. I looked at him, puzzled. I licked the ice cream melting on the side of the cone and he called me a tease. I giggled when I finally understood what he meant. Ashton sighed before he took the ice cream from my hand.

"Hey! That is mine!" I tried to take it back from him.

"There are more in the fridge. You can get some again tomorrow." He removed my hand from his.

"But I've already—" Ashton already took a bite before I could finish my sentence. "Gross."

Ashton slowly turned his head toward me, his eyes wide. He swallowed the ice cream and asked, "What did you just say?" Then he smirked.

I moved away from him, feigning sadness. "That was mine."

He offered the rest of the ice cream back to me. "Eww, no."

"Eww? Did you say eww?"

Ashton seemed offended. But he laughed as he finished the rest of the ice cream. When he was done, he pulled me in and attempted a kiss. Our lips touched but I quickly pushed him away.

"No, not in front of my friends." I laughed. I wiped the ice cream in the corner of his mouth.

Ashton smiled and then kissed the tip of my nose. He put an arm around my shoulder and asked, "What were you thinking just before I came here?"

I turned my head to him, "Hmm. I was thinking about my 16th birthday."

Ashton seemed surprised. Then he furrowed his brows, "What about it?"

I sighed, "Nothing much. I just remembered it when I saw you with the bouquet earlier."

Ashton nodded his head as if he remembered something else. I continued speaking when he did not say anything.

"Did you know I thought you'd forgotten my birthday then? I thought you wouldn't come." I smiled recalling the memory. "Then you came when the party was almost over. I am not sure, but were you even drunk then?"

Ashton's eyes glistened. For a moment I thought that he was about to cry. "I am not drunk. But I did drink." He sighed. "And yes, I originally planned on not going. But I changed my mind at the last minute."

I wanted to ask why, but words just don't come out of my mouth. Instead, I stared at him and waited if he'd tell me.

"Do you remember what I told you then before I left? Have you ever heard of it?" Ashton took my hand and clasped it with his.

"I heard you, but I am not sure if I heard you correctly," I admitted, almost shy to say what I thought he said that day.

He nodded, "I asked you to wait for me." He swallowed. Ashton is about to cry, though I do not understand why.

I laughed. "You are joking, right? You asked me to wait and then you ghosted me for weeks." I tried to laugh away the pain. "Then when you returned weeks later, you were with Bianca."

Ashton stuck out the tip of his tongue and pursed his lips, and tears started to fall on his face. He propped his elbows on his lap and buried his face in his hands. His shoulders moved in between his silent sobs. He has turned emotional, I assumed he was quite drunk.

"Hey..." I moved closer to him and brushed my hand along his spine. "What's going on? Are you okay?"

Ashton nodded. "I.. uh..."

Ashton tried to clear his throat. I used my robe to wipe away his tears.

Ashton squeezed me into a hug. He told me he was sorry, though I still don't understand what he felt sorry about. I rubbed his back until he calmed down. His face became serious when he composed himself.

"Do you remember how often we hang around weeks before your 16th birthday?" Ashton asked.

I nodded my head. How could I forget those times? We were always together then. Ashton picked me up from the house to take me to school and pick me up from school to take me home. He always helps me with my homework and studies for my exams.

During weekends, I meet him to play video games, and we go to the mall and watch movies together. Sometimes we hang out with friends, other times it is just the two of us. I remember Ashton got scolded a lot because he always hung out with friends who were younger than him.

Ashton thinks like a natural businessman. That's what I always hear from my father. But he certainly doesn't want to act like one. He was childish and irresponsible. He understands how a business works, but prefers someone else to do the tasks. Ashton used to be carefree, he was a lot of fun to be with.

Apart from his looks, he does not make me feel like he is way older. And I recognized all those negative traits too. But maybe because I was young, I still liked him anyway. Thinking about it now, I don't think my present self would fall for the old Ashton. His overall personality seemed like a total jerk but then.

Ashton sniffed. His voice still cracked when he spoke. "I did not want to admit it at first, but I think I have started to like you then."

Ashton took a deep breath, then he looked up. I imitated what he did. The sky is clear above us but I only saw a few twinkling stars because lights surround us.

"That night on your birthday, I was conflicted and overwhelmed by all those emotions. I felt insecure and undeserving. I felt old and even disgusted at how I started to see you that way. God, you were young, Tasha. Why were you too young for me?"

I slowly lower my gaze. I realized that Ashton was staring at me.

He reached out his hand and brushed my face. "I don't want to come but decided at the last minute that I don't want to miss your birthday.I shaved my beard in a hurry and even hurt myself. I shaved the beard I've maintained and grown for years because I do not want other people to notice how I am too old to hang out with you."

Tears rolled from his eyes again. "I have no intention to come. I did not even buy you a gift. But I found myself driving and wishing the party wasn't over. I just picked a flower from the decorations at the entrance that night, hoping you wouldn't notice."

Ashton looked down and sighed. "And Bianca... I have also treated her unfairly. Maybe it was my fault that she cheated. She told me that every day I was with her, I made her feel that choosing her was a mistake on my part."

Ashton started to sob loudly. Some of my friends have begun to look our way. "I'm sorry. I'm sorry you don't deserve me."

I never expected that Ashton also felt that way about me. I have always assumed I heard him wrong that day. Or maybe, he told me to wait for him jokingly and interpreted it with bias on my part.

I hugged Ashton and allowed him to rest his chin on my shoulder. I understood the past better now. Maybe it's because I have aged quite a bit, but I understood where he was coming from. I don't know how much he drank but Ashton got too emotional.

Maybe he bottled up those emotions for too long that he blurted everything in one go. I wonder why he did not even talk about it when we had that talk two weeks ago.

A few minutes later, I saw my friends getting ready to leave. I held Ashton's hand and pulled him up. Then we approached them. Ashton cleared his throat. He squeezed my hand as if asking me to speak with them.

I gave a small speech and thanked my friends for coming over. I told them which room they would use, but I reminded them again just in case. We all said our goodnights, except for Tim who I thought had the most to drink. His voice was slightly slurred when he said goodnight.

"Goodnight, Tash! I wish you a happy birthday sex!"

Everyone including Ashton laughed, while my face warmed. Vea tried to cover Tim's mouth, but it was too late. Tim has always been tactless. Tim would still say those out loud, regardless of whether he's drunk or sober.

"Thanks, Tim. I will make sure she'll have that." Ashton said as he pulled me close to him.

But, that is something Ashton will not say out loud. I held my breath in embarrassment and pulled Ashton away from my friends.

"Oh, she couldn't wait!"

Tim and Ashton both said at the same time. It drew even more laughter from my friends, who were right behind us, getting inside the house.

Meanwhile, outside Ashton's house, a pair of brown eyes lurked in the dark, watching everything discreetly.

DATE NIGHT AND UNEXPECTED ENCOUNTERS

I was alone in Ashton's room when I woke up the next day. I went to the kitchen and saw that Ashton was busy preparing my breakfast in a tray and was hanging out with my friends.

"Hey, why did you come down? I was supposed to serve you your breakfast in bed."

I kissed him on the lips and joined them. Lindsay and Derek weren't there, so I assumed they must have left early. I remember Lindsay said she has a shoot today. I noticed that Vea and Camille exchanged glances with each other as if they wanted to ask something but didn't know how to say it.

Ashton understood it quicker than I did. He sighed, "It was supposed to be a surprise, but yes. I have plans with Natasha, but they won't happen until tonight. So wherever you want to go, be sure she'll be here at five." Ashton put the plate in front of me.

I looked at Ashton. Last night's celebration and his confession were more than enough for me.

"I am taking you out on a date. Don't ask for anything more, the rest of my surprise will be ruined too." Ashton smiled at my friends, then kissed my forehead.

"Sorry!"

Both of them said, Vea giggled while Camille looked more apologetic.

After Ashton left the kitchen, I heard Tim's and Derek's voices. It seems like both of them are having fun.

"Are Derek and Lindsay still here?" I took a bite of my PBJ.

"Nah. Lindsay already left an hour ago," Camille answered, but she kept her eyes on her phone.

"Why didn't they go together? Did they fight?" I asked.

Camille was supposed to answer again, but I heard another laughter from upstairs. This time, Ashton joined them.

I caught Vea rolling her eyes. "Your boyfriend has the latest game console and they're all in the game room."

Camille nodded her head. "Do you see how Derek was following Lindsay all night?"

Vea and I laughed.

"Who would have thought that the only thing that could separate him from Lindsay was a video game?" I answered.

Camille put her phone down and then narrated how things went between Lindsay and Derek this morning.

"Hmm. I guess boys will be boys." I took a sip of coffee and then wondered who Camille was texting. "And Mark? Is he upstairs too?"

"Ah, Nah. Mark did not stay over. He left last night too." I sensed the finality in Camille's voice. And as Tim always says, when Camille began channeling her inner lawyer, you wouldn't want to argue or ask her any more questions. So I decided to leave the topic as that.

I turned to Vea. She shook her head and nodded as if she could hear my thoughts. "How about we shop for a dress and watch a movie?" she suggested.

Camille readily agreed so that's what we did. We just went to my room and planned to watch a comedy film before going out to shop. We were in the middle of the movie when Tim knocked. He said they would order lunch and asked us what we wanted. Then he said he and Derek would leave after lunch.

The girls and I decided to do the same. We all had lunch and left together. Tim and Derek drove their respective cars, while Ashton dropped me and my friends at the shopping center.

We mostly spent time looking around and rarely buying anything. Tonight will be my first proper date with Ashton and I feel like my stomach is in knots. I told the girls about it.

"Ashton knows you very well and cares a lot about you. I am sure your date will turn out fine." Vea assured me.

After some time, we decided to have an afternoon snack at a café nearby. As we were walking towards the place, a man bumped into me. I am uncertain if I was seeing things but I swear there was something creepy about how the man looked and said "Sorry".

I couldn't place it well in my memory. But I know I have seen him somewhere. I looked at my friends. Both of them are busy chatting. They did not seem to notice something odd, so I decided to shrug it off. Maybe I was overthinking too much.

But the way the guy looked at me got me a little distracted. I couldn't even remember how I finished the cake I was eating. I guess the girls noticed it, so I told them about the guy.

"What? Is the guy still around? I mean do you still see him?" Camille asked as she looked around discreetly for the guy I described.

I started looking for him with my eyes too. "No. I don't see him anywhere."

After that, we all decided to come home. Ashton was in the living room watching some TV program when I arrived home.

"Hey, baby! Did you have fun?"

"Yeah... so... date night tonight, huh?"

"Yeah. So how much time do you need before we are ready?"

I shrugged my shoulders. I have no idea what to do. "I guess I'd be ready by seven. Would that be okay?"

"That would be perfect." He pulled me in for a quick hug, then he asked me to go and prepare. "I laid your dress on your bed. I hope you'll like it."

I took a quick shower and did my makeup. I have been watching makeup tutorials since I started working. And I guess it helped that I've been doing my makeup every day, I was pleased to see how it turned out. As for the hair, I decided to let it down.

Ashton chose a navy blue, sleeveless dress running just below my knees. The style of the dress complimented my body type and fitted me well. I wondered who helped him choose it. I matched the dress with a pair of sapphire earrings from my parents.

I laughed when I realized my mom probably asked Ashton to buy me these earrings. And Ashton might have intentionally decided on the dress to match their color.

I am ready before seven. I found Ashton already standing in the hallway. This isn't my first time left alone with Ashton, but I am nervous. He looked at me intently, then he offered me his elbow.

It felt unnatural.

"I have never seen you wearing this makeup before, babe. You did well. It enhances your already beautiful facial features."

I told him to stop. Then I fanned my face. We'd been together for weeks, but Ashton could still make me blush. My chest started to heave faster as I breathed.

"I am the luckiest man tonight because I will be dating this beautiful woman." Ashton kept on teasing me.

"Shut up. You're making me shy." I turned away from him. Then I whispered to him, "You look handsome too. And I love the perfume you are wearing."

Ashton's laughter echoed in the living room. He studied me then he smiled.

"Well, you look fine. Except that, I think your outfit isn't complete."

I gave him a worried look. I picked up my phone from my purse, opened the camera app, and looked at my reflection.

Ashton chuckled. Then he slid his hand into mine and pulled me closer.

"I think you are missing this."

On his hand is a black, leathered box from the same brand name as my earrings. He opened it and revealed a rose-gold necklace with a small sapphire pendant.

"Happy birthday, babe." The pendant glistened against the light when Ashton held it to show me. He went behind me and put it on my neck. The necklace has enough length that the sapphire sat elegantly above my bosom.

"Ah, this is what you meant. You got me worried for a second." I touched the pendant and gave Ashton a quick peck on the cheek. My lipstick left a mark on it. I laughed. I took out a small scarf from my purse and wiped his cheek.

"I am thankful. But babe, you don't have to do this. What you're doing every day is enough. You are enough."

Ashton shook his head. "You deserve that...and more." He cupped my face and then kissed my forehead. "Now, shall we?"

He offered his arm again and I gladly took it. Then he led me to the car where Max was already waiting. It was less than an hour's drive until the car pulled to a stop. When I looked outside, I noticed that we were at the port. I saw a couple boarding a yacht and I glanced at Ashton.

"Are we having a dinner cruise on the yacht?"

"Maybe."

A man in formal attire approached us as soon as we headed toward the yacht. Ashton gave the man his name.

Romantic music filled the air as the man led us to an elegant table set for two. I noticed that there were only a few couples on board and that there was enough space for each couple to have their privacy. I laughed inwardly as I remembered a random conversation with Ashton days before.

Ashton asked how I preferred our first date. I recall telling him I was okay with a not-so-fancy dinner date, as long as I was with him. Ashton disagreed. He did mention spending time on a yacht, but I scolded him because I thought spending too much would not be necessary. So here we are, still on a yacht, minus the glamor Ashton has initially planned.

When we claimed our seats, a waiter approached us to hand us the menu. Ashton did not even glance at the menu when he said his order. He ordered all I wanted to have too. I wondered if he had pre-ordered everything on this dining cruise many times before that he already memorized the menu.

Sometime after the yacht started cruising, our orders were served. We talked about my plans after graduation. He also mentioned talking to our parents about moving in with him, permanently. He hesitated, but the way he smiled told me he wanted to tell me something else. Ashton was sweet and caring throughout our dinner date.

Once we were done with the main course, the waiter approached us again. He brought me a heart-shaped cake with a candle on top. Following the waiter was a violinist. He first played a birthday song, followed by what I guess were romantic love songs. The other couple nearby clapped their hands. It was a bit embarrassing, but flattering at the same time.

"Thank you, Ashton. This is my best birthday ever."

He kissed my cheeks before he whispered to my ears. "Always, baby. Whatever will make you happy. I'm glad to do it for you."

When the music ended, we chose to stand by the railings, and Ashton hugged me from behind. We enjoyed in silence the beautiful skyline, the blinking lights from the city buildings, and moving cars. It was almost a two-hour cruise, but the moment seemed so fleeting. I found myself craving more when the cruise ended.

We found Max already waiting for us in the car. I thought I saw someone's shadow moving from a distance, but when I looked, there was nobody there. I decided that maybe my eyes were playing tricks on me after almost half an hour of looking at the blinking city lights from the yacht.

Soon, we reached home and continued our romantic night in bed.

NATASHA'S ABDUCTION

Today is my university graduation day. My parents arrived two days ago for my college recognition and graduation ceremonies. I have been staying in my old bedroom for two days, but I was still disoriented and thought it was a dream when I heard my mom knocking on my bedroom door this morning.

Ah! I missed this morning's routine!

My parents said they would only stay in the country for two weeks because they would return overseas. They do not know yet when they will be back here for good. It makes me sad to think about how short the time that we're going to spend together before they leave again.

I promised myself I would treasure and make the most of their stay. On the other hand, I also miss hanging around with Ashton. I grabbed my phone and then I sent him a text.

Me: Good morning, babe! I miss you.

I did not wait for his reply and headed straight to the bathroom. When I came out of the bath, Ashton had not replied yet. I wondered if he was still in bed. I made my way out of my bedroom and almost jumped when I opened my door and saw Ashton there, leaning against the wall.

"I thought you were never coming out."

I jumped to embrace him and he pulled me into a kiss.

"Oh, boy! I don't think I can get used to that!"

My dad looked as embarrassed as we were. He turned his back to us and headed back towards the stairs. "That's enough, you two. Breakfast is waiting and we still have a graduation to attend."

Mom's laughter filled the kitchen. Dad has told her what he saw. We all had our breakfast. I noticed how my dad seemed a little bit uncomfortable. Maybe that's why he kept telling random stories from their business trips abroad.

After breakfast, I returned to my room to brush my teeth and change. I decided to blow dry my hair and applied some light makeup. We reached the university about an hour later. All my friends and their families are there too. The graduation ceremony took hours, as there were speeches and presentations.

When it was over, my friends and I took more pictures together before we headed out with our respective families to celebrate. We decided to meet tomorrow morning to prepare for the after-graduation party with some of our friends tomorrow night.

THE NEXT DAY
TIM'S POV

My head still aches from the drink I had with my family last night. But I woke up early because I still had to fetch Vea and accompany the girls to buy some of the things needed for the after-party later. Soon, I drove to Vea. Then we headed to the mall to meet Tasha and Camille. We saw that Ashton and Tasha were already waiting for us when we arrived.

ASHTON AND I GOT A little closer since the night of Tasha's birthday. I found out that although Ashton is many years my senior, we have a lot of things in common. Ashton, Derek, and I have even hung out once, without Tasha and the girls. Since I am the youngest, I have found two older brothers.

"Hey, as much as I want to go shopping with you, I have work waiting for me in the office." He said as soon as we reached them. Ashton tapped me on the shoulder. "I'll leave Tasha to you."

Soon, Camille arrived and we all went to the Supermarket. It was about lunchtime when we were done shopping. We decided to eat at the mall, but there was a long queue of people in every fast-food restaurant we saw.

Tasha suggested that we load the bags of groceries in the car while Camille and Vea ordered our food. That way, without the shopping bags, the four of us can either fit at a small table in the fast food restaurant or dine in and not feel awkward in a high-end restaurant.

The both of us went to the parking lot located underground. We loaded the bags into the car when suddenly, a black van screeched in front of us.

Things happened too quickly, I had little time to react. The next thing I knew, two men got out of the van and they tried to take Tasha with them. I noticed that the two men were not carrying weapons. Since I knew some martial arts, I put up a fight. I punched one of the guys, while my foot contacted the face of the other.

I somehow managed to knock them down on the pavement. I grabbed Tasha's hand. We started to run towards the mall entrance when two men on a motorcycle blocked our way. The back rider drew his gun and pointed it at me. The two men from earlier got up and ran toward Tasha. They struggled to take Tasha as she kept on resisting.

I didn't have time to think. I ran after them, and then I heard a gunshot. I couldn't process what happened until my shoulder felt heavy. Then I fell on my knees. Soon I got overwhelmed by the burning sensation on my shoulder. I was shocked. I couldn't breathe. My shirt started to get soaked with blood gushing out of my body.

"No, Tasha..nooo.."

I wanted to get up but I couldn't even feel my knees. My vision got blurry. I saw one of the guys cover her nose with a handkerchief. Tasha's body became limp, then they carried her away in the van.

Who are those people? What will they do to Tasha? They're getting away...no, no, no.

"HELP!!!! SOMEBODY!!!!"

I don't know how long I was screaming when two shoppers approached me. Then I lost consciousness.

NATASHA'S POV

TIM AND I GOT TO THE car park to load the bags of groceries in the trunk. It didn't take long before a van stopped in front of us. Then suddenly, two men grabbed my arms from behind and forced me to get inside.

Tim tried to stop them by throwing punches and kicks. When we thought he knocked them down, Tim grabbed me and ran towards the mall entrance. But then, a motorcycle blocked our way and the back rider drew his gun and aimed it at Tim.

I automatically raised my hands. "No! Please, don't"

My heart thumped loudly against my chest. I knew the guy was ready to shoot at us, anytime. I wanted to scream, but my tongue seemed to leave me. Hot tears rolled down my cheeks as the two men from before got up and grabbed me again. I tried to resist, even when one of the men began to grab my hair.

I had a glimpse of hope when I saw Tim running after us. Then I heard a gunshot ring in the air. Tim suddenly stopped in his tracks and his eyes were filled with shock. I saw him fall to his knees as the pain registered on his face. The last thing I saw before someone covered my nose and mouth with a handkerchief was the blood spreading on Tim's shirt. Then I lost consciousness.

I don't know how long I was out. When I woke up, my hands and feet were both tied in a rope. A pungent smell, a mixture of pee and sweat, filled the air. The room seemed small and poorly lit. When my eyes finally adjusted to the surroundings, I learned that I was not alone in it.

"B-Bianca?"

"The one and only." She answered dryly.

THE CALL FOR RANSOM

ASHTON'S POV

Amanda rushed to the room while I was in a client meeting. Her face spelled worried, she could not even steady her trembling hands. I excused myself from the very understanding client.

"I am sorry if I interrupted you, Mr. Greene. But Mr. and Mrs. Collins wanted to talk to you." Amanda took a deep breath before she continued speaking. "They said it was an emergency."

I studied her face and she looked like she was about to cry. Beside Amanda was Christian Kramer, Jeremy's assistant. "Mr. Collins has already instructed Mr. Kramer to take over this meeting."

I nodded at her. Cold sweat suddenly washed over me. Whatever the emergency is, I feel like it is not something good. Jeremy has even sent his assistant to take over the meeting. I briefed Christian Kramer in the corner before I left to meet the couple in Jeremy's office.

I opened the door to Jeremy's office and Julia called my attention. "Ashton, they are in the conference room." I noticed that her eyes seemed red from crying and her voice still shook.

My hands trembled as I reached the knob. And when I pushed the door open, I found two police officers talking to Jeremy, who suddenly looked ten years older. Beside Jeremy was Camille, who was crying and talking to the same police officers. I probably turned pale when I suddenly realized what the emergency was about.

It's Tasha! Something bad has happened to Tasha!

"What is going on?" My angry, frustrated voice echoed in the room, making everyone silent.

When no one answered, I turned to Camille. She was with Tasha at the mall.

"Camille, tell me. What is going on?"

Camille started crying loudly, making me more worried.

"Where is Tasha? What happened to her?" I tried to soften my voice so as not to frighten her.

Jeremy pulled my arm. "Ashton, sit down," he guided me to a vacant seat.

"What happened to Tasha?"

It took long before Jeremy found his voice. He ran his hand through his hair. His lips trembled when he said, "Honestly, we don't know."

"W—what do you mean?" My knees suddenly felt weak. I couldn't make sense of what was happening.

Camille explained in between sobs and frantic crying what happened at the mall from the time when Tim and Tasha went ahead to the mall's parking lot to the time that they received a call from an unknown person telling them that Tim was shot and was left bleeding at the parking lot.

"T—Tim was shot? How about Tasha? Where in the hell is Tasha?" I was trying hard to control my anger.

"We don't know either. Tasha was no longer there by the time we reached the parking lot. The witnesses said she was taken into a van." Camille started to shake, Julia gave her bottled water to calm her down.

Julia got my attention and narrated what Camille had probably told them earlier. "Tim was still unconscious when Camille left the hospital. Vea was left to look after Tim's needs while they were waiting for his parents." Then she started sobbing too. "According to the person who called them, Tim said some men kidnapped Tasha. Someone kidnapped my daughter."

I felt lost. My mind suddenly went blank. I could hear them talking but I could not process the whole conversation in my head. Then a police officer entered the board room, carrying a USB stick.

"Sir, I have secured a copy of the footage from the CCTV at the mall's parking lot."

We all took a seat and watched the footage on the flat screen. We saw Tim and Tasha loading the bags of groceries in the car before a van stopped. Two men suddenly grabbed Tasha from behind, and Tim tried to put up a fight. We saw everything: the motorcycle, Tim getting shot, and the van taking Tasha away.

The police officer also showed us a clip from the gas station where the van stopped before the abduction took place. The mood lightened up when the second clip showed the kidnappers' faces. The police asked us if we knew any of them, but no one came to mind. One of the officers could not hide the disappointment on his face. Then, he assured us that, at least, they had a lead to work on. The police officers said they would only need to run it in their database to see if they would have a match.

"We're already doing what we can to identify the owners of these vehicles. We've checked all the CCTVs within their possible routes and followed their movements to locate them." He looked at Jeremy, and then at me. "If they kidnapped Ms. Collins for ransom, we are sure that the kidnappers would call any members of her family anytime soon."

I tried to ring Tasha's phone only to realize Julia was holding it.

"She dropped her phone while struggling against her kidnappers," Julia said as she raised the phone in her hand.

I nodded. I tried to stay calm, but I was raging with anger inside. I have never felt so useless in my life. For the next couple of hours, we cannot do anything other than stay in the conference room. Soon, the authorities had set up the equipment they needed to track Tasha's location, in case her kidnappers would call to demand money.

'At about six in the evening, my phone rang. It was an unknown number. My heart thumped loudly in my chest when I answered it.

"Hello? May I know who's calling, please?" I tried my best to speak politely.

"Ashton. I have Tasha with me."

I know that voice very well.

"Bianca? Was it you? You kidnapped Tasha?"

Bianca sniffed. Then she laughed dryly.

"No, Ashton! Do not listen to her!" I knew my eyes widened in shock when I heard Tasha's voice. "She's -—AHH!"

I heard a bang from the other end of the line followed by Natasha's whimpering.

"Natasha!" My hands started to shake. "Bianca, please. Do not hurt her."

I can see the worried faces of Julia and Jeremy in the corner of my eye. The others were also listening intently to the call. The officers signaled me to continue talking and stalling. Julia sobbed quietly at Jeremy's chest, trying not to make a noise.

"I won't hurt her if you follow my demands," Bianca spoke through gritted teeth. In the background, the sound of Tasha's crying can be heard.

"Okay. Tell me how much do you want?" I let out an exasperated sigh. "I will give it to you. Just please, do not hurt her, okay? Let's talk."

"I need twenty million dollars. You only have 24 hours to prepare it. I will call again later to tell you how and where I should get them."

Jeremy's tightened fist landed on my jaw as soon as the call got disconnected, I didn't have time to react. The impact sent me backward until my back hit the wall.

"It was your fault!" The police officers and Julia were quick to get a hold of him. "You drag my daughter into your problem with your ex!"

Julia pulled her back to sit in the swivel chair. He desperately ran his hands through his hair, while Julia stood behind him, trying to calm him down.

"If anything happened to my daughter, only God knows what I can do to you, Ashton!"

"Honey, stop! Please. Fighting and putting blame won't get us anywhere." Julia said in between sobs. Then she turned to the police officers. "What shall we do?"

"One of the officers signaled us to come closer to the monitor. "We are fortunate to have tracked the location of the call. We will now organize a team to rescue your daughter from her kidnappers."

"What if they change their location?" I asked worriedly.

"Then we will have no choice but to wait for them to call us again. Then we will set forth with the entrapment operations." The police officer let out a sigh. Then, he confidently said, "Our priority is to save Ms. Collins. The ransom will only be our backup plan to lure them to meet with us."

The back of my head started to ache. This is going to be the longest 24 hours of our lives.

THE FACE BEHIND THE SHADOWS

NATASHA'S POV

"B- Bianca?" I wanted to rub my eyes, but my elbows and my hands were tied together behind me.

"The one and only."

I tried to get up, and I realized that my feet were also tied with a rope from my ankle to below my knee. Every movement creates friction between the rope and my skin, resulting in small cuts and burns. It was just too hard and too painful to move.

Bianca's voice sounded dry and coarse. She slumped her body in a corner and I noticed her clothes were torn. Although the light coming into the room is dim, I can see her swollen eyes. Bianca can't even open one of them. Fresh blood oozed from the cut on her lower lip, and I could smell the foul odor coming from her body.

It doesn't make sense. What am I doing with Bianca in this small, stinky room? Why was I kidnapped with her? I studied her situation and wondered how many days she had been here. Her hands and feet were not tied, but I noticed something odd about her left leg. Was it broken?

My head throbbed again in pain. Then I felt some liquid dripping from my forehead running down the side of my left cheek.

Am I sweating? Am I bleeding? Did they hit my head? Panic started to creep into my system. I cannot stay here. I needed to escape.

I looked at Bianca. I was hesitant at first but my curiosity took over.

"W—where are we? Why are we here? Who are the people who took us? What do they want from us?"

"Hush yourself. You would get both of us hurt if they heard you."

Just then, the door burst open. A man appeared from it.

"Finally! My salvation is awake!"

I couldn't believe my eyes. Although I saw him only for a brief moment, I can't be mistaken.

"You???"

In front of me stood a six-foot, 50-year-old man. He has brown and gray hair that runs loose to his shoulder but is thinned on the head. The man looks like someone who hasn't shaved his beard for months, and his skin looks dry, dull, and dusty like he hasn't bathed in days. He wore a gray button-up shirt that exposed the hair on his chest.

My eyes widened when I realized he was the same man I bumped into on my birthday when I went out with my friends! He pulled a chair from outside the room and sat on it. He propped his elbows on his lap and placed one hand under his chin, the other rubbing and tapping his knees. The man smiled, exposing the cavities in his front teeth.

"I know you have questions you wanted to ask me." He leaned back on the chair and waved his hand in front of his face. He does this to show that he has changed into a new character. Then he imitated a woman's voice. " Who are you? What do you want from me? What am I doing in this room with this bitch?" He pointed his other hand toward Bianca.

He clapped his hand as if dusting off dirt and smiled creepily. Then in his normal voice, he said, "So let us do the introduction, shall we?"

He offered his right hand, "My name is Brian Scott." He looked at his hand and then he sarcastically laughed. "Ohh, right. Your hands are tied. My bad." He tapped my cheek twice.

His name rang a bell. Horrified, I glanced at Bianca.

This is Brian Scott who was the reason Bianca left Ashton?

"Yes, the bitch at the corner is my wife. And you are here because of her."

"What? I—I don't understa—"

Brian slapped me hard on the face, making me fall on my side. I groaned. For one, I felt a sharp pain in my shoulder when I hit the floor. Then I thought about how a struggle it would be to pull myself up in a sitting position again.

"SHUT UP! YOU CAN ONLY TALK WITH MY PERMISSION!"

I trembled at the sound of his angry voice. I curled my body when I thought he was going to kick my torso. I uttered thanks in my head when he didn't.

"Now, listen. If the bitch here had only successfully done the job I asked her to do, you wouldn't be—."

Bianca's weak and trembling voice cut him out. "I loved you. I left Ashton for you. Why are you doing this? Why are you hurting me?"

Brian got up and went over to Bianca. I could not help but wince when he slapped her twice. Then he grabbed her by the hair and shouted at her face.

"That was when the problem started!" He then held Bianca's face, squeezing the sides of her mouth. "I never loved you. I have only wanted you for sex and to have access to Ashton's money!" He pushed her away as he pointed his index finger at her. "But you were so dumb to admit our affair and even dared him to file a divorce!"

"Then…Then why did you marry me?" Confusion flashed across Bianca's face.

Brian let out a sarcastic chuckle.

"I am asking myself the same thing. Why did I marry a good-for-nothing-and-dumb-bitch like you? Why did I marry you when I can leech off what you got from the divorce, even without marrying you?"

He slapped Bianca's face again.

"I married you because I thought you were carrying Ashton's son and that I could use the boy to extort more money from his dad!"

"What—-what do you mean?"

Brian let out a grunt and then slapped her again. I wanted to stop him. At that moment, I wanted to protect Bianca from him but was too scared to move from where I was.

"You know what? Maybe I have learned to love you too. But I was disgusted when you returned from Ashton and told me about the DNA test result."

"I... I don't understand." Bianca started to cry hysterically. It looked to me like she was having an emotional meltdown.

Listening to their conversation made me confused too. Brian seemed sure about Ashton being the father of Bianca's son. But the gravity of the situation makes it harder for me to process Brian's words.

He adjusted the waistline of his pants and took a deep breath. He let out a fake laugh before he said, "I know Jonas is not mine."

Shock and confusion registered on Bianca's face.

"I have done the DNA test too, months after he was born. That was why I asked you to marry me."

He then grabbed the chair, sat on it, and crossed his legs. "I thought I could use the both of you to milk more money from Ashton. I thought he wouldn't resist his child." He laughed like a maniac when he said these words, "Oh! How I love to control Ashton through his child."

Brian slapped his hands on his lap and it startled me and Bianca. "But damn! Damn! I guess he knows you that well, right? He might know from the start that the child isn't his."

He gritted his teeth, walked closer to Bianca, and grabbed her by the hair.

"The bitch that you are, I still did not think you would go around fucking other men while you were cheating on Ashton with me."

I couldn't help but gasp. I closed my eyes when I saw Brian turn his head toward me. I prepared myself for what was coming. But instead, I heard a loud thud.

He pushed Bianca and spit at her face."I thought about selling you to the syndicate for sex. But do you still have any worth?" Brian reached for his pocket, held out a piece of paper, and tapped Bianca's face.

"How am I supposed to pay the syndicate back?" He smiled creepily at me. "Since this bitch has lost his spell on Ashton, I need your help, Ms. Collins."

Bianca grunted when Brian grabbed her hair. She whimpered in pain.

"Read this note. Then call Ashton to ask for ransom for his hot chic. Do you understand?"

Bianca nodded her head, and tears began to roll down her face. Brian pushed Bianca's head as he let go of her hair. He dialed a number on his phone. Moments later, I heard Ashton's voice. He sounded calm, but I sensed panic and anger in his breath.

"Hello? Who is this?"

Brian pinned Bianca's head on the floor as he held the phone near his mouth. Bianca swallowed before she spoke.

"Ashton, I have Tasha with me."

"No, no, no..." I heard the frustration in Ashton's voice. "It was you? You were the kidnapper?"

I knew it was stupid, but before I had the moment to think, I couldn't resist but speak.

"No, Ashton! Please do not listen to her! She is –"

Brian took three huge steps and a loud bang sounded in my head. His palm made contact with my face.

"AHHHH"

I tasted blood coming from the corner of my lips.

"Natasha!" Ashton screamed over the phone.

I looked at Brian. He placed his index finger across his lips, asking me to keep silent. Then he went back to Bianca.

"Bianca, please! Do not hurt her," Ashton sounded desperate.

Brian grabbed Bianca's head and pinned it again against the floor, making her talk through gritted teeth.

"I won't hurt her if you give in to my demands."

"Okay, okay. Tell me. What do you want? I will give it to you. Just, please. Please, Bianca! Do not hurt her. Okay? Tell me. Talk to me. What do you want? How much do you want?"

"I need twenty million dollars. And you only have 24 hours to prepare it. I will call again later to tell you how I would get them."

Brian ended the call. He lifted Bianca by her elbow until she was seated. Then he pushed her into the wall. When Brian turned to smile at me, disgust crawled under my skin. I cringed when he winked at me.

"Reserve your energy for later."

He closed the door behind him when he left. I wasted no time and scooted next to Bianca. I struggled but I got near her with effort.

"Hey..."

Worry flashed across her bruised face. "What are you doing? Do not come near me or he might hurt you too."

Just then, we heard a boy crying outside the door.

"Mamaaaaaa..."

"Jonas, son? A—are you...are you okay?"

Bianca became frantic. I know she wanted to stand up to rush to the door, but she winced in pain for every slight movement she made.

"Brian? Please do not hurt my son. I beg you."

The door opened and someone pushed the boy inside. Though in pain, Bianca crawled to reach out for her son. The boy couldn't be older than six years old. I caught sight of bruises on the skin exposed by the rip and torn in his clothes.

Oh, God! Did Brian hurt the child too? That heartless bastard!

"I'm sorry, son. This is all my fault." Bianca carried his son into her lap. She wiped his tears using her hand and kissed his cheeks.

I used to loathe Bianca. But now, seeing her pitiful situation and the poor little kid, I suddenly felt sorry for them.

"Do you know how many people there are?" I whispered, fearful that they might hear me outside.

"There were probably at least four people—I know Brian and Jerry, the driver" Bianca looked at the door and we both listened to the noise coming from outside.

Jonas whispered something in Bianca's ear and Bianca softly repeated them, as if in a play. Jonas said there were seven men outside, but not everyone seemed bad. He mentioned Aris, who turned out to be the youngest and the kindest.

"Aris isn't bad. He fed and played with Jonas when Brian was away." I heard the kid say. He looks so innocent as he narrates what happened in the third person. "But the man they call Jugger, he is scary and bad. He hit Jonas in the head." Jonas touched the back of his head.

Bianca looked scared and worried for his son. I think Jonas was about to cry too. But Bianca hugged him and she kissed the back of Jonas' head. She promised that she wouldn't let it happen again.

Jonas hugged Bianca and he smiled. I envy how quickly he seemed to forget the situation we were in. "Aris got hurt because of Jonas. He tried to stop Jugger. Jugger punched him in the face."

"Oh, my poor baby." Bianca cried as he hugged his son.

Jonas has witnessed and experienced too much violence at such a young age. I feel sorry for him for the trauma that he has to go through after this. My eyes started to water and my sight get blurry from the tears. I closed my eyes to make the tears fall off. When I opened my eyes again, Bianca leaned against the wall as Jonas climbed onto her lap, facing his mother. Then he rested his head against Bianca's chest. Bianca hummed a lullaby, trying to put his son to sleep.

As I watched the two of them, I realized why Brian thought the kid was Ashton's son. When Jonas came in, the light from outside reflected his face for a moment and I saw he's got blue eyes. His hair is dark and wavy too, just like Ashton's.

The kid even twitched his mouth to one side when he smiled. The resemblance is too much, if I didn't see the DNA result, I would think too that Jonas is, indeed, Ashton's son.

After a while, Bianca whispered, "The driver isn't like the rest. Somehow, he was also being held captive. I know he owed Brian something. Though I did not bother to ask about the details."

"Do you think we can trust him?" I coughed after I talked. My throat felt dry, my lips were starting to chap.

"I am not sure. Maybe we can trust him. But I cannot say if he is reliable." Bianca kept on stroking Jonas' back.

"What do you mean?"

"Well he is kind-hearted but he fears Brian so much. He would tell Brian if he caught us doing anything."

"Do you know the way around here?" I grunted as I tried to sit up.

Bianca let out a dry, coarse, laugh.

"I would not dare to escape if I were you." She said, pointing to her leg. "They are probably having dinner at this time. No one will be staying right outside of this room. It was about this time when I tried to escape. But there isn't any way out."

Oh. She tried to escape and hurt her leg. Or did they hurt her?

I shuddered at the thought. Outside, I cannot hear anyone talking. No movements. No whispering. Nothing. Bianca is right. They leave the post at this time. But how can I escape? Bianca interrupted my thoughts.

"I know Ashton will save you. Like he always does." Tears flowed from her eyes. "I am sorry for causing this, Tasha." She looked up as if trying to suppress her tears. Then she wiped them away using her fingers. "I wish I could turn back time."

I wanted to calm her, but it was too hard to move. The wound in my elbow, my wrists, and my legs burn. Bianca sniffed, and then she looked at me. What she said next surprised me.

"I knew Ashton has always liked you." She shook her head as if trying to forget something that had crossed her mind. "That was why I told you those hurtful things when I heard you confessing to him."

Tears filled her eyes.

"You were too young then. And I knew too that the only reason why Ashton stayed with me was that he couldn't have you. I was so afraid that Ashton would leave me when you reached the legal age."

Although I have already heard everything from Ashton, Bianca's side of the story has still left me dumbfounded. There I was, all those years thinking about how lucky and confident Bianca was. I did not know how she battled with her demons and how much time she wasted overthinking things that were not happening yet.

"When I came to his office that day and saw how he rushed to your side to protect you from me? I realized that my fear was valid. That they had come true."

"If you were that afraid to lose Ashton, why did you leave him for another man?" I was uncertain if it was the situation, but I got too emotional. Tears began to fall from my eyes again.

Bianca answered me with a laugh. Then she kissed the side of his son's head.

"Ashton was my first serious relationship. Before him, I used to sleep around with men. But when I met him, I was happy with how he treated me. I knew he cared a lot about me. I can feel it in every little thing he did for me."

She shifted her position. I thought her eyes glowed with a hint of happiness for a second. "I was even happier when he proposed to me. Like I can't believe my luck that a man like Ashton was happening to me." The smile on her face vanished when she looked at me.

"Ashton became very busy with work. Suddenly, I felt that he had no time for me and I got pushed to the side. I became demanding and irrational. I fight with him when I can't get him to do what I want. I became very selfish and mean."

I nodded. I guessed she was referring to when my parents' business was about to flourish. My parents were too busy during those years too, and that was also when Ashton officially became a co-owner of the company.

"Ashton was often out of town leaving me behind. I'd like to believe that he also loved me. But I felt neglected. I became jealous thinking he flies constantly to spend more time with you and your family."

When she looked at me, I got a feeling that what she was going to say would make me feel uncomfortable.

"Then every time he got home, he always talked about you. Natasha this, Natasha that."

I can hear the bitterness in her voice. I shifted uncomfortably, thinking maybe I should stop her from oversharing. But then, she just continued.

"It was too tiring, you know? I was there with him while he kept talking about this young woman who did not want to have anything to do with him. Though Ashton doesn't want to admit it to himself, I knew deep down how much he longs for you. So we will start fighting again."

Bianca continued to recount the memories of how she often caught Ashton stalking my social media accounts and how he always denied it even when caught red-handed. She said how they grew apart until the day Ashton went home drunk, blabbering how he thought I got a boyfriend.

Bianca started crying uncontrollably. I thought there was anger in her voice... anger that was directed at me when she said "I didn't mean to. But Ashton pushed me to go back to my old ways. I began sleeping around with different men whenever Ashton was away. I did that until I met Brian."

She started laughing again at her memories. She recalled how Brian made her feel loved and pursued her, and how he made her feel so important. When Ashton started to notice, Bianca thought he would be afraid to lose her. That is why she dared him with the divorce. And that was her fault. Ashton agreed without giving it much thought. In the end, Bianca had no choice but to choose Brian.

All these things that Bianca had confessed to me made me feel guilty. I felt like I had caused their break up.

"Do not be like me, Tasha. Maybe if I had been more understanding, we would still be together. Or maybe if I had let him go sooner, there would not be all these problems and drama", she hugged her son tighter.

I wanted to stop Bianca. But I think she needed to let those parts of herself go too. Maybe she has bottled them up for too long and now is the only time she has to open up.

"Looking back now, I think about every little problem that Ashton and I had. I always chose to fight about it rather than have it resolved. Maybe that drove him to spend more time out of town than with me. Maybe my insecurities have changed me into the worst version of myself. I had him but I pushed him back to you."

I don't know how long we have been talking. Everything is still silent outside. So silent that I thought I could hear waves crashing from a distance. I closed my eyes and imagined the shore, the people, Ashton, my parents, and my friends.

Tim!

I wonder what happened to Tim.

My stomach rumbled and I remembered that I had not had the chance to eat lunch. I haven't even drunk anything. I swallowed but even my mouth was dry.

"How long have you been here?" I asked Bianca after a while.

"I don't know. Two days? Three days?"

"Do they feed you? Were you allowed to drink?"

I did not bother asking about being allowed to pee. The pungent smell of urine in the room answered that one.

"Yes, they do. They will bring us food later. Are you hungry?"

I nodded my head. "I am starting to feel weak and dizzy too."

"Try to get some sleep. I know it's hard in this situation, but it will help. You will need it to stay alive."

I followed her advice and lay down. I hated getting dirty but that is the least of my concerns now. My thoughts drift back to Tim and the scene of him getting shot. I pictured the blood oozing from her shirt. I truly hope he is fine. I wondered how my parents were taking all of these. And my friends... Vea... she must be worried about Tim. And Ashton, I hope he finds me soon.

I was so tired that I drifted off to sleep.

THE RESCUE MISSION

ASHTON'S POV

Jeremy and I decided to go with the team that would rescue Tasha since we wouldn't feel at ease waiting for updates.

Julia chose to stay at the hospital together with Tim and his family. Tim is now out of critical condition. Although Natasha was kidnapped, Julia still feels guilty about what happened to Tim.

On the other hand, Vea and Camille were advised to stay at home and rest. The girls were obviously in a state of shock too. I contacted my friend Alex and asked his team for some help. They have already coordinated with the police officers regarding the operations.

The authorities asked me and Jeremy to wear a bulletproof vest before they allowed us to get in the car. They have located the hideout in an old abandoned resort two hours from where we are.

I couldn't stop my hands from shaking. Too many things may happen in two hours. I wonder how much Bianca is capable of hurting Tasha. I still can't get around the thought that she was Tasha's kidnapper. Bianca isn't perfect. There may be things that she is lacking. But I can't see her being the violent type. I've never seen her hurt or cause harm to anyone.

Has she changed for the worse? Or did Brian influence her to do it? Brian!

"Four men abducted Tasha, right?" I turned to Alex who went together with us in the car.

"Yes, though the identity of those riding the motorcycle was still unidentified. Why?"

"Bianca does not have too many connections. Not unless of course, she got the help of Brian. I also do not see any reason why she would need my money. She got a hefty amount from our divorce." I ran my hands through my hair. "If she's doing it, I am sure she got Brian backing her up."

"There is something I wanted to tell you."

"What do you mean?"

"Before Bianca cheated on you, can you honestly say that you have not met Brian before?"

"Yes. Why?"

Jeremy sitting beside the driver's seat shifted in his position too. He looked at us through the rearview mirror, his face filled with curiosity.

"Do you remember when you were still suspecting Bianca? You asked me to profile Brian. But I do not think you ever read the report I gave you, as she already admitted the affair and asked for a divorce, right?"

I nodded my head at the thought. I was so mad then, that I cannot even remember whether I kept or threw the report in the trash.

"Yes. I was hurt. I did not see the importance of the report at the time. We were separating anyway. Bianca chose him."

Alex cleared his throat. "Well, you and Brian went to the same school from middle school to senior high."

I furrowed my brows. "How was it possible? Isn't Brian older than me?"

Alex shook his head. "Brian is only a year older than you. His drug addiction made his features appear older." Alex turned on his tablet, browsed something on it, and handed it to Ashton.

He showed him a photo of Brian from when they were still students. Alex was right. The guy in the picture looked familiar, but he could barely see the resemblance with Brian.

"But his name doesn't ring a bell. Even if I didn't recognize his face, I should have, at least, remembered his name."

"Brian has changed his name. The reason isn't mentioned, but I suspected he got bullied a lot because of his old name. He also decided to use his maternal grandmother's surname." Alex swiped the photo and showed me a page from a high school yearbook.

"Dick Herman! Of course! I remember that name!"

I didn't mean to shout his name. But it drew a laugh from everyone in the car. And it was the same too when we were in school. Although not everyone has seen or met the boy, everyone knew the name Dick Herman back in middle school. And judging from the laughs the name got even now, it is only reasonable for him to change his name.

"And people knew how much he envied you since you were in middle school. They said he wanted to be like you. Or was it more apt to say that he wanted to be you? You were rich and popular for your looks, while Brian struggled with money and was popular for all the wrong reasons. Some people claimed that's what pushed Brian to join the drug syndicate."

I shivered at the thought. Jeremy might be thinking the same as he repeatedly shook his head in disbelief.

"Does he have some problem with his mental health?" Jeremy voiced the thought running in my head since a while back.

Alex shrugged his shoulders. "Probably. But I am not an expert. There was no record of him visiting a mental health professional."

Alex showed me again a scanned copy of all the records he had in his hands. "The guy was obsessed with living your life, he even made his way to date and sleep with most of the girls you were involved with in the past. It seems he's been keeping a tab on you and Bianca long before the split and he might have been doing the same with Natasha."

Alex's face became more serious. "I hope I was wrong, but this could be more than just kidnapping for ransom."

"Jesus Christ!" Jeremy exclaimed as he punched his fist into his leg. "This is on a whole new level of awkward and crazy."

Jeremy looked at us through the rearview mirror. "How much more time before we get to my daughter?"

The thoughts of Brian touching Tasha suddenly crossed my mind and I can't help but curse under my breath. Jeremy's face turned red. The same has probably crossed his mind too.

Jeremy threw me a dagger look before he buried his face in his palms and was continuously cursing at me. But my mind was already worrying about Tasha. Camille said they were about to eat lunch when she was abducted. The only thing she ate this morning was her granola bar. Are they even feeding her?

Then I thought about Brian. Fuck him! I cannot forgive myself if something bad happens to Tasha. We had been traveling for about an hour but to me, it felt like the car wasn't moving at all.

NATASHA'S POV

I felt something moving across my thigh. I immediately thought about whisking it with my hand, but my movement was restricted. The pungent smell hit my nose and then I remembered where I was.

A bug! A bug!

That was the first thing I thought about. I wiggled and tried to sit up but two hands grabbed my shoulders and forced me down on the floor. I opened my eyes and my heart was filled with terror when I realized that Brian was on top of me, smiling like a maniac.

I tried to scream, but he gagged me by putting a rolled fabric on my mouth. I couldn't do anything but whimper and cry. Brian walked away and disappeared from my view.

I heard a muffled cry from the corner and that's when I saw that Bianca also had his wrists and ankles tied together. Like me, she also has fabric in her mouth. Jonas is lying beside Bianca. The boy was also crying but was too afraid to make a sound.

Bianca shook his head, based on the muffled noises that she made, I could tell that she was screaming. Then she moved near Jonas and tried to cover his son's view. I knew my face mirrored the fear I saw in Bianca's eyes when I realized what was happening. I began to scream and cry, while I tried to wiggle away from Brian.

Brian grabbed me by my foot, then he rolled me to my stomach. He pinned my head on the floor. I couldn't do anything but cry when I heard him unzip his pants. I turned my head and looked at Bianca, desperate for some help. She put her tied wrists to her forehead as if asking for my forgiveness.

Bianca and I tried to scream until Brian snapped and told us to stop making noises. Brian kneeled on my side and grabbed my hand. I closed my fists when I realized what he was trying to make me touch. He grabbed me by my hair. The force lifted my head a little from the ground. I groaned from the pain. I closed my eyes and more tears fell from them.

I opened my hands and Brian let go of my hair and pinned my head on the floor. I thought about one of the defense lessons I had with Tim. I couldn't move my head. And as much as I hated it, I tried to visualize what Brian lay on my hand. I felt the loose skin of his balls.

I grabbed them and squeezed them as hard as I could. Brian started to scream and began pulling on my hair. I squeeze harder until he lets go of me. He moved away holding his crotch area.

"Bitch!"

I rolled to my side and saw that he was lying on his back, his hands covering his mouth, instead of his balls. I saw another opportunity. I ignored the pain, raised my feet high in the air, and landed them again on his crotch area. I aimed and crushed it. Brian grabbed my feet and then put himself in a fetal position. He kept on cursing me as he winced in pain.

I followed his gaze and realized that he was looking at the gun he placed on top of the table. It will take him a few steps to get it, but it does not seem impossible. I looked at Brian and he was still curled on the floor, holding his crotch. I mustered my strength, aimed my feet at his calf bone, and kicked him. It was hard and painful for me as I felt the rope rubbing against my skin. But I got to fight.

I only stopped when we heard the gunshot which echoed in the air.

For a moment, I saw Brian start to panic. "Conrad! Conrad! Get inside and grab the girl!"

I felt the rope in my feet getting loose. I kept on kicking until my feet were free. It must be my adrenalin, but I was ready for whoever Conrad was. At the back of my head, I also knew that the gunshot was a sign that Ashton had come.

Brian screamed for Conrad again, but nobody came. Brian struggled to stand. I knew his calf still hurt because he kept on rubbing it. I bet his crotch felt much worse, judging from how he kept his knees together as he stood.

I heard Bianca's muffled scream, while I wiggled and scooted to where they were. I lost all my bravery when I saw that Brian had finally grabbed his gun. Bianca and I moved and squeezed her son between us. I can feel our bodies trembling in fear. I closed my eyes and waited for my fate. But instead of aiming his gun at us, Brian struggled to make his way out of the room. He kept on calling on to Conrad.

Then there were more gunshots. Jonas started to scream but neither I nor Bianca could move to hush him. I might be hallucinating but I thought I finally heard Ashton's and my dad's voices just outside the room. That was when a man entered the room. Thinking it was Conrad, I closed my eyes and accepted my fate.

ASHTON'S POV

The resort seemed deserted. Alex said no more than ten people were guarding the place. They got a hold of the driver who denied his involvement with the kidnapping. He was still arrested by the police, nonetheless.

Soon shots were fired. Alex signaled to us. He found another way at the back of the resort. The police stated that we should stay in the car, but I begged Alex. So here we are, running towards the other entrance, taking cover, and trying to be safe. I spotted Brian. He was coming out of a room with a gun in his hand. He was naked from his waist down.

"Shit! That's Brian!" I couldn't help but exclaim.

"Oh no! Why is he running half-naked? Are we too late?" Jeremy's face turned red from anger and the heat of the moment.

Brian couldn't walk straight. He kept on brushing his calf with his hand. I am not sure if he was walking with his knees together to cover his nakedness, or because of something else. But I knew he was in immense pain.

The police cornered him. He threw his gun, but instead of raising his hands, he used it to cover his maleness. Two police officers grabbed Brian by his arms and gave him something to cover his member. It was when Jeremy advanced toward him and punched him in the face. I winced. I knew how that punch felt. Alex and I stopped Jeremy from further assaulting Brian.

"What did you do to my daughter?"

Jeremy's voice echoed in the place. Brian just laughed hysterically at him, like a madman. The way he laughed made me angrier at him. I tried so hard to restrain myself as I shouted at him.

"Fuck you, pervert! What did you do to Tasha?" I looked around the place, wondering where Natasha was.

The sound of his laughter annoyed me. I saw the envy burning in his eyes.

Saliva came out of his mouth as he screamed and pointed his finger at me. "Fuck you too! We are both perverts!"

Then he shifted his gaze to Jeremy. "Fuck that girl! She has a tight grip. She does not need to be rescued!" Brian kept on cursing and spewing nonsense.

Then he looked at me. "Why are you always so lucky, Ashton? Why do you always get what you want? You always have the girls crawling at your feet, begging you for sex. You are rich. You have nice company and are having wild sex nightly with the young daughter of your business partner right here."

He poked Jeremy on his chest. Then he wailed like a lunatic. "I wasn't even able to touch her brea—"

Jeremy kicked his crotch area before the police were able to grab him. He winced and he fell on his knees bowing down. Brian cussed again. We heard a boy crying out from one of the rooms. We followed Alex as he came rushing in and were greeted by a pungent odor.

I found Tasha trembling in the corner, her eyes closed. I fell to my knees when I saw how she looked. Tasha jolted and started screaming when I touched her. I hugged her tight and told her it was me. I rushed to remove the cloth from her mouth and she frantically shrieked. Tasha only stopped when she heard his father's voice. Jeremy hugged her daughter and rubbed her head.

When she finally calmed down, I realized that sitting next to her were Bianca and her son. Bruises and fresh wounds covered their bodies, their clothes were torn. And like Tasha, she was also gagged and tied on her wrists and ankles.

Since Jeremy was already untying the rope on Tasha's wrists, I came to help untie Bianca. When both of them had been untied, they spent the minutes hugging and crying, releasing all the tension they must have felt after all those hours. Alex removed his jacket and put it on Bianca's shoulders.

"It's over... I cannot believe it. It's over." Tasha laughed and cried at the same time. Bianca wiped Tasha's tears even when she was crying too. "We are alive. We are safe now."

Tasha nodded her head. Then she scooted closer to Bianca and pulled Jonas into a tight hug. Then she started crying again. She kissed Jonas on the head and apologized to Bianca when she realized what she just did. Bianca told her it was okay and they both squeezed Jonas in a hug.

Alex called the paramedics. Soon both of them were carried on a stretcher and were both examined by the paramedics. Tasha only had cuts on her forehead, lips, wrists, and ankles, while Bianca had a sprained ankle, and possibly a few broken ribs.

Jonas also appeared to have more bruises and some cigarette burns on his thigh when they stripped his clothes off. But thankfully, he doesn't have any broken bones. The paramedics decided that all of them must be rushed to the hospital. We decided to take them where Tim was admitted, and the paramedics approved.

The police wanted to get Tasha's statement right away, but we decided against it as Tasha was still under a lot of stress and shock. When we were about to leave, Jeremy tried to hop on the ambulance but the paramedics stopped him.

"I am sorry, sir. But we can only allow one person to accompany her."

Jeremy gave me a dagger look. "Ah! You have snatched my daughter away from me."

I gave him a wry smile. "I am sorry, man! See you at the hospital!"

UNTOUCHABLE

My eyelids felt heavy minutes after they had inserted an IV into me. I felt relatively calm too. I assumed they had injected me with some medication to calm down. The last thing I remember before falling asleep was my dad being told to go with Alex.

I slept the whole time I was being carried to the hospital. When I woke up, I heard the voices of Ashton and a female nurse. I felt a little groggy and could not even manage to open my eyelids.

"Hello, sir. I am Sarah. We need to transfer your sister into a bed."

Her voice was a little high-pitched. Even without seeing her, I can tell that she swoons and tries to flirt with Ashton. Ashton squeezed my hand.

"Hello, Sarah. Sure. Let me carry my girlfriend and lay her down on that bed."

"Ohhh. Okay. Let me grab her IV bot—"

"Here, honey." It was the paramedic's voice.

Though a bit blurry, I saw that the paramedic smiled at me and said, "You'd be fine, Ms. Collins."

When a doctor came to examine me, I realized that I was already in the ER. He also studied the record that the paramedic handed to him. Not long after, my mom came rushing to my side and hugged me tightly. Ashton excused himself and talked to someone on the phone.

"Oh, sweetheart! I am glad you are finally here. Do your wounds hurt? How do you feel, honey?" She checked my arms for wounds and bruises.

"I am fine, mom. Just a bit shook and feeling weak too."

My tears fell again when my mom started crying. Then the doctor came.

"Hello, Mrs. Collins. I am Dr. Raul Gonzales." He introduced himself before he continued. "She's been dehydrated so the paramedic inserted an IV into her. She needs one to two more after this. Her wounds will be cleaned too so they won't get infected."

Dr. Gonzales paused and then looked at me and my mom. "Although Ms. Collins looks fine, we want to do X-rays on her. We will also schedule her with a psychiatrist, Dr. Anderson, to address her PTSD."

"You have been under a lot of stress. I was told you were shaking and quite frantic earlier. You could be suffering from Post-Traumatic Stress Disorder and Dr. Anderson can help you better deal with it."

After the doctor left, my mom turned to me. "I have asked them to have your room ready, honey. Do you want to go to your room now?"

"Yes, please. I badly want to take a bath too. Can I take a bath? There is no way I will lie on another bed without taking all this dirt out of me. I feel sticky."

I couldn't stomach how I stink when I tried to smell myself. I thought about how I hugged Ashton and my parents. They might have felt disgusted with it too. I winced at the thought.

"And mom, can I see Tim after bath too?"

"Let me check if he is still awake, honey."

Just then, Ashton returned.

"Ashton, you can go and bring her to Suite Room 305. All her things are there. Here is the key to the locker in her room."

"Thank you, Julia."

Ashton opened my locker and got my bag for me. I still find it difficult to move around, because of the IV inserted into me. Ashton offered to do it for me. It is not like he has not seen my underwear, but somehow, it is a little embarrassing as I watch him go through the clothes that my mom packed for me.

"How come I have never seen you in these?" Ashton held a lacy underwear. Then a naughty smile curved on his lips.

I snatched the underwear from him.

Ugh! My mom is something!

I am spending a night at a hospital and she packed those tiny lacy things instead of just some normal underwear! I bet I am as red as the underwear I snatched from him.

"Now, let us wash you."

Ashton gently held my elbows and offered to carry me to the bath. But the moment that he touched me, memories from the abduction flooded my thoughts.

I remembered how Brian's hand crawled on my leg, his creepy smile and the cavities on his teeth, how he laughed like a maniac, his nasty smell, how he grabbed my hair, and even the sound of his voice.

I couldn't help it. I started to shake as if my body was being controlled by someone else. Ashton isn't helping, because the more he tries to hug and calm me, the more my body remembers the trauma. It got overwhelming, I fell on my knees crying. Ashton offered his hand to help me stand. But I suddenly whisked his hand and screamed at him.

"Get your filthy hands off me!"

I saw the pain in Ashton's eyes and the words were not even meant for him.

"Ah—I—" I wanted to retract what I said, but it was too late.

Ashton sat on the floor in front of me. The grim expression on his face told me that he was processing my words. "Did he—Bri—"

"Please! Don't even mention that name." I hugged my knees and started to cry uncontrollably.

Ashton didn't dare to touch me again. He just sat there, helplessly watching me cry. I heard his breathing getting heavy, and he couldn't do anything but sigh. We were at that moment when the door opened.

"Hey! What are you two doing on the floor?" My dad looked surprised at first and then he became worried when he heard me sobbing.

Ashton got up from the floor. He can't even begin to tell my father what just happened. He pointed at me, the clothes, and then he sighed. My father nodded his head. I sensed his hesitation when he walked towards me and then stopped to move a step backward.

Then finally, my father decided to call the doctor and take me to Ashton. Before he closed the door, he asked Ashton if he knew where my mother went.

Moments passed, and I had already stopped crying. But I remained in the same position when my father left the room. On the other hand, Ashton kept pacing the room, uncertain what to do with me.

At that moment, I felt helpless too. I don't want to be a burden and an inconvenience. But even if I wanted to, I can't stop myself from breaking

down. I can hear the footsteps of people coming and leaving the room. I heard voices whenever anyone attempted to talk to me. I am responding to them. But I am unable to use my mouth. I want to look at their faces too, but all I do is stare at my feet and the floor.

"Honey?" I automatically raised my face when I heard my mom's voice. I clung my hands to her neck as if I was afraid to let her go.

My mom hushed me as she repeatedly stroked my back. On the other hand, Ashton can't do anything but curse under his breath and leave the room. Soon, they realize that I only talk comfortably around women.

ASHTON'S POV

I helped Natasha get settled in her room. I held her elbow to guide her inside the bathroom when she snapped. She doesn't want to be touched. Her body started to tremble, leading to a nervous breakdown.

She slumped on the floor and started crying. I offered my hand to help her get up but she slapped it. I saw fear and disgust in her eyes when he screamed.

Get your filthy hands off me!

I knew those words were not directed at me, and that was the worst part of it. I couldn't help but think about Natasha's terrible and terrifying experience with Brian. I wanted to hold her, but I would only make it worse.

Jeremy came and she did not even talk to him. Natasha stopped crying after some time but remained seated on the floor, hugging her legs. Doctors and nurses came and went, but she did not pay them attention.

Only when she heard her mother's voice did she seem to have gone out of a trance. Soon, they realized a male's touch triggered her PTSD. The doctors advised that only female nurses could come to her room.

It took hours before Natasha returned to her usual self. I know what happened has worn her parents more than I did. I wanted them to take more rest but I could not just volunteer to be left with Natasha. So we asked her many times if she wanted me to stay with her, and I was glad when she said yes.

The nurses have given her medication. Soon after her parents left, she had fallen asleep.

NATASHA'S POV

I slept at around three in the morning. When I woke up, I saw that Ashton was already awake.

Or did he even sleep?

I noticed the coffee cup on the table. I wondered how many coffees he had. Ashton seemed so deep in his thoughts that he had not even noticed I was awake.

Someone knocked on the door and I saw Ashton jolted. I laughed. His face lit up when he realized that I was awake. He seemed to have forgotten the door.

"Come in," I said.

A female nurse poked her head first. She asked Ashton if everything tasted okay. By everything, I think she meant to ask if I am fine having other males around me. I nodded my head and she went back outside. She was with Dr. Raul Gonzales and another young doctor when she returned.

"Paul?" I couldn't suppress the smile on my face.

"Good morning, Tasha! I am happy to see you again too."

Ah, that voice.

I tucked my hair behind my ears. I couldn't take my eyes off Paul. Then Ashton cleared his throat.

I glanced at him and noticed how he straightened up from his seat. He furrowed his brows and it created a crease on his forehead. He may not show it but I know he was studying Paul and is probably thinking about how we know each other. My thoughts were interrupted by Doctor Gonzales' voice.

"Good morning, Tasha. I see that you and Doctor Anderson do not need an introduction."

We both nodded. I am uncertain about Paul, but meeting him again took me to the moment I first saw him.

I met Paul three years ago while hanging out with Tim. According to Tim, Paul was their team captain at the time and the one who scouted him to be a part of the varsity basketball team.

Tim introduced us for only a brief moment, but Paul has always been warm and understanding toward me.

I blushed at the memories that flashed across my mind. Then I felt mortified when I remembered that I had not seen myself in the mirror and hadn't even brushed my teeth.

Dr. Gonzales caught my attention.

"As I have mentioned yesterday, Doctor Anderson practices psychiatry. You may need to have a few sessions with him. So even after you get discharged, you need to visit him so he can help you cope with the trauma."

I noticed how Dr. Gonzales was too careful not to touch me. He moved aside when the nurse took my temperature and blood pressure. Then Kat, the nurse, checked my IV and gave the chart to Dr. Gonzales.

"Well, you seem to be in a stable condition. You can be discharged once this IV bottle is empty. For now, I will leave you to Doctor Anderson."

Doctor Gonzales left with the nurse while Paul remained. He looked at Ashton and then at me.

"So do you need some...privacy?" Paul asked me, though it was obvious that he was referring to Ashton being in the room.

I felt quite an aversion toward Ashton now. While I did not intend to feel that way, subconsciously, I thought that what happened to me yesterday was all because of him. I knew it was wrong to resent him, but at present, that's how I feel toward him.

On the other hand, I knew too that Ashton did not mean for me to experience that and I do not want to hurt his feelings. I am aware of the things he did to save me. I felt secure and safe knowing he was within arm's reach, but seeing him reminded me of his role in what happened.

"It's okay, Tasha. Take things slowly," Paul said after a while. He pulled one of the chairs and positioned himself near my bed. I gazed away from Ashton and told Paul I was good to start.

Paul started with pleasantries, about how he remembers me in the past, how he's been doing, and how he met Tim and Vea yesterday. I didn't notice how smoothly he transitioned the conversation to the events that led here.

Unlike the others who seemed to be walking on thin ice whenever they had to mention what happened yesterday, Paul spoke directly to the point. The tone and intonation of his voice were warm and friendly, but it also kept me focused on what he was saying. His voice made me zone out of my surroundings as if putting me into a calming trance. I forgot that Ashton was in the room with us at some point.

Paul made me narrate my side of the story. Whenever I stop or pause, he asks what I was feeling and why I think I was feeling those. When I don't answer, he does not push the question. He made me feel as if it was me who was leading the direction of the conversation.

From time to time, I can hear the sound of paper rustling. Paul would pause, smile at me, and continue to ask questions. After a while, Paul clapped his hands and I blinked. He got up from his seat, reached for the tissue box, and handed it to me. That was when I realized my eyes and cheeks were wet with tears. I saw Ashton standing from my peripheral, but he remained where he was.

Paul helped me wipe my tears, and then I felt him brushing his hand on my back. "You've done well, Tash. You made me proud."

Before I knew it, Paul had again, smoothly transitioned the conversation. He talked about the sessions we'll have after I get discharged, and how we'll contact each other. He casually asked about Vea and Camille, and what I am doing now. I felt his hand patting my head and heard him say,

"That's my girl."

I looked up at him and saw the tenderness in his eyes. My mind flashed the occasions from the past whenever he told me that. I felt my cheeks get warm. I bowed my head again and I felt Ashton's presence by my side.

When I looked up again, Ashton stood in front of me, reluctant if he should also pat my head. Ashton's expressions were soft and gentle. Behind him, Paul said his goodbye and left the room.

PAUL'S POV

I met Natasha four years ago when she was only a freshman in college and I am in my final year. Our first meeting was brief, but I realized the instant connection. She's always been fun to be with. She's kind, compassionate, spontaneous, smart, and beautiful. Like I have always told her, she has all the qualities I want in a girlfriend.

We did go out on a couple of dates. We did some of the things that boyfriends and girlfriends would do. If anyone would ask me, I would say she was my girlfriend.

But while I could feel that Natasha liked me, I knew her feelings weren't the same. Though she was warm and affectionate, I could always feel her reservations. It's as if I was there, but her feelings were intended for someone else. I confirmed it when she refused to label what we are.

Other people have always found it easy to confess and share personal things about them. And Natasha is among those people. Little by little, I met Ashton through her stories. And I realized that it was him—why Natasha couldn't open herself to me fully.

When I graduated from college, she naturally just drifted away. Our 'relationship' lasted for about seven months, but my feelings for her lasted longer than that. But the more I reach out to her, the more she seems unreachable.

I hear rumors from my circle about guys asking her for a date. A handful of them got rejected, while others have only gone as far as holding hands, or kissing on the cheeks. Of those guys, Natasha refuses a second or third date.

I don't talk to other people about it, but in my mind, I want to brag that we have gone a little further than that. I've held her in my arms. I knew what her lips tasted like. But more than the physical connection, I knew that Natasha sincerely liked me too. Not as much as I did, but I know she also had feelings for me.

I hadn't heard from Natasha or her friends for over a year until yesterday. A nurse handed me a chart of a familiar patient, Timothy Clarkson. I didn't talk to Tim right away because he was unconscious for hours. But I did hear from the police officers who frequented his room about the incident.

My heart ached when I heard about how Natasha was still being held captive at the time. I prayed for her safety and promised myself that if she made it out alive, I would do everything I could to help her get through her PTSD.

When I saw her, everything I used to feel about her resurfaced. However, I met Ashton in the flesh for the first time today. And his presence made all the difference. While we were talking, I realized that Natasha still trusted me.

Although Natasha seemed to be in denial, I knew he currently resented and blamed Ashton for what had happened to her. Dr. Gonzales even told me earlier that her PTSD was triggered when his boyfriend touched her elbow.

I wasn't on duty last night when Natasha was admitted. But I told them to limit her contact with the male staff. I wasn't sure but based on my experience with previous patients, most of them get more comfortable and it lessens the triggers if they are around the female staff.

Natasha's case seemed a little different though. When I brushed her back earlier, I confirmed that her aversion isn't from every male. It was just Ashton. From her confession, it's easy to understand why.

I know Natasha is at her most vulnerable now. If I want to, I can even use my profession to manipulate her emotions and shift them toward me. I know I can snatch her away from Ashton. But should I?

NEW RIVAL: DR. LOVE

ASHTON'S POV

Natasha constantly stirred and talked in her sleep. Dr. Paul Anderson called earlier when Natasha had a breakdown and had already warned me about this. While he said this would be normal, he told me to alert the nurses only if Natasha becomes difficult to handle.

I thought I heard the surprise and worry in his voice when he learned that I would be staying with Natasha the whole night, instead of her mother. He reminded me to avoid any physical contact that triggers Tasha's PTSD. I found it odd because I thought the doctor was too concerned about Natasha as if he knew her.

I couldn't sleep well because I was too worried I wouldn't be ready if Natasha needed help. I had my second cup of coffee, by the time the sun had risen. I saw today's newspaper at the nurse's station earlier. I took one and brought it into the room. I got so engrossed in reading that I didn't notice it when Natasha woke up.

I jolted when someone knocked on the door and Natasha told them to come in. The female nurse came in first. She went in, talked a little with Natasha, and came out again. The nurse returned with Dr. Gonzales and another doctor who has a striking resemblance to Chirs Evans.

My head turned to Natasha when he called the new doctor by his first name. I watched the color rise to her cheeks and how she tucked her hair behind her ears. This time, I knew my hunch was correct. Something about the way he smiled and how she reacted tells me

I wasn't just overthinking and overreacting as I did with Tim and Derek.

When Dr. Gonzales and the nurse left, Dr. Anderson subtly suggested Natasha have their first private consultation. For a moment, Natasha seemed to agree. Although I understand, I really should probably leave, my feet are planted where I am.

Natasha struggled to answer until Dr. Anderson acknowledged they could do the consultation in my presence. He walked toward me to get a chair, nodded, and then proceeded with their consultation.

When I met Tim and Derek for the first time, they both acknowledged the age gap. Although they talked casually to me, they were both respectful and somewhat regarded as I was older. They made me feel old.

Dr. Anderson is different. I bet he is the same age as Derek. But he treated me like his equal, which I find more disturbing. There is something about him and how he made Tasha smile and blush that I find intimidating and dangerous.

He asked Natasha if he could put their conversation on record. Natasha hesitated at first. But in the end, he made her agree. And while he started with pleasantries, he did not beat around the bush. The moment he started talking, he got all of Natasha's attention. I have the feeling that she has even forgotten I am here.

Dr. Anderson asked about the most sensitive topic and made Natasha open up. And in certain instances when she paused and appeared reserved, he rephrased his question until she gave him an answer.

When Natasha started talking about the physical abuse she experienced from Brian, I noticed how Dr. Anderson gritted his teeth and tightened his grip on his pen. Yet when he spoke again, his voice sounded calm and his face looked tender and warm. Unlike me, he can mask his emotions rather well.

Tasha began to cry. This is the first time I heard her version of what happened yesterday. Instead of comforting her, Dr. Anderson gave her the moment she needed. He just sat there, taking notes on his tablet. He did not interrupt or ask her to stop. He just let her be. Soon, Natasha narrated the story on her own until the part when she got rescued and was brought to the hospital.

Dr. Anderson asked how she felt when anyone touched her. Natasha clearly stated she did not like it and that it made her skin crawl. He asked more questions and Natasha tried to evade most of them. He did not pressure her to answer.

When Natasha turned silent, he'd say something he remembered about Natasha in the past, and then Natasha would be more open to answering again. I'm not sure how he did it. But somehow their conversation always led Natasha to answer his previous questions indirectly.

That's when he would paraphrase his original question and Natasha would answer more openly. It's as if he knows well how Natasha's mind works and he tricked her to give him the information he needed.

More than an hour has passed. Listening to how the conversation went, I am sure the session is almost done. Dr. Anderson talked about brighter things not related to what happened yesterday. He clapped his hands once and I saw how Natasha blinked. It's as if he put her in a trance. Then he stood up, reached out for the tissue box on Natasha's bedside table, and handed them to her.

Natasha even looked surprised that she cried. She felt her cheeks before she accepted the tissue from Dr. Anderson. I stood up to stop him when I saw he was about to brush his hand on Natasha's back but Dr. Anderson just raised his other hand to me telling me to stop.

I snorted. He just commanded me and I followed.

Why? How?

He tapped Natasha's head and I heard him say, "That's my girl."

Natasha did not flinch. His touch did not trigger her PTSD. Instead, Natasha wrinkled her nose and gave Dr. Anderson a warm smile.

I WANTED TO RETALIATE, but Dr. Anderson raised his hand again and motioned for me to come closer. Which, again, I did. When Dr. Anderson left, I found myself standing where he was standing. But unlike him, I hesitated if I should touch Natasha or not. Natasha looked up at me. She smiled drily and lay down and turned her back on me.

"Tasha?" I called her name, uncertain if she wanted to talk or not.

Natasha just answered with a short, hmm.

"How did you know Dr. Anderson?" I hesitate to sit at the edge of her bed.

"Uhm... what do you mean?"

She wanted to evade the question. I shook my head when I began to think about how Dr. Anderson played his 'tricks' on Natasha. I decided to handle it my way.

"Babe, I am neither deaf nor blind. You blush the whole time. You kept on fixing your hair. You cannot look him straight in the eyes. Your voice was a little octave higher when you greeted him."

Natasha remained on her side, facing away from me.

I sighed, "Do you... like him?"

Natasha turned her head towards me. The color of her cheeks confirmed what she wanted to deny.

"You like him." I sighed.

"W—well I—He—," Natasha stuttered. She cleared her throat. "We sort of dated for seven months."

Natasha talked too fast, her words were almost inaudible. Then she went back to lying on her side. She even pulled her blanket up to cover her face.

I get it, she doesn't want to talk about it.

"Huh! You dated, but it lasted for seven months. Cute." I murmured, "And how about us? It's barely been a month since we started dating." but I guessed she heard it.

"Why don't you ask Paul if you don't believe me?"

I WANT TO ASK, BUT that puts Natasha in a bad mood. A little later, I asked if she wanted to eat. Dr. Anderson also asked her earlier, but she said she wasn't in the mood to eat. Natasha said the same now, I doubt she isn't hungry because she hasn't eaten anything yet.

I got back to the corner table and got her something to eat. Someone knocked on the door, then it opened. It was her friends. Both of them did not notice and they went straight to Tasha.

Tasha sat up, and she excitedly hugged her friends. They didn't ask her anything, but they were worried about her.

"OMG!!! We were so worried about you," both keep telling Natasha. Then they fell silent for a few moments. Camille and Vea exchanged glances, as if doubtful whether they should tell Natasha something or not.

"What? Why are you guys looking like that? Come on, tell me." Natasha was holding both of their hands.

Camille broke the ice," You will not believe who I just saw. AHHHH!"

Natasha just smiled. Of course, by the exciting look on her friends' faces, I could tell exactly what they meant.

"OMG! Paul works here. He is way hotter than he used to."

There it goes. It's about Paul. I rolled my eyes. Then I noticed how Tasha gave her friends the 'do-not-say-anything-else' look.

Camille then joked about wanting to date the 'hot doctor' and she asked Tasha if she'd allow it.

Plates clinked on the table and they all turned in my direction. Vea looked guilty and embarrassed, while Camille just shrugged her shoulders.

"I am sorry. But why does 'my girlfriend' need to have a say on whether you should go out with the hot doctor or not?" I wanted to act maturely, but I couldn't hide my irritation.

"Ashton, listen okay? Paul is in the past." Camille said dismissively.

"Right. It's obviously in the past." I didn't intend to, but it came out sarcastically.

"What can I do? I've got a pair of clear eyes and I know how to appreciate his handsome face and hot body." Natasha murmured.

I felt ashamed to have this conversation with her friends, but I could not stop myself. And so I asked her.

"What if he suddenly asks you out on a date?" I walked to her bed and handed her a sandwich on a plate.

"First I doubt that he would do that." She took a bite, chewed her food, and swallowed. Her friends asked her to eat slowly. "I know Paul. He's always been kind and helpful. I know he only wants to help me professionally."

"Wow, seriously?" I arched my brows.

"Yeah, really," Tasha assured me.

"Now, that is settled. Paul is just trying to be professional. Tasha and Ashton have feelings for each other. So there is no point in fighting over Paul." Vea tried to be funny and tapped my shoulder.

But I noticed how Tasha winced as if Vea said something disgusted.

"Now let us change topics, shall we?" Camille agreed. Resigned, I returned to my seat, continued reading the paper, and allowed the girls to talk.

"How are you feeling, Tash? Were you hurt?" The worried glances are evident on her friends' faces.

"I am fine now. I need to have some sessions with Pa—" Natasha suddenly changed the topic. "Hey! I have not seen Tim. I wanted to go and see him."

"Tim is fine. We went there before we came here. Hey, have your breakfast first. We also know how awful hospital food tastes, so..."

Vea got the container out of the paper bag. The smell of the pasta and its sauce mixed in the air when she opened it. Vea and Camille took turns to feed Tasha, who seemed to enjoy it.

Vea gave the fork to Tasha. "We were so scared yesterday. We thought we were going to lose you and Tim."

When they were finished feeding Tasha, Vea turned to me. "I guess we shall leave you to Ashton. We will go back to Tim. He is on his own because his parents went out for a while. See you there in a bit?"

Tasha nodded her head before she hugged them. "Thank you for showing you care. I love both of you too. See you there later."

After the girls left, I sat on the edge of her bed.

"I have one last question."

Tasha rolled her eyes.

"I know what you are going to ask. So listen."

I laughed at how she had a ready answer before I could ask her.

"I did not mention him during the "truth night" because I forgot about him. Or maybe he crossed my mind too. But he wasn't important to me at that time. You know, out of sight, out of mind." Tasha made the quoting gestures with her fingers. "Now can we please stop talking about Paul?"

That doesn't sound convincing enough, but I let it slide.

"Right. Now about last night—"

"Well, I.. Uhm.. Ashton. I'd rather not talk about last night now. It makes me feel more anxious." She tucked some hair strands behind her ear. She cracked her knuckles.

"I understand." I pursed my lips and decided not to say anything more.

"Well. I wanted to go to the bathroom to tidy up a little. Can you help me, and then let us go to Tim?"

"Of course."

I cannot help but compare her to Bianca. Though Natasha tends to be difficult to handle at times because of our age gap, she always chooses to see things objectively. Sometimes, Natasha acts impulsively.

But once I gave her the time to sort her thoughts and feelings, she reflected on it and acted more maturely. When I look at her like that, I know, she is more emotionally stable and mature than Bianca.

I offered to help Tasha to see Tim, but she refused. Later, I asked for a nursing aide to help Natasha get into a wheelchair. Surprisingly, they sent a male aid instead of a female. I tried to help the aid when he bent down to carry Natasha. But he respectfully stopped me.

Then the aid asked me to go to a corner. The aide whispered and said," Dr. Anderson told us that we should be careful about letting you have skin-to-skin contact with Ms. Collins. He said only your touch triggers her PTSD."

I snorted. Somehow, I felt like the doctor was using his job to sabotage my relationship with Natasha. On the other hand, I don't want to risk it too and trigger her PTSD. So I just nodded and allowed the aid to do his job. I gasped when Natasha did not flinch nor complain when the aid began to carry her.

Tasha burst into tears as soon as she saw Tim.

"Tim! I am so sorry you were hurt because of me. And I am thankful for what you did."

Seeing how Tim was reluctant about whether she should hug Tasha, I guess Tim was not briefed yet on the 'new protocol'. He seemed speechless when Natasha held his hand and exclaimed, "Oh!"

Her friends helped Tasha to sit at the edge of Tim's bed. Natasha carefully put an arm around Tim, so as not to hurt his wound. He looked unsure and awkward. He looked at me as if asking about Tasha's triggers. I shrugged my shoulders. What should I tell him when I don't understand how the trigger only comes from me?

"Hey...I am sorry too if what I did was not enough. I am glad we were both safe." Tim said after a while.

Tim, Vea, and Camille looked at me, asking. I don't know what to tell them. I just pursed my lips and shrugged.

"I owe you a lot, Tim. You have risked your life in trying to save me." Tasha held Tim's hand again.

After spending some time with Tim and their friends, she decided to rest some more in her room. When we got there, her parents were already there waiting for us.

"Did you go to see Tim?" Jeremy was the first to ask.

Unlike Tim, he's now more comfortable around Tasha, but more cautious about me being around his daughter. I assumed the 'hot doctor' had talked to Tasha's parents.

"Yes, Dad." Tasha gave Jeremy and Julia a kiss on their cheek.

"Ashton, I went to the billing station earlier and learned her bill has been settled. Thank you."

I smiled and nodded.

"So what did the doctor say?" I sat together with Jeremy on the couch.

"The bottle should be empty by 4 pm. Then she can be discharged." Jeremy crossed his legs.

I waited for him to say more, but he didn't. Instead, he took out his phone from his pocket.

"Uh-huh. And what about Dr. Anderson, what did he say?" I reluctantly asked.

"It was you." Jeremy glanced up at me, then returned her eyes to his phone. "You are Natasha's trigger."

Jeremy did not look at me again. I wanted to ask him why but realized the trigger would be me.

Everything started with me. She met Bianca because of me. Bianca left me and cheated on Brian because of me. Natasha met Brian because of me. And Brian. Fuck the psychopath! He used and hurt both Bianca and Natasha because of me.

That explains it. Natasha talks to me and hangs around me, but whenever I get too close, she becomes alert and aloof. I trigger her anxiety. I trigger his trauma. My touch reminds him of Brian and what she did and almost did to her.

But how do I make her forget it? I wanted so badly for Natasha to stay with me. I was about to open my mouth to ask but Jeremy gave me a dagger look.

"My daughter is coming and staying with us until we return abroad." He said as if reading my thoughts.

Julia suddenly laughed, her face almost turned red. She is by Natasha's bedside peeling and feeding her with oranges. Natasha smiled at her mom, while Jeremy and I were both puzzled.

"I'm sorry..." Julia said, and then she laughed some more. "You two look funny. I mean Ashton, I know you are eleven years younger than us. But whenever you guys talked about Tasha, he treats you like a little kid and you act like one.

I chuckled. I admit what she said was true and it is a little embarrassing to be treated that way in front of Tasha. But since they came back, I felt like walking on ice around Jeremy. I am so scared to offend him, that he would forbid me from seeing Tasha.

On the other hand, Julia was easier to get along with. She has been very supportive of my budding relationship with her daughter.

"Ashton, you can stay with us while we are here. You know, just like the old times." She put a slice of orange in Natasha's mouth.

Jeremy rolled his eyes. Julia ignored him and continued, "And since you are already consenting adults, I do not mind if both of you would choose to stay in the same room."

"Julia! You knew what Doctor Anderson said!" Jeremy couldn't help it.

"Mom!" Tasha blushed. Then he turned to his dad. "Wait, what? Did Paul—I mean Dr. Anderson tell you anything?"

None of them speak. Natasha grabbed his mother's arm. "Mom!"

"What?" Julia just looked at her daughter. "Do not mom me. I believe you need to be together to overcome your triggers." She put oranges in her mouth, chewed, and then spoke again," Besides, I don't care what Dr. Anderson said. I do not trust him."

Ah, Julia is so modern, she even kept on teasing her daughter. She swallowed, and then she spoke again. "I knew both of you have gone further than kissing and petting. Don't take me for a fool."

Tasha covered her face with a pillow. And while the temperature in the room was low, I felt so warm that I started sweating. I looked away when Julia looked at me. I know the teasing is coming in my direction. And then she said it.

"I know Ashton would also find a way to sneak out in the middle of the night, and then return to his room before the sun comes out." She let out another laugh.

I chuckled. Yeah, Julia was right. I would do that if we were put in a different room. I scratched the back of my head.

"OMG! We are not talking about this."

Tasha looked too cute when she covered her head with the blanket. On the other hand, Jeremy covered her ears. He decided to leave the room to "get some fresh air".

Julia followed him out and left her daughter to me. She told me to 'sort it out'. I understood she meant her triggers, but how do I do that?

THE PROPOSAL

A *SHTON'S POV*
After Natasha was discharged, she stayed home alone with their parents. While I wanted to stay with her, I do not think it is appropriate. For the most part, it also felt like Natasha isn't ready to spend 24/7 with me, after her kidnapping incident.

While I do not put a hundred percent of my trust in Dr. Anderson, I agree with him when he said that we should not force Natasha when she isn't psychologically and emotionally ready.

Natasha started going to therapy twice a week with Dr. Anderson soon after she was discharged from the hospital. Natasha did not go alone in those therapy sessions. Dr. Anderson has created a schedule for her family and friends to accompany her in those sessions.

Natasha has yet to complete all twelve of her sessions. I was with her in the first two of those sessions, which just revolved around the underlying issues Natasha has for me, starting from the past to the present.

From those sessions, I understood how Natasha sees and values me from her standpoint. I realized her fears, hopes, what-ifs, and what could have been. I learned about her non-negotiables, the events that gave her the greatest pain, and those that made her the happiest. Somehow, those sessions have made me understand myself a little more too.

I am aware that Natasha and Paul have met once or twice out of their scheduled sessions. It bothered me, to be honest since I have witnessed how close and trusting Natasha is when it comes to him. But I don't want Natasha to think I do not trust her. Not especially when I am what triggers her PTSD. So even if I wanted to ask her to change her doctor. I remained silent.

Despite my jealousy, I acknowledge the doctor's ability. I understand now how at a young age, he is considered among the best in his field. It's only been two weeks since she started the session, but Natasha has already improved. She is slowly getting back to her normal self around me too. She has become less aloof even when I am nearby. We have even started to hold hands again.

Jeremy and Julia are supposed to be coming back abroad by this time. However, they have decided to extend their stay because of what happened. In return, their unfinished business dealings and activities fell into my hands.

Now, here I am in my room packing my things. I'm going to leave tomorrow morning. Natasha told me she had mixed feelings about the situation. Of course, she's happy her parents are staying here with her. But she's also sad that I will be the one to leave. She cried when she learned that I would be gone for two months. Natasha came earlier to hang around. By dinner time, she told me she was going to leave.

"Hmm. Can I do that for you?" She asked shyly. She's been sitting on the bed, where most of my clothes are scattered.

"Do you want to?" I took my luggage out of the closet.

She nodded her head. She only asked me to put out everything I needed to bring and she'll pack it for me. I did as she requested and sat on the bed. In about half an hour, she organized my toiletries and nicely folded clothes that she neatly tucked inside my suitcase. I was impressed. I do not remember when Bianca packed my things for me. With Tasha, she just did all these little things and she easily made me feel loved.

"Marry me."

Natasha began zipping my bag slowly, and then she stopped. She just stood there, her back to me. And then she turned around slowly to give me a questioning look. I know she was trying to figure out if she heard me correctly. And if she did, she's probably thinking if I am pulling a prank.

"What did you just say?"

I am stunned I said it too. But it felt like that was the most natural thing to say. I walked to the closet and retrieved a dark blue box from the drawer. I felt the weight of Tasha's stare behind my back. I knew she was watching my every move and probably knew what would happen next. True enough tears glistened in her eyes as her hands covered her slightly opened mouth.

"I was supposed to give this to you on your birthday while we were on board that cruise. But I hesitated. I thought you might think it was still too early. So instead of this, I gave you the necklace." I took a deep breath and then I continued, "Then you were kidnapped and I feared that I might not have the chance to be with you again."

I opened the box but instead of looking at the ring, she kept staring at me. Happy tears began flowing from her eyes.

"With the absence of all the grandeur, the fireworks, the candle-lit dinner, and all the fancy little things, I am asking you, Natasha Collins. Will you marry me?"

I don't know how long she planned on staring at the ring. I started to feel nervous. The room fell silent until I could hear the clock ticking on the wall.

"I'm sorry—"

My heart sank. But I still waited for what she was going to say.

"But can you ask it again?"

For a moment, she got me confused.

"Please, Ashton?"

She smiled and I laughed at myself. Of course, she wanted to hear it again.

"Natasha Collins, will you marry me?"

Instead of saying yes, she hugged and kissed me passionately on the lips. I felt tears staining my cheeks. My happiness skyrocketed when I realized that Natasha initiated the physical contact.

"Yes, Ashton. I will marry you." In between kisses and her sobbing, she continued, "I have been dreaming of this. Well, not exactly this, this. But—.well—I guess I don't care as long as you want to marry me."

I was scared that bad memories would snatch the moment, but Natasha seemed fine. She did not tremble. She did not cry. She did not zone out. But I know she's only halfway to healing, so I treat her with extra care. I wiped the remaining tears from her cheeks.

"You can even propose without this ring, and I would still say yes." And then she buried her face in my chest while she excused herself from blabbering things she thought were nonsense to me.

I kissed her lips again. Then I slipped the ring on her finger.

"I love you, baby"

"I love you too, Ashton."

"I love you more." I kissed the hand with the ring on.

She laughed and said, "I love you first."

"You're not sure about that. But I am sure that I will love you always." Then I pulled her again for another kiss.

WE ARE ENGAGED!

N I cannot believe that Ashton has proposed to me just now. I know that our relationship is still young and I am not prepared to have kids yet, and all that. But I have been waiting for him almost all my life and this – the two of us standing here in silence, in the middle of his bedroom, with nothing fancy or grandeur except maybe for our feelings for each other – is more than a perfect proposal for me.

Ashton kissed me on the lips. His hands explored the territories on my body that belonged exclusively to him

"You made me very happy. I do not want us to end." He said in between kisses.

Then he lifted me and put me down in bed. Ashton started showering me with kisses, though his movements were gentle and slow. I felt that his actions depended on how well I would receive or initiate intimacy.

We haven't touched each other for weeks. And I know that much separation was enough to build the sexual tension that is now trying to burn and consume us. I can feel his thirst and hunger and am just as ready to match it. Soon, our bodies intertwined, moving to the rhythm only we could hear.

Exhausted, Ashton lays his head on my arm as I wrap them around him. He buried his face in my neck and wrapped his arms around my waist. If it's up to me, I would remain in bed. I wanted to savor every moment we have before Ashton leaves tomorrow. But we promised my parents we would be home for dinner.

Arthur and Edith, Ashton's parents, would be there too. Ashton has one younger sibling, Monica. But she is currently in Spain. Arthur and Edith have always been nice to me. But not her sister, Monica, who is only five years older than me. We should be close, but Ashton said Monica had always been jealous of me. She sees me as a rival in gaining Ashton's attention. Thus she has always kept her distance. I know Ashton is close with her sister. Monica is his only younger sibling that's why I understand where she's coming from.

I held my hand in front of me and admired the ring on my finger. Ashton knew me too well. The ring looks modest and elegant, the gold metal is thin and is accentuated by a small diamond in the middle.

"My parents are going to freak out." I tightened my hug around his neck.

"Mine too," Ashton murmured against my skin. "Julia and Edith would be elated."

I winced. I hurt my ears just by thinking how happy and loud they would be. "I think Arthur would be happy too. But my dad. I am not so sure about my dad."

"I guess I need to prepare my jaw. I did not know Jeremy was capable of throwing a solid punch." Ashton chuckled. He touched his jaw as if a punch had just landed on it.

"What do you mean?" I loosened my grip and moved my face away to see Ashton's face better.

"He punched me that day. You know just after Bianca ended the ransom call."

I shuddered at the memory of Brian hurting Bianca before and during that phone call.

"Heeey," Ashton tightened his arm around me, and then I felt his hand brushing my back. "I'm sorry for reminding you. Are you okay?"

I nodded my head, then I let out a nervous laugh. I focused on the image that emerged in my head—my dad throwing a punch that landed on Ashton's jaw. I thought about my dad's possible reaction when he heard the news. I am sure he'd throw a fit.

He has proven many times how he can be immature when it comes to my relationship with Ashton. He'd probably ask the reason why we want to marry since we have just started dating. An old soul that he is, my dad would probably ask if I am pregnant.

Pregnant. Wait, what? Shit!

I got up from bed and looked for the condom's empty packet. Ashton looked at me and asked if I was okay.

"Where is it? Where did you put it?"

Ashton reached for my purse and took out my medicine. He must be thinking I am having an episode and looking for my medications. I whisked his hand and lifted the comforter, exposing his nudity. Ashton got up earlier. I saw him throw something in the bathroom.

I rewound what happened in my mind. Then it sank in. We did not use a condom. We had unprotected sex. My anxiety started to crawl in. My hands trembled as I reached for the medicine that Ashton offered me earlier.

"B—babe, what's wrong?" Ashton isn't sure whether he would touch me or not.

I turned my head slowly toward him and asked, "Did you put on a condom?"

He stuttered. I slapped him on his chest. He knew! He realized it before I did and he did not tell me.

"Ashton!"

He caught my hands, hugged me, and wrestled me back to bed. Ashton tried to soothe me and assured me that nothing would happen. I started to cry and Ashton hushed and calmed me until I fell asleep. I woke up two hours later. Ashton laughed at me because the first thing I did when I opened my eyes was panic.

"Babe, calm down. I already told them you fell asleep. Besides, we have enough time to prepare."

It was around eight in the evening when we reached our house. I rang the doorbell while Ashton held my left hand and kissed it. The front door suddenly opened revealing my dad. He looked surprised, then just shook his head after.

"Honey, they are finally here." My dad gave Ashton a darting look. His eyes widened when he noticed the ring on my hand. "What the hell is that?"

He couldn't help but ask. My dad started making a scene. Sitting in the living room and watching baseball, Arthur suddenly rose to his feet, curious about what my father was saying. Edith and Susan came rushing from the kitchen too.

"Hey, what happened?" My mother looked at my dad and then at us. "Why are you guys standing by the door?"

"Come on in. Dinner is ready." Edith walked towards us.

Edith put her hands on my arm and guided me to the dining. We walked past my dad who was still standing by the door.

"Hey, honey! Come on!" My mom wrapped her arm around my father's waist and grabbed Ashton by the elbow. Then she pulled them together to the dining area.

Arthur and my dad took both ends of the dining table. Ashton and I sat together on one side, while Edith and my mom sat on the other side, beside their respective husbands. My dad looked grumpy and kept glancing at Ashton.

Jeremy let out a heavy sigh just about at the same time when I heard Arthur, who was seated on my left, gasp loudly.

We all looked at him. He had his hands covering his opened mouth.

"I am sorry. But I just can't—" He motioned his hand toward my ring.

I bowed my head and hid my hand under the table. Ashton did not say anything and just smiled. I guess our reactions have made both of our mothers more confused.

"I'm sorry. What is going on?" They asked almost at the same time.

Arthur turned to Ashton. "Congratulations, son!" And then he asked me, "Are you sure about your decision, Natasha?"

He clasped his hands in front of him, then he leaned closer to me. He whispered, but his voice was loud enough for everyone to hear. "If I were you, I would choose the hot doctor. I heard he's a lot more good-looking than my son."

I did not expect what he said and he threw me into a half-nervous laughter. I laughed so loud and I naturally and casually covered my mouth with my hands. That's when my mom and Edith noticed the ring.

"Oh my God! You guys are engaged?" Tears dwell in my mother's eyes. "This soon? I mean I am happy for both of you, but honey. Oh, my God!" She began fanning her face, then she turned to hug Edith.

"We will truly be a family now." Edith is now in tears too. She let go of my mom's embrace and then screamed, "Aaahhh! We're in-laws!"

Both of them got up to hug me, and then Ashton.

"So when are you planning to get married?" Ashton's mother asked.

Ashton and I looked at each other.

"Wait, honey. You are not pregnant, are you?" My father dropped his fork when he asked me.

"No, of course not!" I said more loudly, making me sound too defensive.

Ashton looked at me. He sensed my anxiety. Then he held my hand.

"No, she isn't pregnant. I proposed to her earlier. We are yet to talk about our wedding plans."

I knew Dad was supposed to say something, but my mother warned him.

"Jeremy, do you remember when and why you proposed to me?" She asked.

My parents met each other at the university. My dad proposed to my mom just a year after they graduated because my grandparents were moving across the states, and they wanted my mom to move with them. My mom had no choice but to agree.

My mom said dad was too afraid to lose her so he proposed. That way, even if they are living far from each other, he already has an assurance that my mom will still end up with him.

"You said you'll stay with your parents for at least two years! Ashton will only be gone for two months! What is he so afraid of?" My father exclaimed, pointing his table knife in Ashton's direction.

"You should ask WHO he is afraid of," Arthur emphasized and then winked at me. His remarks sent some laughter on the table.

"Dad, I am not afraid of anyone." Ashton put a chunk of meat in his mouth. "I trust Natasha."

My father rolled his eyes. He was about to say something, but my mother put some food in his mouth.

"You followed me to my parents' house just two weeks after we moved!" my mother grabbed some napkins and wiped the corner of my father's mouth. I am sure he felt embarrassed by what my mother said because we all laughed, and his face turned red.

"Fine! Ashton can marry my daughter. But now, let us eat." He finally conceded "We waited for you for hours, now it seems clear why you were late for dinner."

My dad still sounded annoyed. Ashton's mother apologized on behalf of his son, but she is as static as my mother does. Shortly after dinner, Ashton's parents decided to leave, while the four of us hung out in the living room to watch a movie.

Dad and mom sat together on a sofa. Dad put his arm over my mom's shoulder while mom hugged him. Ashton and I were on another couch. Ashton's head was on my lap while I placed my right hand on his chest. From time to time, I ran my other hand through his hair.

"Ah, this feels awkward." My dad said after a while. Mom just laughed at him.

"They are not awkward. They are cute. They remind me of how we used to be."

"Yes. But at least we are of the same age. And your dad was way older than me too. And we don't hang out with our parents like this."

"I'm sorry, Dad." I somehow felt disappointed with myself.

"Hey, honey. No, I didn't mean it like that." Then he sighed again. "I guess we will just continue watching in our room. You guys have fun and make yourselves comfortable."

My father patted Ashton on the arm and kissed my forehead. "As long as my princess is happy, I am happy too. Good night." He turned again to Ashton, "Good luck, and take care on your flight tomorrow."

Then we are alone in the living room. "Hey, don't be sad. I know your dad too well. It will take time but he will get used to this."

Sometime later, my phone rang. The screen registered Derek's name and number. I looked at Ashton, he nodded his head.

"Hey, it's been a while."

"Hey, doll! We have heard from Vea. I am sorry we weren't able to visit you at the hospital. We were out of the country and just came back." Derek sounded apologetic.

Lindsay was just as worried, "How are you? Are you okay? My God! We were so scared for you!"

"Hey, I miss both of you. Yeah, I am fine. I got little scratches from here and there, but I am fine." If they have heard from Vea, they know that Tim and I are currently undergoing therapy.

"We are glad too that you and Tim were fine. We were so scared for both of you when we learned what happened." It's Derek again.

"Were the kidnappers caught?" Derek and Lindsay asked almost at the same time.

I looked at Ashton. I realized I had no idea what happened to the kidnappers too after I was taken to the hospital. I don't even know about Bianca's condition. Ashton just scratched his head and then he gave us some information.

"Yes, they were taken under the police's custody and our lawyers are taking care of the case." He paused for a while. And then he said, "Lindsay, can I ask you a question?"

"Yeah, sure!"

"You are a very talented photographer. Do you also do prenuptial photo shoots?"

I opened my mouth in surprise. I can't believe he blurted it out in front of my friends just like that. I hit him on the chest.

"Yeah, I—wait a minute. Who is getting married?"

I looked at Ashton and he smiled like an idiot.

"I—uhm—am asking for a friend. But do you do those kinds of photoshoots? Engagement announcements, prenuptial kind of photoshoots?"

Derek's laughter echoed from the other line. Their voices became soft as if they stepped away from the phone and were having a conversation. But we can still hear what they were talking about.

"He is not asking for a friend. I can tell it's them." Derek said.

"You think so?" Lindsay answered.

"Charge them a hefty amount. Both of them can pay." Derek laughed hard.

"Hey, we can hear you," I told them.

Ashton and I laughed at their conversation too.

"Oh, right! I am sorry. OMG! I am excited for you!" Lindsay exclaimed.

"What? Why? I did not say it's us." Ashton continued bluffing.

"Oh, cut it. We are sure it's you." Lindsay seemed a little annoyed. "Anyway, yes. I will do it for you. Let us just set a schedule when you are ready and let us discuss the details in the schedule and everything."

"Okay. I will tell my friend what you said." Ashton said.

"Shut up, man!" Derek said.

I laughed at how they seemed to get closer now.

"Thank you guys for checking on me. I appreciate it." I moved closer to the phone.

"Of course, anytime." Lindsay sweetly answered.

"Bye, doll!"

I looked at Ashton and then I laughed.

"Bye, beast!"

Derek growls.

"I hate it when he does that." Ashton frowned.

We heard Derek's and Lindsay's laughter. Then they said goodbye together. Ashton ended the call and we got back to watching the movie.

When the movie ended, I told Ashton he should probably get home. It's getting late and I want him to have a good rest. But he refused to leave just yet. He told me he could spend the whole flight sleeping. But I doubt that. I know he cannot sleep when he has work to do.

I realized I won't be able to send him off to the airport tomorrow. Sadness engulfed me when it hit me that this moment right here, is the last time I'll see Ashton. And he'll be gone for two months. We hugged each other tightly for one last time.

UNEXPECTEDLY YOURS
NATASHA'S POV

It's been more than two months since the kidnapping. Ashton and my parents made sure that the lawyer they hired would do everything to put Brian and his men behind bars. We also learned that Alex decided to take care of Bianca and his son. Bianca and Jonas had also gone under counseling with Paul and we have seen Alex going with them at the clinic a few times.

Ashton said Alex has talked to him about Bianca. Alex has begun to develop feelings for Bianca since they started to see each other more often about the case. But he has been too cautious to make a move out of respect for their friendship.

Alex felt heartbroken when he saw Bianca's condition during the kidnapping, and Ashton thinks it all started from there. Then maybe, all is good then. While I have only seen Alex a few times, I can say that he is also a good catch and a much better choice than Brian. Bianca also deserved another chance at love. I honestly wish her the best, in life and love.

Everything was also going well with my life. The news about my sudden engagement shocked my friends, but they were all happy for me.

Though Ashton and I have not chosen an official date yet, Vea and Camille have excitedly started to look for possible photo shoots and wedding venues, dress styles for the bridal entourage, and even the best honeymoon places!

I have also started to have a full grasp of how our family business is operating. My parents decided to gear me to become the Director of Marketing, which I will fully take on in a year or two.

Time has gone by too fast, I cannot believe it has already been more than six weeks since Ashton left. He informed me yesterday of the probability of him going home earlier than planned. But instead of counting the days until Ashton got home, I devoted my time working in the office.

Two days ago, Amanda introduced me to Vincent Mendez. He is a half-Spanish young lad and the son of Gustavo Mendez, one of the board members. According to Amanda, Vincent is only a Grade 5 student and wanted to accompany me for a week for a school project.

His father also said that Vincent has great visual presentation skills. He said he wanted his son to experience the gist of how marketing is done in real life and requested me to guide and allow his son to work on one of my business presentations.

I've worked with Vincent for two days, and I can tell the guy is enthusiastic to learn. He's also responsible, quick-witted, and has a great sense of humor. I won't be surprised if one day, I'd see him working as one of the top executives in our office.

As usual, I woke up to the sound of my alarm at six in the morning. I slept rather early last night, but I still felt overly tired. I even counted the hours I slept and knew it was more than eight hours. I wonder why my body felt so heavy and tired.

I reached for my phone that was lying on top of the bedside table. I have missed four voice calls and six video calls from Ashton. I wondered if anything bad happened because there were missed video calls from Mom and a handful of unread messages from Ashton, Mom, and my friends. I checked most of their messages, and they asked the same thing: where am I, and if I am okay?

I wondered why my parents texted me, then I remembered that they went on vacation out of town to celebrate their anniversary. I will be home alone until the weekend. I laughed at how they could comfortably leave me on my own now.

I scrolled and checked my calendar. I groaned when I saw that I have one meeting out of the office later today. It was the meeting that I said I would take Vincent to observe. I felt too lazy to go. I laughed when I thought about sending Vincent alone. I headed to the kitchen and prepared something to eat. I munched on an apple, then my phone rang.

It's Ashton.

"Hey, babe. Good morning." I answered lazily.

"Hey, I have been calling you since last night. Is everything well?" Guilt washed over me when I realized how worried Ashton might be.

"Yeah. I am sorry. I just felt tired yesterday, I fell asleep as soon as my head hit the pillow. How are you?"

"I am fine. I just missed you so much. I wish you were here with me." He paused. I heard some papers rustling from the background, and then he asked," Are you all set to meet with the client later?"

"Yeah. I've told you about Vincent, right? He asked if he could do the visual presentation. Initially, I was hesitant, but when I checked his work, I only did minor revisions. The kid is talented and smart. I will take him with me later so that he can observe what we do."

"I trust you, babe. I know you can do it. I love you. I gotta get going too. I will call you again at lunchtime."

"I love you too. Talk to you later."

I ended the call and felt my stomach turn upside down. I ran to the lavatory and threw up.

"Oh no, not today", I sat on the chair for a while. When I felt better, I dragged myself to the bathroom to shower.

I met Vincent at the office and reviewed the presentation before meeting the client. It could be the stress, but I felt like throwing up again as soon as we reached the lobby. I excused myself and went to the comfort room. I felt fine after a while.

But during the meeting, I had to excuse myself again. I felt embarrassed towards Vincent because I had to leave him alone with the client. I smiled when I realized that Vincent had the floor. The client seemed entertained and hadn't noticed how long I had been gone.

I sighed when the meeting ended and the client left. When I stood up, I felt my surroundings sway. Vincent noticed and he quickly ran to my side and asked me to sit down for a while.

"Hey, Tasha! Are you alright? You look pale." He waved at the waiter and asked for some water.

"I am fine. I feel a little nauseated though. Thank you for covering for me earlier.

"You do not have to thank me for that. Are you sure you are okay? I can bring you to the hospital if you want to."

"No, I am fine. And please, do not mention anything to Amanda. I know Ashton would call her about the meeting, and she's bound to mention this to Ashton and my parents if she knew. I do not want anyone to worry. Understood?"

He nodded, and then he took my purse. "Okay. Let us take you back to the office then." He helped me stand and held me by my elbow as we walked.

I sank onto the sofa as soon as I reached my office. I checked my schedule on my phone's calendar. When I looked at the date, I stared at an icon I use to track my period."

"F*ck! My period was almost two weeks late!"

I got up and ran my hand through my hair. I walked back and forth thinking about that night before Ashton's flight. Just then, Amanda's head poked at the door.

"Dear, Ashton is on Line 2."

She was about to close the door when I called her back.

"Amanda, wait!"

"Yes, dear?"

"Please tell him I am out of the room."

She looked puzzled, but then she said, "Okay, dear. I got it."

I hate him at this moment. Though I learned weeks ago that I could be pregnant when we did it, it still feels different when it is finally sinking in. The anxiety is eating me away.

OMG! I just turned 24! I have a lot of plans, and getting pregnant this early is not one of those!

My phone rang. I knew it was Ashton. I turned it off and went back to the sofa. The next thing I knew, I was crying and sobbing. I felt so confused. I do not know what to do. I grabbed my bag and then I went to Amanda's desk.

I asked her if there was anything urgent that required my attention. I was glad when he said that there isn't. I told Amanda I was having my lunch out and that I might be returning a little late. Once on the elevator, I turned my phone back on and called Vea.

"Hey, are you free to have lunch?"

"Hi. I am heading out to that Italian restaurant near your office. Do you want to meet up?"

"Great! See you there in a bit."

ASHTON'S POV

Tasha avoided my calls. Whenever she does it, I can only think of two things: I did something that made her mad at me, or she was having that time of the month. Whatever her reasons are, I know it would be smart if I let her come to me on her own rather than bug her. So I decided to wait for her to call or text me.

But the whole day has passed and I have not received any call or text from her. I could not think of anything that I had done wrong. So I assumed she was on her period. I felt a little bit of sadness.

Though I did not intend not to wear the protection that night, I was hoping I would get her pregnant. I cringed at how selfish my thoughts sounded. But I wanted to have a son with her. Although I figured out that maybe having a little Tasha running around the house would be fun too.

Damn!

I must be getting old thinking about babies and kids.

This is unlike me, but my thoughts suddenly drifted into creating my little happy family with Tasha. I wanted to have more than two kids. But if she only wanted one, I would concede to her happily. I am just hoping that we could have a kid together. And I promised I wouldn't stop her from achieving her dreams if I got her pregnant.

I remembered that Tasha mentioned this morning that she wanted to invite her friends and stay overnight at my house. She told me she missed me, but did not want to stay there alone. I laughed and said she did not need to ask for my permission. I have told her she should refer to it as our house, but she's still awkward to say it.

NATASHA'S POV

I ordered my favorite pasta but I could not eat it. I felt like I would throw up anything I ate.

"Hey, what is wrong?" Vea asked. Worry is etched on her face.

"I think I am pregnant," I whispered through my breath. She did not catch what I said.

"What? Can you speak a little louder?"

I just shook my head.

"I wanted to spend the night at Ashton's. But I don't want to stay there alone. Will you please stay with me at his house for a night? You and Camille. Please?"

"It is okay with me. I will call her later. Are you sure you are okay?"

I nodded my head.

"I'm sorry. But I need to go back to work. You know it is only my second week and I don't want to mess up."

Vea has just started as a curator at an art gallery two blocks from here.

"Sure. I will see you, girls, later." I bid her goodbye.

"Take care!" We both said at the same time.

I waited until Vea was out of my sight. Then I went to the pharmacy to buy pregnancy test kits. I bought all the different testing kits they have just to be sure. Then I head back to the office. I decided to do the test later with the girls, but the thought kept me more anxious, and I could not focus on the report I was reading.

So I grabbed two kits and went to my office's comfort room. I felt like my world crashed when I finally saw the results. Two lines have formed slowly in two kits in front of me.

OMG!

It's confirmed. I am pregnant. I am carrying Ashton's child...our child. I wrapped the kits in bathroom tissue and tucked them inside the brown paper bag before I shoved them inside my bag.

I know other girls would consider me lucky. Ashton decided to marry me even before learning about the pregnancy. And I know I should have started on pills early on. But I am still mad at him. I wanted to blame it on my hormones. Or maybe it's just me. I don't know.

Ugh! I hate him!

I looked around when I saw Max in the lobby. Ashton gave Max a vacation since he's out of the country and I went back to my parents anyway. Max waved at me.

"Max! What brings you here?"

"Good afternoon, Ms. Collins. Ashton told me to fetch you today."

Max's smile faded and changed into worry. "Are you alright, dear? You look rather pale."

I told him not to say a word to Ashton. I am glad that he understood and maybe he assumed that I was just tired from the job and need not worry Ashton. Martha, Max's wife, and Ashton's house helper was also home. Martha said Ashton requested her to look after me and my friends.

MARTHA ASKED ME IF I wanted to have anything for dinner. Ashton prefers to cook for himself and only asks Martha to clean the house while we are in the office. Maybe that was why he asked Martha to cook for me.

I sighed before I answered, "I don't know. I have been throwing up everything I put in my mouth since this morning."

I absentmindedly put my hand on my stomach and did not notice when Martha took a glimpse of it.

"I guess I should prepare something healthy." she just said. "This would take a while, dear. You look sick. You can go to your room and rest. I will call you when it's ready."

"Thank you, Martha."

Half an hour later, Martha asked me to come down. She told me to sip the broth soup first. To my surprise, the broth seemed to calm my stomach. I tried to eat, and fortunately, did not throw up.

After I had dinner, Max arrived with a plastic bag full of fruits. Martha offered to peel them for me, but I refused. Both of them also offered to stay with me until my friends arrived.

I looked at the fruits Martha placed on the table and craved for some grapes. But something seemed to be missing. I texted my friends and asked them if they could buy some yogurt for me.

A little later, the doorbell rang.

"Hey, girl! I heard you are sick?" Camille said the moment I opened the door.

"Uhm, no. Not really." I absentmindedly rubbed my tummy.

"Then why do you suddenly crave these?" Vea took the yogurt from the paper bag.

I waited until Max and Martha had left. Then I returned to the sofa and took out all the other pregnancy test kits I bought earlier. Their eyes widened.

"No way!" Both of them exclaimed.

I went to the bathroom next to the kitchen and used all three remaining kits. I knew what the results would be. But somehow, I still hoped that they would turn out negative. When I came out, their faces were full of anticipation. I lay all three kits that show the confirmation of my pregnancy in front of them.

"OMG!" They both exclaimed at once.

Then I took out the two other tests I had in the office earlier. They looked happy and excited, but I broke down and cried. Both of them do not know what to do. They asked if I already told Ashton, and I just shook my head.

"Hey, we get it that you are worried. But Ashton loves you so much. He won't let you down." Vea said. She ran her hands over my back.

"I am sure you just have to talk to him about your fears and he will surely understand." Camille hugged my arm as she placed her chin on my left shoulder.

"And we are here too. We will never leave your side."

Both of them wiped the tears from my cheeks. We all pulled each other for a hug. Later, we all decided to watch Netflix. Vea took a snap of us and we all put up the same photo on our Instagram accounts. It hasn't been long since I saw Ashton put a heart on my post. I sighed and put away my phone. Just twenty minutes into the movie, I was out. My friends decided to wake me up later, so I could sleep well on the bed.

TWICE THE TROUBLE

NATASHA'S POV

Three days have gone by fast. I completely ignored his calls while I answered most of the texts and chat messages. I have also limited our conversations to office-related things. It sounded so immature, I know. But I couldn't bring myself to talk to him about the baby.

Today is Friday and Ashton is coming home tonight. I felt nauseated when I woke up. I can barely stand, so I decided to call in sick to the office. I asked Amanda if she could move the 10 AM meeting to Monday next week. Whenever I move, the world seems to sway with me. I didn't bother to wait for Amanda's reply. I crawled to the bathroom and vomited.

I heard when Martha came and called out my name, but I felt too exhausted. I slumped myself by the door and leaned against the wall.

ASHTON'S POV

Tasha must be too busy to take my call. I also noticed that while she texted and chatted with me on social media, everything she said was about office work. I am glad that my business trip ended sooner than I expected. Now, I am bound home to be with Tasha again.

It was already past eight when my plane landed at the airport. So instead of heading home, I went straight to the office. However, it wasn't Natasha that I saw on her desk, but a worried Amanda. Vincent stood behind her, equally anxious. They did not notice me as they were busy finding files on the newly created data filing system. I tapped the desk and they both looked up at me.

"Ah! Mr. Greene! I have never been so glad to see you!" A look of relief washed across Vincent's face.

"What is wrong? Where is Tasha?" I searched for her in the room but did not find her.

Amanda answered quickly, "She called in sick today. She asked me to move the meeting but the client was so difficult. He said he can only meet us today."

"Natasha is sick?" I rolled my sleeves and pulled my luggage to my desk. I dialed her number but she did not answer.

"I think she has been sick all week," Vincent retrieved the printed documents from the tray. "She must have been too stressed the past few days. I told her she might need to go to the hospital and have her blood pressure in check."

Vincent scratched his head. He told me that Natasha did not want me to know and asked me to act like I still didn't know. I nodded and thanked Vincent for his information. I dialed Martha's number, but she's not answering either.

"Mr. Greene, this client..." Amanda hesitated.

"What time is the meeting?" I put my phone back in my pocket.

"At ten this morning." Both of them answered.

I looked at my watch and realized we had 30 minutes to prepare.

"Call the client. Tell them we will proceed with the meeting. Vincent, come with me." I told Amanda to call Martha and check on Natasha for me. I told her to inform me right away if anything went wrong with her.

Before the meeting started, Vincent took my phone from me. He noticed that I was getting distracted, waiting for a phone call. I snorted and couldn't imagine a 14-year-old boy ordering me and telling me what to do.

I did what I could to finish the meeting as early as possible. An hour and a half later, I reached home and knocked in front of Tasha's room.

"Hey, baby?"

I opened the door and found Natasha curled on the floor near the bathroom. She's lying on the comforter, her eyes closed and she is hugging a pillow.

She tied her hair in a messy bun, and I noticed the droplets of sweat on her forehead. I approached her. She must be too tired to walk, she trembled as she crawled back to the bathroom. She vomited as soon as she reached the toilet seat.

"Hey, what is wrong?" My nose caught a whiff of a sour odor coming from the bathroom.

"Get out! I don't want to see you"

Natasha tried to close the door but I blocked it with my body. And because she was too tired, she couldn't use much force. She went back to vomiting and I sat beside her. I ran my hand on her back to soothe her and helped her get up when she tried to wash her face. I felt her forehead, Natasha winced and turned her face away.

Her temperature seemed normal. I asked her about the last thing she ate. She did not answer. I looked around her room and noticed the fruit bowl on her study table.

"Max! Get the car ready! We are bringing Tasha to the hospital."

"I do not need to go to the hospital. Go away!" She pushed me away. I took a few steps from the bathroom door as she sat on the toilet seat.

"Hey, do you want something warm for your tummy? Hot tea? Coffee?"

Although looking frail, she reached for the drawer beside her. He took me by surprise when she threw five different sticks at me. "I can't just drink coffee, you idiot!"

"Natasha!"

I did not mean to shout at her but was more surprised when he called me an idiot. I said sorry. She also bowed her head as if admitting her mistakes. I bent down to pick up one of the sticks. My eyes widened in shock when I realized what I was holding.

She's pregnant!

I gathered all the sticks that fell on the floor. All of them have lines indicating a positive sign.

Tasha is pregnant!

I couldn't contain my happiness, but was torn when I realized Tasha was crying. Guilt overcame me. How can I want the baby so badly and see her all worried and sick because of her pregnancy?

I stood there like a fool, not knowing what to do. The door opened behind me and there was Martha, holding a tray.

"Mr. Greene, I am sorry I failed to take your call."

One look at Martha, and I knew why. She looked haggard today, and I can tell how much she worries about Natasha. I nodded my head. She was carrying a tray with a small pot and a bowl. I took the tray from her hand and put it on the table. I smelled the chicken broth as soon as I opened the pot. I smiled when I saw that she also put some vegetables on it.

Martha helped Natasha get back to the comforter. I scooped some soup into a bowl and sat beside Natasha, carrying the bowl in my hand. Martha took more pillows from the bed and stacked them by the wall behind Natasha.

I scooted next to Tasha. I noticed that her hair tie got loosened so I put the bowl down and I helped her tie her hair again. The soup was still hot so I scooped a spoonful and blew onto it before I fed them to Natasha. However, she insisted on bringing the whole bowl close to her mouth. I helped her blow onto the soup to cool them, then she sipped from the lid.

Natasha let out a long sigh the moment she tasted the soup. She looked much better and relaxed after she finished the content. She leaned her back on the wall and closed her eyes again. I wanted to hug her but I did not want to make her feel more upset.

A little later, Natasha asked me to minimize my movements. She said she still feels nauseated. I got up slowly and sat on the edge of her bed. I ran my hand through my hair and stared at the pregnancy kit scattered by my feet.

"Babe, are you still upset with me?."

She didn't answer, but I saw the tears that fell from her eyes. I have heard from my male friends before how women's hormones messed with their emotions when they were pregnant. So I tried to be more patient with her. I moved closer to her and put my arm around her shoulder. Though she asked me not to move too much, she welcomed the gesture.

I put my hand on her tummy. I could not wrap my head around the fact that my flesh and blood were growing inside her. I could not even explain how I was feeling. I kissed her hair.

"Have you gone to the hospital for a check-up?"

She whispered, "No."

"Do you want us to go together?"

She did not answer.

"Are you scared?"

She said, "Yes." Tears started to flow from her eyes again.

"Baby, I am scared too. But we will get through this together, okay?"

Natasha wrapped her arms around me. She buried her face in my chest and I ran my hand through her hair and back.

"Hey, stop crying. Our baby would be sad too." I hugged her tight. I thought about the things that might be worrying her about the pregnancy. "Are you worried about your career?"

She looked up at me. I helped her wipe her tears. "Yes. I have only just started. But now suddenly I have a baby to take care of."

"Hey, I am here. I will help you raise the baby. You don't have to stop working if you don't want to. We can even hire nannies to look after our baby if you want."

"But I do not want to leave my baby under someone else's care."

Her answer stunned me. I understood her now from her point of view. She wanted a career and success. But she also wanted to be a hands-on mom. Natasha wanted to have the baby, but maybe later when she established her career.

I bit my lips and scolded myself for being too happy about the situation, without considering Natasha's feelings.

"We will find a way, okay?" I wiped her tears. "I won't hide that I badly want to have the baby. I do. But I do not want to compromise your happiness. So let us find a solution that would work for both of us, okay?"

She just bowed her head. I convinced Natasha to go and see a doctor. Then I carried her to the bathroom and washed her. After she had washed and put on her clothes, we made our way to the dining area.

Martha is busy preparing some lunch for us. Natasha said she still feels full. Martha offered to prepare her a snack we could bring. Natasha thanked her. Then she apologized for the trouble that she caused her for the last four days. Martha shook her head, then she rubbed Natasha's back.

Martha and Max met late, so they could not bear children. Martha even thanked Natasha for allowing her to experience having a daughter. Then she went to the kitchen to prepare Natasha's snack.

Max finished his lunch ahead of us. He already got the car ready by the time we went out. I held Natasha's hand until we reached Dr. Rebecca Clark's clinic.

Rebecca is a long-time friend of me and Bianca. She couldn't hide her surprise when she saw me visiting her clinic with a much younger woman.

"Hey, Ashton! It has been a long time. What can I do for you and your...friend?"

"Hey! I am glad to see you too. This is Tasha, she is my fiancée. She is pregnant so we would like you to check on her."

"Wow!" Rebecca looked even more dumbfounded. She kept looking at me, and then at Natasha before she spoke again. "Congratulations! Let me prepare what I need and I will call you into that room, okay?"

Rebecca left to call her assistant. Minutes later, she called us to go to a room. I felt a little bit nervous and I knew that Tasha was too. Rebecca handed Tasha a white blanket before she asked her to remove her underwear and lie down. Natasha seemed confused. Rebeca smiled and explained to her patiently.

"Your baby might be too small to be seen using the standard ultrasound. So we are doing a transvaginal ultrasound." She held the device in front of Natasha.

"Oh! Wow! Uh—okay."

Rebecca left to give her privacy. When she was done, we called Rebecca back. Rebecca put a blanket over her waist. She held out a stick that was attached to the ultrasound device and put what looked like a condom on it. Then she began to examine Tasha.

My heart leaped when we saw an image on the screen. My eyes widened at the two bean-like images she flashed on the screen. Tasha seemed to be more worried too. And who would not? I know she can tell what we were seeing as she covered her mouth with her hands.

"Okay. So these ARE your BABIES." Becca said as she emphasized and confirmed what we already know."Congratulations! You are going to have a twin."

She turned to Tasha. "Do you know the last time you had your monthly period?"

"I am not sure. I would say about six to seven weeks ago?"

"That is about right. According to this, you are about six weeks and four days pregnant. The babies are in healthy condition and their heartbeats are strong."

Rebecca clicked something and we heard two racing heartbeats as the monitor started to show the blinking dots.

"I will prescribe folic and iron supplements for you. Start eating more healthy food. As for the coffee, avoid it and drink milk instead. If not, limit your intake to only one cup per day."

Rebecca moved her chair to a small cabinet in the corner and got one booklet from it. She started writing on it as she explained some things to Natasha.

"I assumed this is your first pregnancy?"

We both nodded our heads and said "Yes" in unison.

"Oh, please, Ashton!" Rebecca rolled her eyes. It's too late to retract what she said because Natasha has already caught on.

"B-Bianca. Bianca got pregnant... and then she miscarried." my voice trailed off at the memory.

"Bianca.. right." Natasha nodded her head and then smiled.

Rebecca turned to me, her stare questioning. I just nodded and then gestured toward Natasha.

"Do you suffer from morning sickness?"

"Yes. I am throwing up everything that I eat."

"Okay. This shall help you with that." She scribbled and prescribed something on the booklet. "While throwing up and getting dizzy is normal, we do not want to get you dehydrated, okay?"

Tasha nodded her head. Becca handed me the booklet before she turned to talk to Tasha.

"It is normal to be worried. Since you are young and you are carrying twins. And also, this is your first pregnancy. I will help you with it, okay? It will turn out fine."

Tasha looked down. And then she nodded her head.

"Let us schedule you for another check-up after two weeks. Do not hesitate to call me should something unusual happen. We want this pregnancy to push through, right?"

It took a while for her to respond, but after some time, she nodded. Rebecca printed a copy of the scan and handed it to me. I could not hide my smile when I stared at the first photo of my twins.

"Okay, thank you, Becca. We will see you in two weeks. And uhm...the..."

Becca suddenly laughed. I got a little nervous when Tasha furrowed her brows.

"Right now, please avoid physical contact. We wanted to make sure that the twins were all right. If they are, wait for the second trimester and you can have steamy sex again."

Tasha blushed when she finally understood what we were talking about. Then she turned to me," Did you ask her that too when you went here with Bianca?"

Rebecca gasped and left me to Natasha in a hurry.

Natasha fell silent until we reached the car. She began to rub her tummy and cry. I pulled her into a hug and placed my hands over hers.

"Shhh.. crying would be bad for them."

I kissed her cheeks. She leaned on my shoulder and soon, she fell asleep. I worried about Tasha but I also could not contain my happiness. I sent my parents and my younger sister the ultrasound photo through a group chat. My parents were happy, especially my mom who has been asking me to give her a grandchild. However, my younger sister does not seem tickled by the news.

Edith: Wow! Are you telling us that we are going to be grandparents? And are those twins?

Monica: Really, Ashton? First, you told us that you are marrying the kid. And now, this even before the marriage?

Edith: Monica! Do not talk to your older brother that way.

Me: Tasha is 24! She is no longer a kid!

Arthur: I am happy for both of you, son. When are you going to bring Tasha over?

Edith: That is right, dear. I understand that maybe Monica still remembers the 10-year-old Tasha who used to spend her family vacation here with us.

Arthur: We hope to see her again before the wedding.

Me: I will talk to Tasha about it. She is still a little upset at the moment.Monica: I would say she is acting immature! That is what you get for having a relationship with a kid.

Arthur: Haha. Look who is acting maturely. Honey, I would say you are just jealous your big brother is getting married again.

Monica: Dad!

Edith: Ashton, have you tried to bring her to the mall?

Me: Mall? No. Not yet. We just came from the OB for her first check-up. Why?

Arthur: Sometimes, shopping is everything a woman needs to feel better. Take it from me. Haha!

Edith: Are you complaining, Arthur?

Edith: Anyway, Ashton. Bring her to the infant boutiques. Do you know those boutiques? Baby things might help to condition her mind into welcoming the babies.

Me: Okay. Thanks, Mom! We will see you soon.

Monica: I cannot promise that I will be good for her.

I closed the chat button and told Max to bring us to the mall. Sometime later, we arrived at the mall's entrance. I gently tap Tasha's shoulder.

"Hey, baby. Wake up."

She opened her eyes and looked out of the car. "Where are we? Oh! We are at the mall?"

I opened her door for her, and then we walked towards the mall's entrance. We held hands as we made our way to the infant boutiques.

I watched her as she went from one section to another. Her face lit up as held the tiny onesies in her hands.

"OMG! Look at these! They are so small!"

I started to feel more excited too. I imagined us, carrying the little creatures we both made. I followed Natasha around. Then she went to the baby headbands and small dresses. I think she wanted to have a girl. A little later, a sales lady came to approach us.

"Hi! How may I help you?"

"We are just looking around. We don't know the gender of the babies yet." I told her.

"Oh, right. I am sorry. But we have gender-neutral items over there. Do you want to see them?" Tasha looked at me. Her eyes suddenly beamed with excitement.

"Sure. Maybe we can see some items that we can buy now."

When we got home, we had three large shopping bags full of gender-neutral baby items and one large shopping bag full of maternity clothes. I still see tears in her eyes, but I know she feels better.

Now I guess it is time to tell Jeremy and Julia. I know Julia will be happy with the news. I am not quite sure about Jeremy though.

THE WEDDING

ASHTON'S POV

Martha waited for us by the door when we returned. She seemed genuinely happy to ask about Natasha's condition. Her eyes got filled with tears when she heard that we were going to have twins.

"Dear, I cooked mushroom soup for you. Come, have some. I also went to the grocery earlier. There are fruits and yogurts on the ref. I noticed how you loved eating them for the past few days."

Tasha hugged her. "Thank you, Martha."

I watched her go to the dining room as I climbed the stairs to put the shopping bags in our room. I thought I would have to turn one of the bedrooms into a nursery now. When I came down, Natasha was feasting on the soup. She smiled at me. I approached and kissed her head.

"How are you feeling, baby?"

"I am feeling better, but a little bit tired. I am sorry for earlier."

I sat down beside her. I cupped her cheeks and kissed her lips.

"When are we planning to tell your parents?" I wiped the corner of her mouth.

Natasha swallowed before she answered, "Maybe later?"

She got up but I stopped her. I asked her what she needed.

"Ugh! I do not know what I want! I am craving something sour." Natasha pursed her lips.

She asked for oranges and yogurt.

"Are you sure about these?"

She groaned. "I don't know."

Natasha went upstairs and told me she'd wait for me in the room. I remained in the kitchen and peeled the oranges for her. I found Natasha in my room, standing by the foot of the bed and staring at the wall.

I put the tray on the table. I moved closer to Natasha and gave her the oranges. I wonder why the way Natasha took a bite and enjoyed the oranges appears tempting. I took one slice but spat it immediately. The oranges tasted too sour. Natasha laughed at me while I was left wondering how she ate those.

"Can we move all my things here?" Natasha asked after a while.

"I told you to move them months ago." I gave her another slice.

"Right. What are your views on co-sleeping?" The juice dripped from her mouth and she wiped it with her hand.

I noticed how she talks about our babies with so much ease now. I chuckled. Now that I think about it, I suddenly realize I would have to share her with those two tiny creatures.

"We will need a bigger bed." She glanced at my bed.

"Or they can stay in a nursery." I tilted my head, referring to the room she was using now.

Natasha shook her head.

"But I hate the thought of not seeing them right away. Like, you know? When they cry in the middle of the night?"

I put the plate back on the tray and inspected the bedroom wall.

"How about we make a connecting door between our room and the other room? We still have plenty of time. We can still get it done."

"Yeah. Maybe we should do that."

Natasha hugged me from behind. Then she handed me her phone and asked me to take a photo with her. She said she would send them to her parents, who were on their way home from their vacation. I saw from her gallery that she took photos of what we bought earlier and the printed ultrasound. She even tried one maternity dress.

Five minutes after we sent the photos, we received a video call from her dad.

"Can you explain what these photos are all about, Ashton?"

"Well, dad," I stressed the word Dad, Jeremy groaned.

"Ugh! Do not call me dad!"

I ignored him.

"Anyway, Dad. You are going to be a granddad soon."

Natasha appeared behind me, said hi to her parents, and showed them her still flat tummy.

"What? Oh boy!" Jeremy started to laugh and cry at the same time.

Julia joined her husband on the call. It looks like she just saw the photos we sent.

"I thought you said she is not pregnant?" she moved her face closer to the phone as if trying to see the bump in Tasha's tummy.

"We only found out about it this week," Natasha said.

I rolled my eyes. "I only found out today."

Natasha picked up the onesies from the bed and showed them to her parents, who were both in tears and smiling.

"So how far along are you?" I can sense Julia's excitement.

"About seven weeks."

Jeremy and Julia exchanged glances. I almost dropped the phone when Jeremy shouted, "You got her pregnant before you left two months ago! You, Ashton!"

"No, no! I did not intend to!" Ashton passed the phone to me as if asking for my help.

"I am sorry to disappoint you, Mom, Dad." I gave them the puppy-eyed look.

"Oh, no. No, sweetheart. Do not think about it that way." Julia quickly appeased her daughter.

"I am still young. I'm sure there are better things that you want for me. I'm sorry."

I knew Natasha did not mean to speak that way, but guilt returned to me again.

"You'll be okay, hon. I was about your age when I had you too. And I did not regret that. You will do fine." tears welled in Julia's eyes again. Jeremy pulled her close and tapped her head.

"You think so, mom?" Natasha smiled and looked down at her belly. "You think I can be a good mom too?" she asked, rubbing them.

"OF COURSE! MAYBE YOU can even be better than me. " Julia wiped her tears. "So how are you feeling?"

"I feel tired and weak all the time. Morning sickness is the worst!" Natasha complained. When she realized what she had done, she looked down at her tummy and apologized to it.

"I am sorry to hear that, honey. But that is not the worst part." Julia sniffed.

"What do you mean, mom?"

"You have to carry the twins for nine months. You will have crazy food cravings, sleepless nights, sometimes you might even pee in your pants." Julia laughed hard as if she remembered something from the past. "And oh! The glucose test! That will make you want to throw up again. Then lastly, the labor pains. But once you have them in your arms, you will feel it's all worth it.

Tasha began to cry. But this time, I can feel that it is out of joy.

"Do not forget to eat healthy food and have plenty of rest, okay?' Then Julia turned to me. "And don't be shy to tell Ashton your cravings. I'm sure he enjoyed making the baby with—"

"Mom!"

Natasha cut Julia, but her mother ignored her.

"What? Don't tell me he did not enjoy it?"

Jeremy grabbed the phone from Julia. I am sure he felt embarrassed too. In the background, I can still hear her say, "It would be fair if you give him a hard time looking for and helping you satisfy your odd cravings!"

"Ah, that's right!" Jeremy nodded in agreement. " I got something for Ashton too." When he laughed, I knew it wouldn't be good. "You better prepare yourself for her mood swings too."

I looked at Tasha and remembered how her mood had changed for the past hours. "Yeah. I think I have already had a glimpse of enough mood swings today."

Tasha punched me in the arm.

"Ah! Whatever you saw today, that is nothing. She would get crazier than that. Pregnancy hormones are the worst!"

"Dad!" Tasha seems annoyed. I laughed.

"Seriously, please care for my daughter...and the babies."

"I miss both of you. I wish you guys were here."

When Tasha cried, Jeremy gave me the 'I-told-you-so' look. I guided Natasha to sit on the bed and I held her close.

"We miss you too, honey. We cannot wait to see you." Julia's voice cracked.

"I miss you too, princess. Now I regret why I agreed to your mom and left you with Ashton." Jeremy removed his glasses and kept wiping his tears.

I chuckled. "Natasha is happy with me."

He groaned again. "But I am not happy with all these. Anyway, we have to go. You guys take care. Bye."

"Bye Dad" I teased him one more time.

"Shut up!" he shouted. And then the call ended.

NATASHA'S POV

The week went by fast. Today is our wedding and I am now 20 weeks pregnant. My bump is showing but I still can hide it with a flowing dress. When we planned the wedding, I told them I wanted to be reminded of the dinner cruise on my twenty-second birthday. So we had the wedding on a yacht. I regretted the decision because when we started sailing, it gave me vertigo. I am glad it went away once I got accustomed to the motion.

I scanned the surroundings and was delighted with the decoration. Vea volunteered and her creativity was astonishing. There were lights and candles everywhere. Even the small pool is full of floating lights and flowers on it. The wedding was very intimate with only about 60 guests. The ceremony was short and simple too.

During the reception, Ashton surprised me by singing *Dashboard Confessional Stolen*. I remember he asked me three weeks ago when I realized I had a crush on him. And I told him it was when I saw him playing the guitar and singing that song.

I cried by the time he finished. And while I blame my pregnancy hormones, I know that his effort touched me. We also danced to *Ed Sheeran's Perfect*. Ashton was surprised when Derek's crew came onto the stage and asked him to sit back and watch.

Ashton glanced at Becca with a worried look on his face. She made an ok sign, assuring him I got her permission for the routine, which we kept light and fun. No matter how simple, our wedding was full of surprises, not just for the guests. Our parents and our friends told the other guests what they knew about our love story.

My mom compiled old videos and photos of us. I think I was only three or four years old in one of the videos that she played. The video was when we went to the beach mom told me that Ashton could not make it. I cried in the video and my dad offered to carry me.

While still crying, I pushed my dad away and said "I don't want you. I want Ashton." My mom said there were other guys in the resort. Still crying I said "But they are not Ashton. I only want Ashton."

I don't even remember that video but I felt embarrassed! Ashton looked amused as he hugged me and kissed my cheeks. All the guests laughed too, including his parents and her sister Monica.

Next was Ashton's mom. She told us Ashton never failed to buy me gifts, even when we drifted apart. She also told us how Ashton learned to laugh again after his divorce when we became together. Edith also shared the conversation when Ashton was trying to fight his feelings for me and how he finally admitted it to himself.

During the dinner, they played the prenuptial videos, photos, and the same-day-edit video of the wedding ceremony. I realized that my friends are great event planners. They have prepared many games and trivia about me and Ashton. The bouquet and the garter toss were also done with games. All the guests had fun and I can say that this has also been the happiest day of my life.

Ashton and I danced with our guests for the last time. Ashton pulled me into an embrace. He rested one of his hands on my protruding belly while I rested mine on his shoulders. I held my gaze into his blue eyes which mirrored my happiness.

"Are you happy, baby?"

He asked and I nodded. My vision got blurry as happy tears flowed from my eyes.

"I love you. You and our babies." Ashton slid his hand to feel my tummy.

"We love you too." I kissed his lips.

We both gasped when we felt the twins move in my tummy. I guessed they were very pleased and glad about all that had happened.

EPILOGUE

I am 33 weeks pregnant but look bigger because I carry twins. Despite Ashton's and my parents' disapproval, I persuaded them to allow me to do my job. I started working from home a month ago and this is the last week before I filed for a leave. I only have a few weeks before I reach my full term.

I went to the bathroom to pee, which has become more urgent most of the time now when the twin keeps pushing against my gallbladder. Although, it felt a little weird this time. I felt like defecating, though I was not sure I was going to. I pulled my underwear back up when I saw drops of blood in it.

Oh no! Am I bleeding?

There are days when Ashton works from home too. But he left this morning to attend the Board Meeting. I am supposed to join them online, but now I do not think I can.

I called Dr. Becca on the phone and explained to her the discomfort I was feeling and the blood that I saw in my underwear. She instructed me to go to the hospital right away, to prevent early delivery, or worse, a miscarriage.

"M—Martha?" My voice cracked.

I found Martha in the nursery. We began stacking baby supplies two days ago, and Martha kept them in storage. A worried look appeared on her face when she saw me holding my tummy.

"Yes, dear? Are you alright? Do you want me to call Mr. Greene?"

"Yes, please. Actually, no. Is Max here? Call him first, please? Tell him we need to go to the hospital, NOW!"

Martha disappeared from my sight in an instant. I felt grateful when I saw that Martha had already prepared the go-bags. I checked if anything was missing, then grabbed and carried them. Martha returned with Max.

She snatched the go-bag from me while Max attempted to lift me. I told him I could walk but asked him to share my weight. The discomfort I felt took us a lot of stops before we reached the car.

Ashton was already in the hospital lobby when we reached the hospital. I found him waiting with Dr. Becca and a nurse. Ashton said he left the meeting as soon as he heard and that my parents would follow shortly.

"Hey, baby. How are you feeling? Hold on, okay?" He asked the man who rode the elevator with us to press the button for us and then turned back to me. He touched my belly and talked to the twin, "Oh, you naughty babies! You are not supposed to arrive yet."

The first thing that Dr. Becca did was the ultrasound. She smiled at me, but I felt like she saw something wrong with it. Then she asked the nurse to bring me into a room where they attached an apparatus. After a few minutes, I could hear my babies' heart beats loudly.

Dr. Becca handed me what seemed like a stress ball and instructed me to squeeze it every time I felt a contraction. Then she left the room and asked Ashton to come with her. When Ashton returned, I noticed that his eyes were red.

Did he cry?

"Hey, babe what is wrong?" I wiped the tears in Ashton's eyes.

She caught my hand and brought it to his lips. "How can you ask me that, when you're lying here?" Ashton sobbed. He lowered his face to me. "Baby, listen. They need to do an emergency cesarean on you. They said that babies are already pushing their way out but the cord was coiled and choked one of them."

I could not process the entirety of Ashton's words. But I understood that my babies were in danger.

"They might need to be placed in an incubator because they're premature. But they would be fine. You would be fine." He started sniffing. "We can do this, okay?"

"I am scared." I grabbed his hand and he squeezed it.

Then we both cried. He held me close. Soon the nurses arrived to inform me that I needed to prepare for my emergency operation. They asked me about many things, got my blood pressure and my temperature, and asked me to change into a hospital gown.

Sometime in the afternoon, I underwent an operation. Though I felt scared, I was awake the whole time. Dr. Becca allowed Ashton inside the operating room. He talked to me and tried to put me at ease. I think more than an hour passed until we finally heard a cry. Becca handed the baby to Ashton.

He then placed the first baby on top of me and put a blanket on it. "Babe, this is Samuel." Ashton sniffed when another doctor took the baby from him to be placed in an incubator. Ashton kissed my forehead and assured me that I was doing fine.

Ashton put the second one on top of me. Ashton's facial expression appeared more calm and smooth than when he held the first one.

"This is Samantha. Oh, my princess!" He took the second baby too soon from my chest, tears glistened in his eyes.

I forced a smile. I think he already has a favorite. That was the last thing that I remembered before I fell asleep.

The babies stayed in the incubator for a month. I chose to stay in the hospital too so I can go and visit them at the neonatal intensive care unit to breastfeed and do some KMC. I felt glad when we were finally allowed to bring the twins home.

THREE YEARS LATER

NATASHA'S POV

We were in our room, getting ready for a company event. Samuel refused to wear his clothes and kept running around the room and jumping on the bed with only his diaper on.

"Hey! I told you to stop jumping and to put on your pants. Come here, let us put your clothes on you." He squeaked when Ashton caught him.

"No! I don't want to put on clothes. I want to jump, jump, jump!" He tried to escape from his father's grasp.

"Are you sure that is what you want?" Ashton put Samuel on the bed and began tickling and biting his sides.

Samuel squealed and asked for my help.

"Dad! Ahhhh!!! Stop!! Hahaha!!! Mom, help me!"

"You are such a baby. Mommy cannot help you. She would be busy putting makeup on me." Unlike Samuel, Samantha is already dressed up, sitting in front of the dresser. She combed her long and Auburn hair.

Ashton and I laughed when she twinkled her eyes and pouted her lips at the mirror. I took the brush from her and brushed her hair.

"Why do you need to put makeup on? You are already beautiful, sweetheart."

She turned to face me. "Because I want to look pretty for Vincent."

My jaw dropped. For a moment, I thought I saw the younger me in her.

"What did you just say, young lady?"

Ashton had just finished clothing Samuel. He put him down and walked toward us. He bent down so he could see his daughter at eye level.

Samantha rolled her eyes. "I said I want Vincent to notice me."

Samantha laughed at me when Ashton dropped her jaw.

AT THE COMPANY EVENT

There were only a few guests in the lobby when we arrived. My parents are in the corner, talking to Gustavo Mendez, Vincent's dad. When Samantha saw Vincent, she called out his name and ran straight to him. Ashton smirked.

"Vincent! Carry me!"

Upon seeing Samantha, Vincent lowered his leg and opened his arms, ready to welcome the kid. Then she swept her into his arms.

"Do I look pretty?" Samantha asked him right away.

"Of course you do, querida."

Samantha giggled and squealed.

"Look, Daddy. Vincent said I am pretty. He likes me, he likes me!"

Everyone found Samantha adorable. But my dad had a loud laugh. He approached Ashton, and in a low voice, I heard him whisper, "Oh, well. I guess karma is a bitch."

Vincent must have heard it too since he let out a nervous laugh. He pinched Samantha's cheek and said "Querida Mia, why do I feel like you are going to get me into deep trouble one day?"

Ashton took Samantha from Vincent. I can't tell if he's serious, but his brows are furrowed when he speaks to him.

"You can make as many excuses as you want. But I won't buy it. I have been there. I have done that. And I will be keeping my eyes on you."

The room erupted with so much laughter.

THE END.